THE PARIS COLLABORATOR

For Carol-Anne and Terence
And in memory of JAn Napiorkowski –
a friend and writer who lived with passion

THE PARIS COLLABORATOR

A.W. HAMMOND

echo

PUBLISHING

echo
PUBLISHING

An imprint of Bonnier Books UK
Level 45, World Square,
680 George Street
Sydney NSW 2000
www.echopublishing.com.au

Bonnier Books UK
4th Floor, Victoria House,
Bloomsbury Square
London WC1B 4DA
www.bonnierbooks.co.uk

Echo Publishing acknowledges the traditional custodians of Country throughout Australia. We recognise their continuing connection to land, sea and waters. We pay our respects to Elders past and present.

This is a work of fiction. Names, characters, businesses, places, events, locales and incidents are either the products of the author's imagination or used in a fictitious manner. Any resemblance to actual persons, living or dead, or actual events is purely coincidental.

First published 2021
This edition published 2023

Printed and bound in Australia by Pegasus Media and Logistics

The paper in this book is FSC® certified.
FSC® promotes environmentally responsible, socially beneficial and economically viable management of the world's forests.

Page design and typesetting by Shaun Jury
Cover design: Debra Billson
Cover images: City view through giant clock tower in Paris, France, by Songquan Deng/Shutterstock; Silhouette of a lady standing in front of the big clock at Museum Orsay, Paris, France, by Andy Tam/Shutterstock; Film noir, detective investigating the crime scene, by Dm_Cherry/Shutterstock

A catalogue entry for this book is available from the National Library of Australia

ISBN: 9781760688035 (paperback)
ISBN: 9781760687021 (ebook)

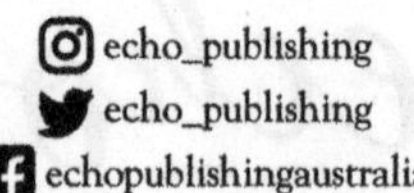
echo_publishing
echo_publishing
echopublishingaustralia

ABOUT THE AUTHOR

A. W. Hammond was born in South Africa and emigrated to Australia as a child. He currently works at RMIT University and lives in Melbourne with his wife and daughters.

The only clue to what man can do is what man has done.
– R. G. Collingwood, *The Idea of History* (1946)

Monday, 14 August 1944

ONE

The body hung from a tree. A warm breeze made the dead man's hair dance in the dappled light. His eyes and the soft flesh of his face had been eaten away. The crows had been busy.

Auguste Duchene stood below the corpse. Around him, a carpet of rotting fruit glistened under a clear sky, and the sour fragrance mingled with the smell of rank flesh. With one hand clasping his nose and the other shading his eyes from the sun, he stepped closer to the dead man.

While his features were unrecognisable, the man's clothes, still damp from last night's rains, betrayed something of his identity. He was dressed in tan trousers and a cotton shirt, and a scarf was tied around his neck just below the rope. He wore only one boot; the other lay on the ground among the fallen fruit. At one time, there had been a knife in his belt, a tool for rural life, but only the sheath remained.

The noose had been expertly tied; the knot that held it to the plum tree was strong. The farmer had been tied to the lowest branch – his feet would have thrashed the grass. Just high enough to die with no effort wasted.

The rain had blurred the handwritten note that was pinned to the body. Perhaps the Germans had killed him, punishing a word of dissent, some act of defiance – all crimes during an occupation. But the hangmen were just as likely to be Resistance, encouraged by the fighting at Normandy to settle old scores.

Only one thing was sure: this man, local and dead at least a week, was not the one Duchene had come to find. He and the woman who travelled with him had fled from Paris only three days ago.

Duchene resumed his walk towards the farmhouse. It was still some distance ahead, occasionally visible between the low-hanging branches of the plums. Between the orchard and the house stood a coop made from stone and wire; the silence of the farm suggested any chickens had long since been eaten. Ivy grew rampant across the farmhouse, concealing where its timber extension joined its original grey stone walls. The dark leaves rustled in the breeze, as though the house was bristling at his arrival.

His leg caught twine strung between two trees. He froze in place.

His eyes followed the length of the twine, fearing that by looking he'd summon a grenade into being.

It was tied to an old can, too full of rainwater to rattle.

He let out a breath, then ducked below a final branch and moved with quiet haste to the chicken coop. He stopped at its corner and knelt on the soft grassy earth. There was no movement outside the farmhouse.

Some milk thistle was growing up against the coop's wall. Keeping an eye on the house, he uprooted the entire crop, quickly rolled it in his handkerchief and tucked it in his jacket pocket.

Still no movement.

Closing his hands into fists, he stepped into the open

yard and started to jog with his head low. In a few seconds, he was up against the farmhouse wall.

He waited to regain his breath before peering through a window into a storeroom, its contents smashed and strewn. Drawers had been pulled open, boxes broken, and old sacks of meal and grain slashed and torn. Thick dust covered the papers on the ground, while the grains had greyed and sprouted in the damp and summer heat.

Beyond an open door was a kitchen.

Keeping his head down, he moved along the wall until he came to the next window. He raised his head just enough to see into the kitchen, his low crouch causing a dull pain in his back. The missing leg of a sideboard had been replaced with a brick, while above the stove a pot rack had been reinforced with rope. Fresh bread cooled on a small table, its surface scratched as if it had been recently overturned then righted on the hard stone floor.

Through the kitchen door, in a living space, a man sat at the edge of a threadbare chaise longue, a shotgun at his feet. He was using a knife to carve a wooden block into a doll.

Duchene examined the man's face; it matched the description he'd been given. He had found the right place.

He ducked below the windows and knocked on the front door. The rap of his knuckles was loud and brief. He paused, as he heard something metallic being lifted from the floor.

'Monsieur Jaubert?' Duchene stood to the side of the door, his back against the wall. 'Monsieur Jaubert, I'm here to talk.'

More silence.

'Jaubert?'

The slide of metal on metal may have been innocuous to some, but it was distinct to Duchene: Jaubert had chambered a shell. 'Leave. Or get shot.'

'I'm afraid I can't do that, Monsieur.'

'Leave.'

'I have come from Paris.'

'You followed us.'

'Yes.'

In the orchard, a large crow came to land on the top branch of a tree. It splayed its feathers and grunted towards the house.

'Open up. So we can talk. Can we at least do that?'

There was another moment, another pause of indecision. He could hear whispering – Jaubert and the woman.

'I'd like to talk to Madame as well, if I may?'

A bolt slid, and the heavy wooden door opened. Duchene stepped back from the wall to face the entrance.

Jaubert was as he'd been described, his beard dishevelled, eyes dark. As with so many during these fraught times, he was struggling, desperate. He held the shotgun, its barrel pointed squarely at Duchene's chest. It had a short barrel, an empty bayonet adapter – it had been reconfigured for close quarters combat.

'Your father's?'

'What?'

'The trench gun. Your father's?'

'I know how to use it.' Jaubert adjusted his sightline, aiming a little higher. Neck or head, it didn't matter; if he pulled the trigger, the blast would hit both.

'I don't doubt it,' Duchene said, raising his hands.

'Weapons?'

'None.' He rotated on the spot, wincing as his back

faced the muzzle. 'Is your wife here?' He nodded past the living room.

'You talk to me.'

'This affects both of you. It would be polite to talk to both of you, no?'

On the far side of the living room was another open door. A woman, petite and wiry, emerged at its edge. Much like her husband, she showed the worn lines of sleep deprivation; unlike her husband, she showed her grief through tears in her eyes and tremors in her hands. She cradled a small bundle, only the faintest of movements suggesting its contents.

'He's sleeping?' Duchene asked.

She stared at him, her hands shaking.

'It's good that he's sleeping. You should kiss him farewell and pass him to me.'

'No,' Jaubert said, stepping forward with the weapon.

Duchene took a step back. 'I'm not here to cause trouble.'

Jaubert stepped forward again. 'You want to take the boy. That's trouble.'

The gun was inches from Duchene's face. 'I appreciate that you see it that way. But I'm here to help you.'

Jaubert whistled through a sneer.

'Shoot him,' the woman whispered from the doorway.

Duchene held his hand up. His heart was racing. Twice now in one day – he doubted it was good for him. Scanning the room, he saw a wooden carving on the ground: a crucifix, the kind that might hang on a wall.

'Wait. Think for a moment. You're good people. People of faith. So let me warn you, give you a chance. Do you know why I'm here? Me, specifically?'

Silence.

'He's ours now.' The woman moved further into the room, keeping her husband between them.

'Madame Jaubert, I can't imagine what you have been through. This war has taken so much from so many. My sincere condolences for your loss. But that is not your child. He needs to be with his own mother.'

'He's fed from me. He knows me.'

'I can see you've made a good home for him. But he can't stay. I'm just the first who will come for him, and the others won't be so reasonable. They won't come unarmed.'

Jaubert tilted his head to one side, his eyes widening. 'Is that a threat? Maybe I should shoot you. Then I'll shoot them.'

Duchene's heart hadn't slowed, the pressure building in his chest. 'It's just a fact.' He breathed deeply, adjusted his tone. 'Think back to when you took him. A brand-new pram pushed by a young nanny? This is a family of means.'

Jaubert's face soured. 'Collaborators,' he spat.

'Yes. And if I don't return with that child, the Germans will be the next to knock at your door.'

'You say that as though you're not one of them. And yet here you are, working for them.'

'I work for myself. I try to help. Will you let me help you?'

Jaubert didn't move. Behind him, his wife adjusted her grip on the child, releasing him a little from her chest, allowing just the slightest of distances between them.

Duchene spoke to her. 'His parents love him. They'll provide for him.'

'Paris is too dangerous for him,' she said. 'The Americans are coming, and the Germans will fight them. The city will be bombed. Michel will die.'

'I appreciate everything you're saying, really I do. But that's not Michel. I wish that it was – too many innocents have died. But the child's name is Jean, and his parents should decide what's safest for him. We just have to do what is right, here and now. That means putting down the gun and giving me the child.'

The wind moved through the house, pushing at the curtains, bringing with it the scent of jasmine.

'Please,' Duchene said. 'You know his mother is distraught, afraid.'

With caution, Madame Jaubert lowered the child from her chest. Her husband sensed the movement behind him and stepped sideways.

Duchene raised his hand to his face, shielding his eyes from those of Jaubert. He stepped past the barrel of the gun into the small house. He held out his hands to the child.

'Let me feed him,' said Madame Jaubert, 'so he's not hungry. Please. One last time.'

'That will only make it harder to let go.'

A tear gathered in her eye. 'I need to remember my baby. Just one last time.'

TWO

Dust rose as Duchene walked back to the truck. The farmhouse was a kilometre behind, and the milk-drunk child slept in his arms. The soft infant, oblivious to the world around him, pressed himself close, seeking to share Duchene's warmth. He was surprised at how quickly the movements came back to him, his arms tilting to make a cradle, his weight shifting to ease his tread into a rocking motion. All his actions focused on encouraging sleep.

Lucien was smoking beside the truck, one leg at rest on the running board. His grin was almost as bright as the sun that drifted towards the horizon behind him. 'You were successful!' he called while exhaling smoke from his nose. 'Or have you been looting from the orchards?'

'I was successful.'

'Then smile, old man. Today you have done a family a great service.'

'And another, a mischief.'

'That's it, I've had enough. Put the child on the front seat, and you get in the back. Even you cannot be so disagreeable.'

'They were in mourning. They were desperate.'

'But they are alive. And that, my friend, is a gift in these dark times.' Lucien clapped him on the back. 'You're a good man, Auguste.'

Good.

That word didn't make sense to him anymore, not in a way that carried any truth.

The infant began to stir, and he patted him on the back.

Lucien held his fingers to his lips and started to walk around the back of the truck to the driver's side.

'What's in there?' Duchene glanced over the wooden palisades into the tray, where dozens of unmarked hessian sacks lay neatly stacked against the wall of the cabin.

'Potatoes.' Lucien smiled, pulling open the door.

Duchene looked back at him. 'Really?'

'Yes. But there's also butter. Ten kilos in an icebox hidden under the bags.'

'Butter?'

'Of course.' Lucien tossed his cigarette aside, took off his suit jacket and hung it behind his seat in the cabin.

'Hiding the butter only makes it more suspicious. Marks you out as a smuggler.'

'But what's the alternative, to let the Germans see it? Confiscate it for their Brötchen? No, thank you.'

'And if we get caught?'

Lucien winked. 'I have you.'

Duchene shook his head. Easy charm and good looks would only keep Lucien alive for so long.

'Don't look at me like that,' Lucien said. 'It cost me to borrow this truck. Gasoline is hard to find, expensive. This trip is an opportunity to make some money, for both of us.'

'You profit.'

'So do you. Compared to those people back in that farmhouse. Besides, look what else I picked up.' In the seat between them was an old apple crate covered by a linen cloth. With the flourish of a maître d', Lucien peeled it back to show the contents: a small knitted dolly and some gingham fabric folded to make a soft mattress.

'How?'

Lucien smiled. 'You know I can get you anything. All you have to do is ask.'

The truck rattled as it accelerated, and Lucien tightened his grip on the steering wheel. Paris was flickering into life on the dusk-wrapped horizon, with points of electric light beginning to punctuate the soft amber glow of the disappearing sun. When Lucien pulled on the stick, the cabin shook. The baby stirred.

Lucien glanced down, then back to the road. 'Sorry. But we need to hurry. Nineteen hundred hours – that's when the guards change shift. We need to be there before that.'

'Why?'

'The old guards have tired feet, they're ready to leave. New guards are more diligent.'

'And where will we meet them?'

'Avenue d'Italie. I know most of the guards there. That will make it easier.'

'Easier? You said it would be no problem getting back into Paris.'

Lucien tugged a cigarette loose from the pack in his shirt pocket and slipped it into his mouth. He nodded to Duchene, who picked up the lighter from the seat to flick a flame under the cigarette's tip.

On the road around them, vehicles were trickling into the city. In recent weeks there were hardly any civilian cars; anticipating things to come, drivers avoided the thoroughfares. Now there were hourly convoys of large trucks with troops and supplies bound for the front. Their camouflage paint hastily daubed on with mops, they rumbled west, hoping to stay clear of bombing raids. Even now, on the road opposite, the tracks of a massive tank shook the ground as it trailed smoke from its tar-blackened exhausts.

Duchene remembered when the German tanks had first arrived, how Parisians clustered around them, awed and intrigued. Now their purpose was all too clear, the markings the crew painted on their steel sides understood by everyone: the number of Frenchmen they had killed.

As Lucien's eyes moved from his watch to the road, he weaved the truck around the slower-moving vehicles, using his horn to make a space in the queue that led to the roadblock. They were crossing into the 13th arrondissement, the border to the city's centre, a boundary well understood by French and German alike. It was no mistake the cordon had been erected so precisely here – the symbolism was overt.

Ahead lay sandbags and a machine-gun emplacement. German guards checked over vehicles with flashlights and short words. Lucien wound down the window and picked up his cigarettes. They waited without speaking, with only the sound of the engine to fill the silence.

The soldiers who arrived at the truck looked young, younger than Duchene when he'd been sent to the last war. One shone his lapel torch through his window while the other leant into the cabin at Lucien's side. 'Your purpose?' he asked in French.

'Good evening, private,' Lucien replied in German. 'We both speak Deutsch.'

'Your aim?' he asked in German.

'We have brought some potatoes to sell. From the ... ah ... *field* ... *land*.'

'... from the countryside,' Duchene corrected. He watched as the second solider shone his torch across the back of the tray. Its light picked over the rounded shapes of potatoes in their bags.

'Potatoes?' asked the first soldier.

'That's right,' said Lucien. 'Cigarette?'

The soldier took it and slipped it into his breast pocket. 'Potatoes?' he called to his companion, who started to tug at the bags. Apparently satisfied by their weight but not their contents, he took out his knife.

Duchene held his expression, trying to calm his racing heart. He reached into his pocket and pulled out his papers. 'If you could look these over, Obergrenadier,' he told the first soldier, 'you will find that we're on business authorised by your command.'

'German command?'

Lucien smiled. 'Not from von Choltitz himself, but yes.'

After taking the papers, the soldier waved a hand at his companion, who walked over with the torch. The top sheet of a typed triplicate bore the Wehrmacht insignia.

Behind the truck, a couple sitting in a Citroën watched in silence through their windscreen as the Germans handed the papers back. 'All right. You're free to proceed.'

'Until we meet again,' Lucien said. He put the truck into gear and pulled off.

Duchene grabbed hold of the box beside him as they lurched down the street.

They continued up the avenue to the Place d'Italie, following the curve of the large traffic circle past the arrondissement's town hall. Between its vaulting arches hung Nazi flags, the occupation reinforced to all who passed by. On the streets around them, Parisians walked: the men in linen suits, the women in summer dresses, all three years out of date. But to do anything less than your best was to succumb to the Germans, to the rations, to the malaise of occupation, so hats were embellished, offcuts were repurposed as scarves while black lines drawn down the back of bare legs imitated seamed hosiery. Where the materials were new and the styles fresh, assumptions could be made about the wearers. And with the Americans now on French soil, it took a certain fatalism or wilful ignorance to mark yourself out as a collaborator.

Duchene and Lucien wound their way onto the Boulevard du Montparnasse, arriving at a tree-lined esplanade from which they could just see the lights of the Eiffel Tower. A wide, grassy island ran the length of the street. Here, the last stragglers of picnics were packing up their hampers and blankets to take their celebrations into the well-lit residences that surrounded them. It reminded Duchene of how little and how much had changed – although picnickers had always been common in the centre of esplanades, these were German officers accompanied by Frenchwomen.

Lucien let the car idle while Duchene stepped out on the cobbled street and turned to take the box.

'What a beauty,' Lucien said. 'He didn't even wake.'

'He's a good sleeper. His parents are lucky.'

'Got to keep moving, find a refrigerator for the butter.

I know a pâtissière who'll pay a strong price, but she won't be at her shop until first thing tomorrow.'

'Until tomorrow.'

'Of course, my friend. Adieu!'

Duchene walked up the stairs to the townhouse opposite. He pressed the buzzer and, after a quick acknowledgement, was let into the foyer. Gripping the box with one arm, he removed his hat and stepped inside. Beneath a large chandelier, a marble mosaic spread across the floor to a curved staircase. It was down this that the woman ran while the man hurried after her.

'Monsieur Vernier. Madame, I –'

Madame Vernier, barefoot with a house jacket thrown over her nightgown, rushed to the box. 'He's all right. Tell me he's all right.'

'Jean is fine. He slept the entire way.' Duchene held out the box while the infant's mother reached in to retrieve him. On being held close to her breast, he roused and burst into tears.

'You've done an amazing thing, Monsieur Duchene, just amazing,' Vernier said as he took the box from Duchene's arms and firmly shook his hand. 'Tell us what you want, and I'll do everything in my power to give it to you.'

Behind the tearful mother, padding down the stairs, came the nanny. She tugged at her sleeves, but not before Duchene saw the bruises on her arms. With the infant now in her arms, Madame Vernier turned her back and walked to the opposite side of the foyer.

'Been difficult times,' Vernier said as he leant close to Duchene, his breath heavy with liquor. 'We were going to dismiss the nanny, but she begged and promised to work for us for free.'

Duchene nodded.

'So, what can I do for you? A new apartment? A car? Nothing is too much for the return of our child.'

'Thank you, but no. Just what I can carry. Some of that cognac you've been drinking, and any cigarettes.'

Vernier turned to the nanny. 'Sophie, a case of Hennessy and three cartons of Ecksteins for Monsieur Duchene.' As she hurried upstairs, Vernier leant forward again to Duchene's ear. 'Give me their address and I'll make it two cases.'

Twelve bottles. Worth a fortune on the black market.

'Sorry, Monsieur. I can't do that. Those were the terms.'

'I know, I negotiated them. But come, my friend, these are criminals. My wife has been frantic.'

'I'm sorry.'

Vernier stiffened and stepped back. 'Of course. We had an agreement.'

Duchene watched as the Verniers took Jean upstairs. He waited, hat in hand, for another ten minutes before the nanny returned. She gripped the box in both hands, carefully moving down the steps. Her hair came free from her bun, and as soon as she handed the box to Duchene, she neatened the loose strands.

'Thank you, Sophie,' he said, then, 'Reconsider. You don't need to stay with them.'

She looked up at him, a frown of worry on her face.

'The Americans will be here soon. You can survive until then. The Verniers will want to flee or stay, and neither is good for you.'

'That was then. This is now. I cannot leave. Without their protection, you know what they do to people who work for sympathisers? People like us?'

'Us?'

Her eyes narrowed in confusion. 'You work for the Verniers too.'

'I did it for the child.'

'Then so do I.'

THREE

The Germans had been busy. Duchene passed new fortifications, the fresh hessian of their sandbags contrasting with the dark cobblestones and limestone walls behind them. Commands and watch houses had their windows boarded up and their doorways reinforced. The smell of timber was in the air.

It was no surprise that the streets were empty, more so in recent days than at any other time during the occupation. In the past, the façade had been maintained – this was Paris, after all – and nights were a time for celebration and culture. But now they were quiet. Even in his own neighbourhood, passers-by didn't raise their eyes to meet his, keeping their hands in their pockets despite the mild weather, moving quickly on to whatever activity had forced them outside.

Duchene turned the key to his apartment building and entered the foyer. He checked his postbox. A habit – it was always empty. He made his way to the first floor, narrow wooden stairs creaking under his tread, seeming to resent the added weight of the box in his arms.

A second key and his apartment door was open. He weaved his way around the stacks of books that lay across a threadbare rug, then cleared a space among the papers on his dining table and was finally free of the cigarettes and cognac. Once he would have carried the case across town with no effort, but his breath left him quicker as he edged closer to fifty. When he looked in the mirror these days, he saw his father's face, the same receding, greying hairline, the lines cutting across his cheeks, and now the bone structure that had started to show once food shortages came in.

He looked across the room at the slow spread of chaos, the migrating stacks: those books he cherished, those he'd struggled to complete. There were more of them in his bedroom and even a few in his small kitchen. But not in the other bedroom. That remained closed; that remained as it had been a year ago.

He took his handkerchief from his pocket and unwrapped the milk thistle from the farm. Careful to avoid its spines, he lowered it into a sand-filled tank that sat on his crowded windowsill. 'Ernest,' he called, peering down into the tank. A cautious head emerged from a black-and-yellow striped shell and swayed from side to side as it sniffed the air. 'For you. From the forest of Fontainebleau.'

At first, he'd had trouble caring for the creature; its presence had summoned too many bad memories. Even so, to abandon it would have meant to betray his life before the war. This was, after all, a simple tortoise, and the memories were his burden to overcome.

Eventually, Ernest crept up on his meal and started to eat.

Duchene stroked the animal's neck.

His duty done, he navigated the drifting library and made his way to the kitchen. In the breadbox was the heel of a stale loaf; toasted, it might suffice. Perhaps food would have been a better payment. In the larder was the last of his butter, two potatoes, some sardines and a can of compressed meat. He strongly suspected the wine bottle on the cupboard beside him was empty – double-checking it wouldn't make it full again.

Duchene rolled up his sleeves and began to wash his hands.

There was a knock at the apartment door.

'I thought I'd heard you come in,' Camille said as she stood in the doorway.

'I've been out.'

A wry smile crossed her lips. 'This much is clear by your standing in front of me.'

'Are you going to come in?'

'I fear I'd topple something. I wanted to see if you've had dinner. I have made a gratin, and you're welcome to share it.'

'I don't have much I could exchange. My cupboard is empty. Unless . . .' He returned to the dining table, lifted a bottle of cognac from the box and held it towards Camille.

She crossed the room, slipping easily between the stacks of books. Unlike Duchene, she had always been slim, keeping up her callisthenics. There couldn't have been more than a year or two between them, but when he looked at her toned arms and calves, and the freckles on her face, it was as though time was passing more slowly for her.

When she noticed him watching her, he turned his attention to the bottle in his hand. 'For after?'

She took it from him. 'Where did you find them? Actually, don't tell me, I don't want to know. You should keep it. Sell it.'

'Let's enjoy it instead.'

'Food, company, drink. Sounds good.'

He locked up, and they crossed the hallway and walked through Camille's open door. No matter the many hours he spent in her apartment, he was always amused by its familiarity and difference. It mirrored his, with the bedrooms at the same end, the kitchen and bathroom at the other. The cornices and mouldings, although in better repair than his, were the same, the inbuilt cupboards and kitchen furnishings identical. However, her decor, unlike his, would have been met with the architect's approval: the statues, vases, and large framed photographs on the wall were as current as possible in a time of war.

On a walnut coffee table between two angular club chairs, the meal still steamed. It smelt of butter, toasted breadcrumbs and cauliflower. Beside the gratin was half a fresh baguette.

'It's just a Dijon roux,' Camille said. 'No cheese, I'm afraid.'

'It's wonderful.'

'Let's get it done, then. I'm keen on that cognac.'

He nodded and held the plates as she served them from the dish. A cooked meal made from fresh food. The gravity of the moment wasn't beyond them, and she had brought out her best dinner service to mark the occasion.

They sat in the club chairs, a fork in one hand and plate in the other. Camille paused and examined her meal, and Duchene watched her in silence. It was as though she was trying to discern something, read the signs. 'Please, start,' she said as she gently shook her head.

He did. But just a small mouthful, so he could ask, 'What's troubling you?'

'This meal. Every meal. Do you know what I mean?'

'Yes.'

'Do you remember when they first arrived?'

'Of course.'

'I remember this officer. He'd seen me playing in a club, learnt that I was a piano teacher, wanted lessons. He'd been learning back in Germany, before the war, and wanted to keep up. I couldn't understand it – this enemy, wanting to make art, to improve himself through creating beauty …'

'A contradiction.'

'It was. But that's not what troubled me the most.'

'No?'

'No. He wanted to pay for his lessons, my full fee, when he could have just forced me to teach him for nothing. To have him want to pay me … It legitimised him. For him it was the polite thing to do, but for me it was frightening. He was here to stay, to live in Paris, to pay for our services. To become one of us – no, worse, we were to become one of them.'

'What did he want to learn? Wagner?'

Camille laughed. 'Not so clichéd. Tchaikovsky. Can you imagine? But enough of that.' She shook her head, her smile lifting the lines on her face and guiding his gaze to her eyes, which gave him their full attention. As Duchene had aged, he had felt slow and sullen, his advancing years like a rot setting into an old stump. Camille seemed to cherish her moments and rise above the malaise of the occupation.

'This is delicious,' he said.

'It's nothing. Really.'

He tried to take his time, but the roux was flawless, and in no time he had eaten it all. He waited in silence for Camille to finish. She nodded to him, and at this signal he collected two glasses from the sideboard.

'I saw Marienne today,' Camille said.

'She was well?'

'Yes. She's invited me to dinner.'

'You can't go.'

'Of course I can.'

Duchene uncorked the cognac, poured generously and handed her a glass.

'She asked after you,' Camille said. 'You should talk to her. Make more of an effort.'

'Cheers,' he said and held out his glass.

She chimed and brought the cognac to her nose before taking a sip. 'And what about Marienne?'

'All right, yes. I'll make more effort.'

'Your daughter still needs you. No matter how angry she gets.'

'I really don't want to talk about that.'

'What shall we talk about then? Your tortoise?'

Duchene sighed. 'When they're little, you're filled with joy at even the simplest things they do, like reading a word. I think because it gives you a sense of their opportunity, of the life that lies open to them. But when they get older and make disappointing choices, so much potential seems lost.'

'Well. She's in love.'

'So you agree with her decision, then?'

'It's not really for me to say.'

'Why not?' he said. 'You're the one she confided in as she grew into a woman. You might as well be her mother. In many ways ...'

Camille shook her head. 'I think it's a bad decision, short-sighted. Look at the world we live in. The Americans are coming. What is to be gained from it?'

'She's stubborn.' Duchene poured another glass. 'Like her mother.'

'Of course she's stubborn. She's like you.'

The yellow glow from the street lamp cascaded through the venetians. It was just enough light to see the half-empty bottle of cognac. Duchene poured another glass. Soon it would be morning, and he would have to face another day.

The tortoise moved in its tank, oblivious to its own significance.

The bomb had landed close to the school. One moment he was teaching English prepositions, a moment later the room shattered.

The bomb is in front of *the building*.

The force of the explosion passed over him and threw him to the floor. With each breath, his ribs tore pain across his chest. Dust filled his lungs, choking him, clogging his mouth with grit and blood. His ears rang, the pain like the stab of a knitting needle.

The room is under *rubble*.

As he pulled himself free, the sun broke through the plumes of dust and smoke. Among the debris was a section of wall. Sitting against it, glinting in the light, was a glass reptile tank. It was undamaged. It was the only thing that remained. A field of rubble lay before him, and small, unmoving bodies lay beneath it. The roof had fallen. The space that had once contained desks, bags and bookshelves was now littered with broken wood and shattered tiles.

The children are among *the dead*.

Tuesday, 15 August 1944

FOUR

A mist had risen from the Seine and refused to fade in the morning light. Autumn had announced its intention to return to the city with a grey chill. When Duchene dragged himself from his apartment, the last tendrils of the night flowed around Parisian and German alike. He wore his winter coat and carried a worn valise.

From his apartment in Quartier Saint-Ambroise he made his way to the river and followed it to the Tour Saint-Jacques; he passed men and women starting their working week. A captured city had to function to prove the legitimacy of its occupiers. To illustrate the point, a large group of soldiers supervised council workers as they tore down posters calling for a general strike. Someone had stuck the notices around the square with flour paste, a sign that not only had the night's curfew been broken, but also that civil unrest was looming. This explained the speed at which people were moving, their heads down, eyes averted. Even the soldiers shifted on their uneasy feet while this challenge to their authority remained.

At the café tables on the square, senior officers sat drinking coffee and smoking. In this sea of grey uniforms was Lucien. He was sharing cigarettes with a young lieutenant and waved to Duchene as he approached.

Lucien stood up, gripped Duchene's arms and kissed his

cheeks. 'You look like hell, my friend.' He turned back to the officer and spoke in German. 'Oberleutnant Ritter, this is Monsieur Duchene.'

Duchene nodded back. 'Oberleutnant.'

The officer reached out a hand, and Duchene shook it.

'The Oberleutnant has the day off duty in the city. I've recommended he visit the Sphinx, but that's for tonight. Since he's been here, he's seen the Louvre, Sainte-Chapelle and Notre Dame. Anything else to recommend?'

Duchene paused. 'Saint-Séverin.'

'Of course. Latin Quarter. A good visit – beautiful mosaics. Get your fill of piety before you head out for a night of sin.'

The lieutenant laughed. 'Got to have a balance.'

'That's right. In Paris we do all things in moderation. But we do *all* things, if you take my meaning.' Lucien clapped his hands together. 'Well, we must go.'

As Lucien said his farewells, more cigarettes were offered, backs slapped, and Ritter insisted on picking up Lucien's bill.

Duchene waited until they were moving back through the square before he spoke. 'You're too friendly with them.'

'Hard to drum up business if you're an arsehole.'

'It looks bad to the rest of Paris.'

'And yet they buy from me too. Everyone knows I'm a capitalist and not a sympathiser. And besides, talking to them lets me practise my German. Should come as no surprise that they're all very keen we learn to speak it. I thought you'd be pleased.'

'You are improving. But it's not for the love of the language.'

'Can you still say that you love it?'

'Times have changed.'

'Obviously. But the language hasn't.'

'The reason for my speaking it has.'

Lucien laughed. 'Take heart, my friend, you have the best of both worlds. The Americans could be here any day now. We're liberated if they win – and, if not, you're in with the Germans and their accomplices. You can't have forgotten yesterday's success already?'

'How can you be so glib? You're tempting fate with the Germans.'

'Some of my best customers.'

'Lucien, I'm serious. Things are going to get more dangerous.'

'What's in the bag?'

Duchene passed it to him. 'Before someone notices.'

'Come on, who exchanges contraband in a public space? We would draw their attention if we slid off down an alley.' Lucien felt the heft of the bag. 'More than one bottle?'

'Three. And a carton of cigarettes. I was paid more than I expected. I thought you should benefit too.'

'You're a terrible businessman – you missed an opportunity to profit.'

'We should share the wealth we're given.'

'First the strike posters and now this. I didn't expect this morning would be filled with so much Bolshevik subversion.'

At the Gothic tower in the centre of the square, Lucien stopped and took a black notebook out of his pocket. Considering the effort he put into his appearance, his faded and dog-eared notebook was a curiosity. With the attention of a bookkeeper, he turned the pages to find his place. The small letters were handwritten with the utmost precision, and the pages were ruled in red ink; it was clearly a ledger, with columns for incomings and outgoings. He held the book away from Duchene's view and made a notation. With a theatrical flourish, he said, '*Cognac – three bottles – Received – M. Duchene*. What kind?'

'Hennessy. XO.'

Lucien raised an eyebrow and amended the entry. 'It's a generous payment. You need to be careful your place isn't robbed – those locks of yours aren't very secure.' He tucked the book back into the inside pocket of his jacket and picked up the bag. 'Just a thought.'

'Noted. Along with all the others.'

'Excellent. Well then, payment received and gratefully accepted. I'm off to Madame Lyon, the pâtissière I mentioned. I've been promised a croissant from that butter I delivered in the small hours of the morning. If you come, I'm sure we can get you one too, before the greedy Germans buy them all.'

Duchene nodded and followed Lucien through the streets, waiting for him as he stopped to offer his compliments and chat to shopkeepers, and sometimes flirt with them. How much of this was business or whim was unclear, but it was enough to keep Duchene's mind occupied while his memories of the bomb that hit the school were still fading. *Not unlike the mist.*

As expected, the patisserie on Rue de Castellane was crowded, mostly with Germans and those few Parisians who still had money. Lucien and Duchene huddled along a glass counter where the morning's baked goods glistened. By the time they made it to the front of the line, Madame Lyon was waiting with a wry smile as she patted her apron straight. 'Hello again, Lucien –'

'I have to admit it's not you I'm interested in at this moment, just how you can make me fat.'

'Do you blame the winemaker for turning you into a drunk?'

'That depends entirely on the quality of the wine. If it is good, like your croissants, then yes. You are culpable in every way, Madame Lyon. This is my friend, Monsieur Duchene.'

Duchene nodded back and smiled.

'You're the one who found the child.'

'He is.'

'It's nothing,' Duchene said.

'It's everything to his parents, and more than most would do.'

'Surely assisting the finest patisserie in Paris is noble work too,' said Lucien. 'Just think of the pleasure I have brought families by ensuring your supply of butter.'

'It's not the same. And you belabour your point – it's gauche. But, yes, Lucien, I have saved you two croissants.'

'Excellent.'

'And Monsieur Duchene, please take a blackberry tart as thanks.'

With a nod, he accepted the gift, then went outside to wait for Lucien, keen to move on from the attention of the queue.

They stopped at a bistro, where Lucien traded one of the croissants for café noir before thrusting the other into Duchene's hand. Lucien removed his hat and they stood outside against a narrow bar top that ran along the edge of the restaurant's window. The owner arrived and placed two small coffee cups before them. Duchene couldn't remember the last time he'd eaten a pastry, and he felt obscene; it was hard to enjoy the rich treat in such lean times.

'You're notable, now,' Lucien said as he chewed. 'People are talking and asking questions. But it won't last long. You should do a tour of all the shopkeepers this close to the Verniers – you'll make a killing.'

'That's just one of the many ways we're different.'

'You should consider it food for a week, and that is a long time in this war. Could be other advantages, if you wanted to seek them out. Madame Lyon is a widow, you know.' Lucien grinned, then suddenly his face fell.

Duchene saw a young woman walking towards them. It took him a second to recognise her. Since he'd last seen her, she'd cut her hair with a fringe. Her blouse and skirt were noticeably new, and she was taller in two-tone heels. He and Lucien were not alone in watching her as she approached them, but she was unconcerned by the attention – yet another thing that had changed.

'Lucien Martin . . . Dad.'

Lucien threw back what remained of his coffee and kissed her cheeks. 'Mam'selle Duchene. A pleasure. You must call me – I have some nylon stockings still in the packet, range of deniers.'

'I'll call you to arrange a visit. And I'll pick up a box of foreign cigarettes too, if you have any.'

'You smoke?' Duchene said.

'It was inevitable. Don't act so surprised. It's an expensive time to start, but there you have it.'

'Well,' said Lucien, 'don't let me impose on this happy reunion. Marienne. Auguste. Adieu.' Placing his hat back on his head, he scooped up his bag of cognac and strode off.

'A quick exit,' Marienne said.

'He doesn't like feeling uncomfortable.'

'Who does?'

They watched as Lucien paused briefly to tip his hat to three women. He alone seemed to enjoy the moment, smiling and sauntering, as they kept walking, their faces set with a grim focus on two Luftwaffe officers crossing the road ahead.

'It's been a long time,' Marienne said. 'Camille told you I visited?'

'Yes.'

'You didn't call?'

'It was late last night, and I left early this morning. I didn't want to disturb.'

'Well, you're here now. Come with me.'

Duchene followed her, half a step behind, as they went down the street. The morning traffic was dispersing with the urgency of the workday. He passed another council worker, under close observation by German soldiers, removing strike posters from the bollards of an old bombsite. Marienne seemed to barely notice it, while Duchene couldn't help but look.

She stopped at a bookstall, the vendor hovering nearby as she scanned the pile. Classics and newer works had been separated into groups, with many German editions strategically placed among them – not separate but integrated, an acknowledgement of the vision of a reconstructed France. Duchene wondered if the seller had a box hidden under the stall filled with American paperbacks, ready to adapt to the demands of the market.

Marienne picked up a translation of *A Portrait of the Artist as a Young Man* and flipped through the first few pages. 'I've finally read Joyce, by the way. *Ulysses*.'

'In English?'

'Of course.'

'And?'

'No. Too wordy. Too obscure.'

'How about Hemingway?'

'He's too literal, with too much machismo. He lacks abstraction.'

'I like his directness, stories told without embellishment. It's clear he thinks about each word.'

Marienne replaced the book and smiled at him. 'Listen to us. Critics who can't lift a pen, arguing about Americans and Irishmen.'

Duchene chuckled.

She gripped his fingers. 'I worry that you're not getting by.'

'I'm fine.'

'You're not teaching. You have no wage.'

'I help around the neighbourhood.'

'Still looking for children?'

'I am.'

'You know you're not responsible. For what happened. You don't have to do penance.'

'It's something I can do, to help. The parents come to me. How can I say no?'

'Do you find them all?'

'Some.'

'Better than none.' She placed a hand on his shoulder. 'I'm not telling you not to do it. Just be safe, and don't blame yourself.'

'I'll be fine. Honestly.'

A frown crossed her face, but she nodded.

'And you? You haven't gone back to *Le Figaro*?'

'Since they returned to Paris? No. I've outgrown their

politics. They may have stood up to German censorship, but their time in Vichy has changed their leaning.'

It wasn't news. He had kept an eye on the paper, scanning for her by-line. She was an excellent writer, especially for her age, but he stifled his disappointment nonetheless.

'I used to enjoy your articles.'

'And I writing them. But freelancing was hard work and I have the money. I'm fine. And besides, I don't want to be the kind of journalist who gets published in Paris, not right now. Anyway, let me at least get you something for lunch.'

'I have this,' he said, holding up the makeshift box from the patisserie.

'What is it?'

'A tart.'

'That's hardly a meal. You know Guillaume's?'

'I've never been.'

Duchene placed his arm in his daughter's as they resumed walking. He tried to enjoy the momentary peace between them, pushing his concerns to one side. This would be the third free meal he'd been given in the past twenty-four hours. Food paid for by others, offered to him as charity.

But the money isn't hers. The money is the blood of French innocents – of young men – of would-be liberators.

The chime above the door to Guillaume's was brief, its ring muffled by the many preserved meats that hung from the ceiling. These drooped so low and were so many in number that the shop had the atmosphere of a cave – they stifled the light, and the air was chilled to help with their preservation. But the smell of dried spices and herbs was enticing, and Duchene found himself regarding the hams and sausages as he speculated on which he might like to try.

The man he presumed to be Guillaume stood behind the counter serving a Generalleutnant who was delighting at the large selection of German-style sausages on offer. Once the meats were wrapped, however, his composure grew strict, and he stared grimly at Marienne and Duchene on his exit.

'This place is very popular with the Germans,' Marienne said as the Generalleutnant pulled the door closed behind him.

'I can see why,' Duchene said.

'Mademoiselle Duchene, welcome,' said Guillaume. He was tall and wiry, his grey hair slicked back from a bespectacled face. He was nothing like the cliché, being neither ruddy nor plump.

'How are you, Monsieur?' Marienne asked.

'I get by. As we all must.'

'We're here to help you do that.'

'You're most welcome to. How can I assist?'

'This is my father, Auguste, an aficionado of confit.'

'A man after my own heart ... Duck or goose?'

'Duck,' Duchene said.

'Anything else?' Guillaume asked.

Duchene retreated from the counter.

'No,' Marienne replied, surely sensing his discomfort. He was her father, not yet elderly but being bought for. Where had she inherited the behaviour of a modern woman? He'd always assumed she'd be a traditionalist, just to rebel against her mother.

'And for Mademoiselle?' Guillaume asked.

'Two saucisson, one sec and one garlic, five slices of chicken galantine, and a pâté – what is good?'

'I've been fortunate to get some apple brandy, and I can't

say where, but it did let me make up a terrine de campagne with thinly sliced apple, not diced.'

'That sounds wonderful – enough for five. And also, some kaiserfleisch and two leberwurst.'

Duchene glanced at her.

'Very good,' said Guillaume. 'Give me a moment.' After gathering the meats, he worked with the slicer. He placed pieces of the galantine onto waxed paper and, with the precision of a surgeon, removed a portion of the terrine from a larger, jellied block. The little finger on his right hand was missing, and Duchene found it hard to imagine any mishap given the skill with which he wielded a knife.

'You are very well stocked,' Duchene said to him.

'I am. I am fortunate that I have patrons who are willing to pay. The Germans love their pork even more than we do, and their pursuit of wurst lets me keep our citizens in terrines and saucisson. It's a sacrifice I'm willing to accept.'

'Paris is a place of pragmatism,' Marienne said.

'Unless you're a German or in the Resistance,' said Duchene.

'Well, that's no one here,' Marienne said, raising a conspiratorial eyebrow. 'Unless you're not telling us something, Guillaume?'

'Oh, I have many secrets, but that's not one of them,' he replied as he finished wrapping.

Marienne paid and said her farewells. They stepped out from the charcuterie into a light rain, and she looked up, letting the drops fall on her face.

'Leberwurst and kaiserfleisch?' Duchene asked as he pulled his collar up against the chill.

'Guillaume is the only charcutier this side of the Seine who sells it.'

'It's for him.'

'Me too. I quite like it.'

'Marienne, I'm worried for you.'

'So that's why you never visit?' she said, handing him the package of confit.

'I don't come because I have to be cautious.'

'Ah, so Max *is* the problem.'

'Of course.'

'But even before the Germans arrived, you didn't visit me.'

'I wouldn't say that.'

'Not properly. You hid away. You didn't have to deal with your loss alone. Your children.'

'They weren't my children.'

'That didn't make it any less tragic.'

The memories of the bombing started to return. He shook his head.

'This is not just a simple disagreement about your lover. You know the Americans are coming. It's not a good time to be living with a German.'

'Max has a plan. I trust him. If he leaves, I will go with him.'

'Really? He's twenty years old. In a war. What does he know?'

'His family will keep us safe. He's already been talking to them.'

Marienne was walking at a brisk pace. Duchene tried to keep up; he had no idea where she was going.

Looking for strudel, most likely.

'You're doing all this for a German?'

'Yes. I thought you at least would appreciate that I honour my commitments.'

'But why? It's dangerous out there. Are you even certain you truly love him?'

Marienne stopped and looked up at him, her eyes a sharp blue like her mother's, the curve of her brows dipping down. 'Listen to yourself. "It's dangerous out there." It's dangerous here. Where isn't it dangerous? What I know is that I trust him, and I enjoy his company, and it makes me sad to think I would never see him again. So yes, I love him.'

Duchene sighed.

'Meet him.'

'Pardon?'

'Come meet him tonight. I've invited Camille. You should come too.'

'To dinner?'

'I doubt you'll see what I see in him, but at least you might get some answers to your questions.'

'I –'

'Come. Promise me.'

After returning the Vernier baby, he was already compromised. What difference could one dinner with a German make?

'All right,' he said.

'Thank you, Papa.' She kissed his cheek. 'See you at seven.'

He watched her walk away through the rain, his mind running over their morning together. That's when it occurred to him.

She ordered food for five.

She had always intended to invite him and had known he couldn't refuse her. But he brought their number to four. There was another guest, someone she had avoided mentioning.

FIVE

A military band was playing in the square outside Saint-Jacques Tower. The conductor used his baton with sharp, confined movements, his eyes showing little joy. The general strike posters had been removed from the walls; all that remained were the ghostly outlines of flour paste. Duchene watched the men play.

Here to exorcise the spirit of the Resistance. Or to assert the city is still theirs to control.

On bollards around the square, council workers were plastering up official posters: in one, a helmeted German stared out over a blood-red sky as workers progressed towards factories. In French, the text read, *They give their blood – give your work to save Europe from Bolshevism.* The posters were a year out of date.

Duchene walked back to his apartment building and knocked on the door of his downstairs neighbours. Monsieur and Madame Junet were elderly and polite, and had more need of a pastry than him. He knocked again and called out their names. Nothing. It was a rare occasion that they went out, but it wasn't unheard of.

He went upstairs and tapped at Camille's door. No response either.

When he turned to place his key in his lock, he paused. The worn brass of the keyhole had been scratched, sharp and clean. Looking at the tip of his key, he considered the frequency with which he'd inserted and removed it.

He stood frozen for a moment. The corridor was too long to run and hope to turn before gunshot or mishap. His heart pounding, he unlocked the door and braced himself for whoever was on the other side.

As he pushed the door open, he saw Lucien sitting at the small dinner table, clutching an unlit cigarette. Two men sat opposite. It seemed that in crossing the room they had toppled several books, and some of these lay open, while others had their pages bent.

Duchene held up the box from the patisserie. 'Glad I have tart. Wouldn't want to come home to company empty-handed.'

Lucien half-smiled before remembering where he was. He lit his cigarette and leant forward. 'Auguste, I've been asked to make an introduction.'

'Close the door,' said one of the men. He was younger than Duchene, his black hair thinning around a widow's peak. His damaged ears and broken Roman nose suggested many years spent playing rugby. The scars were a contrast to the delicate silk scarf and woollen cardigan he wore, and his voice betrayed a city education despite his damaged features. 'Please sit down, Monsieur Duchene.'

'Of course. And you may be?'

'Philippe Angevine. And this is Armand.' He indicated the smaller man beside him.

Armand tipped his fedora, a size too big, which only accentuated his diminutive height.

'Please, take a seat,' Philippe said.

As Duchene sat at the table, the strangers shifted to

face him, and the pistol tucked into Armand's belt became clearly visible.

'Lucien has a lot to say about you,' Philippe said.

'He does?'

Lucien gave a tight smile and stared at the table, spinning his lighter between two fingers.

'Oh yes.' Philippe nodded. 'You are perhaps wondering who we are, Monsieur. Why we are here. Let us start with that.'

'Both good questions.'

'We would like *you* to answer them for us. Consider it a demonstration of your skills as an investigator.'

Duchene leant back in his chair, its creaking the only sound in the room. 'I don't perform tricks,' he said.

'No,' Philippe said. 'I don't imagine you do. Tricks are frivolous. But this is not a frivolous situation.'

'The stakes are high,' Armand said. 'Very high.'

Duchene looked at Lucien. 'This is absurd.'

'Auguste, please, just go along with it. This is important.' The movement would have been subtle, perhaps, under other circumstances, but here in this room, surrounded by these men, Duchene noticed that Lucien's cigarette hand was trembling.

Duchene stiffened in response. 'You're Resistance. You're an educated man, Parisian. That Sorbonne badge on your lapel says you were an academic before the university closed, well placed to lead a cell in the city. Armand has come from the country, a maquisard who fought in the Normandy hinterlands during the landings – his revolver is an Enfield No. 2 from a British airdrop. You're here because you want me to find someone, obviously, because this test is to demonstrate that I notice things others wouldn't. You know that families ask me to find their missing children. They've been doing this for almost a year now. As you're Resistance, I imagine the person you want me to find is not a child. Is that enough?'

Philippe's face lit up. 'Wonderful.'

'You speak German?' Armand asked, his eyes narrowed.

'Until last year I was a German and English teacher. I've spoken German since I was young. You can be loyal to France and speak other languages.'

'Yes, yes,' said Philippe. 'Don't take Armand to heart. He's just committed.'

'Clearly.'

'It's a valuable skill when finding people in a country occupied by Germans.' Philippe took out a packet of Gauloises, offered one to Duchene, then paused, waiting to see his reaction.

It wasn't their dedication, the desire to see France free of the Germans, that was Duchene's concern. Far from it. He shared their goal and was impressed, almost awestruck, by their ambition. It was the other side to that coin, the fanaticism, the unwavering belief in a simple answer – with us or against us – that caused his fear. The box of cognac sat on the floor under the table. He was glad he'd already placed the German cigarettes inside with the last two bottles and closed it; it was unlikely Philippe and his men would approve of where it had come from.

Duchene took the cigarette and held his face towards Philippe's lighter.

'You're quite correct,' Philippe said. 'I'm here to make use of your services.'

Duchene placed the pastry bag and the wrapped confit on the table, and tapped his cigarette into an old porcelain saucer he used for an ashtray. 'I'm not sure I can help.'

'Manners,' warned Armand.

'We need you to find someone,' Philippe said.

'Who?'

'For the specifics, we would need you to agree. And explain your hesitance.'

'Do I need to? You're Resistance. Associating with you is a death sentence if the Germans find out.'

'But aren't you doing that right now?' Philippe asked, indicating the four of them at the table.

'You broke into my home and are carrying guns.' Duchene looked straight at Lucien, who turned his palms upward.

It was easy enough for Duchene to imagine how his friend and the Resistance were connected. But he refused to speculate on what had led Lucien to bring them to his door; later, when they were alone, he would demand answers.

'I'm not sure if the Germans would see it that way,' said Philippe. 'Nuance does not interest the Gestapo.'

'You're probably right. But this is as far as it's gone, right now. I'm having a conversation that would mark me out as a political opponent. It's one occasion, in a private room. However, if I start walking around Paris in search of your missing person – well, I'm not sure how I can conceal that from the authorities and their informants.'

'True,' said Philippe. 'But, Monsieur, your thinking is flawed.'

'How's that?'

'You've assumed you have a choice.'

'You just told me you won't reveal who the missing person is until I agree to help you.'

Philippe held up his large hands to emphasise his point.

'Before the war, no one thought Parisians would need to be convinced to aid in overthrowing foreign fascists, but there you have it. When liberty falls, fraternity is quick to follow.'

'People are frightened. Afraid for their lives.'

'You'd be a fool not to be, but that's no reason not to act. The fear of death, well, that I can understand. But look at Armand, he's testament to the fact that if you are clever, you can survive.'

Armand grinned.

'So, what's your threat?' Duchene asked.

'I'm sorry?' said Philippe.

'You said I don't have a choice.'

'I don't have threats. Just an observation.'

'Feels like semantics.'

'Perhaps. But it helps me to get by.' Philippe used the tip of his cigarette to light a second, then stubbed it out in the saucer. 'You have a daughter, a traitor.'

And there it was. A numbness crept through Duchene, a lethargy and futility – he was useless to do anything of consequence, he had no threats to counter, was capable of no violence to bring this sham conversation to a decisive and bloody end.

From the moment his daughter had taken a German lover, consequences had awaited her. Duchene couldn't even summon the effort to blame himself. His paternal influence had been lost a long time ago, when her mother had left, and in that moment he'd felt a similar futility. He would always bear Marienne's blame for not having done more to change that part of their lives.

'Well, do you understand?' asked Armand.

'He does,' said Philippe. 'Let the man be. Let him think on this.'

'How can you truly fight for all of France if you're prepared to murder one of your own?'

Armand spat. 'Not one of ours. A traitor.'

Duchene snatched up the pastry bag. 'What about her, the woman who bakes for the Germans? What about the workers who sweep the streets? The police who maintain order? Are these our enemies too? Must Paris cease to function so its citizens can be spared your accusations?'

'But we're not talking about them,' said Philippe. 'We're talking about Marienne.'

'A whore,' spat Armand.

'Armand, please. Monsieur Duchene, your daughter is sleeping with the enemy. She may well be young and foolish, but there she is and here we are. We can't change history, as much as I wish every day that I could.'

'What would you have her do? Stab him to death in his bed?'

'One less German,' Armand said.

Philippe tilted his head. 'But that's not what we want. Can we move on?'

During their exchange, Lucien had made himself as small as possible – wrapping his arms around his waist, crossing his legs and pulling his feet under the chair. The cigarette in his mouth was unsmoked; it hung there as it burnt to ash. His head was turned from Duchene as much as possible without putting his back to him.

Duchene locked eyes with Armand and placed the box back to the table. He made a sharp gesture with his open hand. *Proceed.*

'We're looking for a priest. Father Bertrand Ramelle.

He's gone missing with the weapons he was hiding for us.'

'So, it's this cache of weapons you're after?'

'Ultimately. But the priest was a friend. We think he might have moved the guns and be in hiding somewhere.'

'From the Germans.'

'Who else would he hide from?' Armand asked.

Duchene felt it was best not to say.

'We'd like you to find him as quickly as you can,' said Philippe.

'By Wednesday, midday,' said Armand.

'That's less than forty-eight hours.'

'We didn't approach just anyone,' Philippe said. 'We came to you. You're the man who finds things.'

Duchene scowled. 'The man with a compromised daughter.'

There was something fragile about the outer shell of civility Philippe tried so hard to maintain. Duchene had seen it many times during the Great War – every part of a man spent until only that shell remained. They clung on to it with desperation, recognising at some level that it stood between them and barbarity.

Duchene broke the silence. 'When and where did you last speak to the priest?'

'Thursday, at his church,' said Armand.

'And you?' Duchene asked Philippe.

'Sunday before last. In the rectory below Saint-Lambert's.'

'So how did you become aware that he was missing?'

Philippe straightened his scarf. 'We went to collect the cache on Sunday afternoon. There were about a dozen parishioners, still gathered since that morning. Ramelle hadn't said Mass – they were concerned about him. So, we spoke to his maid, and she hadn't seen him in two days.'

'Why had the parishioners only just become concerned?'

'He shares his responsibilities with another priest. But on Sundays there are several Mass times, and he failed to show for the later service.'

'Did this other priest know about the cache?'

'No,' said Philippe. 'Only Ramelle. He is part of the Resistance.'

'You realise that when I look for him, I will ask questions of people, and they will begin to suspect something.'

'Tell them you're a concerned citizen. You're looking for the priest on behalf of the parishioners.'

'Any parishioners who can vouch for this?'

'I'm sure we can find some,' said Armand.

'Describe for me this cache. How large, and what was it packed into? How many men does it take to move it?'

'Six crates,' said Armand. 'Rough wood. It would take two men to move a single crate without dragging it.'

'And in them?'

Armand paused.

'He's needs to know if he's going to find them,' Philippe replied.

'One crate of Bren machine guns, three crates of Lee-Enfield rifles, a crate of grenades, and one of Webley pistols.'

'British weapons. These were from an airdrop?'

'Yes. They were costly to retrieve. Lives lost – good French lives.'

'How did you get them into the city?'

Armand glanced at Lucien.

'Of course,' said Duchene. 'That much should have been obvious. So, from what you are saying, if this priest,

Ramelle, moved the crates and went into hiding with them, he probably had help. Or could he alone have dragged them? I'm assuming you went to where he hid the weapons. Were there drag marks?'

'No,' said Armand.

'So, he must have had help, or …'

'Or what?'

'He's dead, and someone else has your weapons.'

'Then find out,' said Philippe. 'If the Germans have them, we need to know where they've been taken.'

'So you can get them back?'

'They're needed,' Armand said.

Philippe held Duchene's gaze. 'And you have forty-eight hours to find them.'

SIX

The shadow from the church steeple fell across the street. Its spire, like a finger, pointed at Armand. To Duchene it seemed an accusation.

Implicated in the abduction or death of a priest.

There was a possibility that Father Ramelle had fled, but it made little sense that he would take the weapons with him.

What does a priest want with guns?

The Church of Saint-Lambert de Vaugirard had made its opinion known, and Duchene was inclined to agree. With its heavy sandstone bricks, imposing tower and narrow arched windows, it asserted its authority. Unlike many Parisian churches, this one had not been neglected. The time on the steeple's clock face was accurate, the paving stones behind its wrought-iron fence swept and maintained.

Armand was standing on the other side of the road, smoking a cigarette. After their meeting, he had loitered outside Duchene's apartment block until he and Lucien emerged, then followed them through the city. The purpose of his joining them was unclear to Duchene – he had already threatened Marienne – but it seemed Armand wasn't taking any chances. Perhaps he feared Duchene might take Marienne and leave the city.

He smiled to himself; he had a better chance of finding the priest than forcing Marienne to leave.

Turning to Lucien, he asked, 'How long have you worked for them?'

'I don't. For the past two years, we've had a deal – I help them, they turn a blind eye when I sell to Germans.'

'And you had to bring them to me?'

'Auguste, please believe me, I didn't get you involved in this. They know you find missing children. It was only a matter of time before they required your services.'

'A service is freely given.'

Lucien rubbed the back of his neck. 'I'll do everything I can to warn you from now on, I promise. But I couldn't say no to them.'

'Did they pay you?'

'Do they look like men who pay? You're not the only one in a precarious position.'

'All right. Show me where you put the guns.'

Duchene started up the stairs to the heavy wooden door under the arched entrance, but Lucien held back. 'So, you believe me, yes?'

Does it matter?

'Auguste?'

'It's fine, Lucien. I know you're compromised.'

The whole of Paris is compromised.

The inside of the church had the same imposing architecture as the exterior. Columns of dark stone rose up to meet a vaulted ceiling and above the entrance door a dark wooden organ looked down at the pews.

In the reverent stillness Duchene was taken back to his childhood, when he'd shared this faith and marvelled that Jesus was present in the thin wafers he ate. Such a ridiculous fiction to him now, but so alive and present when he was young. He recalled the last time he'd taken Communion, and betrayed both God and himself. He had lost his belief long before then, but in that trench in Verdun, when it seemed that hell was all around him, he took the army chaplain up on his offer as he made his way down the line of mud-encrusted men. Two shells later and most of those men were dead, blown to pieces or suffocated under the earth that had once protected them.

Lucien whistled at Duchene from the far side of the church. 'This way.'

He followed as Lucien led them around the side of the altar and into the sacristy. Here a walk-in closet contained robes and vestments while a locked cupboard probably housed other articles of worship. The smell of incense lingered in the air from a metal censer that hung from a hook in the wall. Duchene touched it. Still warm. 'Mass just done?'

'At midday. Come.'

A narrow spiral staircase led down into the priest's office and the rectory. These stood on the ground floor, suggesting the foundations of the church proper had been raised and incorporated into the natural rise of a hill.

'Madame Noirot, are you about?' Lucien called.

Duchene scanned the office while they waited. On a heavy oak desk were stacked neat piles of paper: christening forms, service guides, a few funeral memorial papers. In the corner of the room was the lithograph that had likely been used to produce them. Behind the desk stood a large glass-doored cabinet with alphabetically arranged books and texts on its shelves, while at its base were religious artefacts and a comprehensive selection of whiskies.

'Hello?' said a faltering voice from beyond the office.

'Madame Noirot, we are here to help find Father Ramelle,' said Lucien with a reassuring smile.

The woman who emerged was only a few years older than Duchene. She was tiny, a little hunched, and seemed to be shivering in the cool of the room. She looked up at Lucien. 'You're here to find him?'

'Well, to be precise,' Lucien said, still beaming, 'this man is.'

Duchene approached her, his arm outstretched. 'My name is Auguste.'

'Anne-Marie,' she said, shaking his hand. Her grip was firmer than he'd expected, but she released him suddenly at the sound of footsteps on the stairs.

He turned to see Armand in the doorway, his hat still on, cigarette smoke lingering around him.

'And you know Armand, of course,' said Lucien, his smile evaporating.

Madame Noirot nodded in silence.

'Take us to the cellar,' Armand said, his eyes locked on Duchene.

The housekeeper nodded again and slid a ring of keys from her pocket. She walked to the other side of the desk, unlocked one of the drawers and reached her hands inside. Their movements produced a soft *click*, and she withdrew a large, worn-down iron key. The bit at the end of its shaft was simple and rectangular.

She led the men into a corridor that seemed to connect a series of living spaces. The smell of a wood fire drifted towards them, and the occasional crackle could be heard from a room beyond. Halfway down the corridor, she made a sharp turn and opened a small door that could have easily been mistaken for that of a closet. This led onto another spiral staircase, far less maintained than the one descending from the sacristy to the office. A musty smell and damp chill rose up from the darkness.

The housekeeper's hand moved to a light switch and revealed a basement below.

Duchene followed her down the stairs into the dank chamber. It seemed older than the rest of the church, its stone a rougher cut, a darker hue. Along one wall, wine racks were falling into disrepair. He observed Lucien's growing disappointment as he scanned the empty bottles; no forgotten vintage awaited discovery.

Along another wall were piled offcuts of wood and marble. Madame Noirot guided the men towards a series of planks. She started to move these, stacking them to one side. Lucien and Duchene joined her, while Armand watched in silence. Eventually they uncovered another door, three-quarters the size of a standard door and covered in iron bands. These and its heavy hinges were fixed into place with large hand-crafted nails.

Duchene whispered to Madame Noirot, 'What is this?'

'A door. That much would surely be obvious.'

'Madame, I mean the rooms down here.'

'I know your meaning.' She smiled briefly. 'This is from the original church. Fifteenth century.' She removed the hefty iron key from her pocket and placed it into the lock, where it turned only after some force was applied and opened into pitch-blackness. 'The crypt,' she announced to Duchene. She felt around just inside the door until she drew back with an old lantern. Assisted by Lucien, she lit it, and Duchene and Armand followed them in.

The chill of the crypt came as no surprise; what amazed

Duchene was its size. The vaulted ceiling was twice the height of the previous room, made all the more impressive by the dark pillars that supported it. Along either wall were the straight lines of unadorned stone sepulchres, behind which deep tombs had been cut into the rock in stacks. Most of these had been sealed, capstones adorned with Gothic script detailing their occupants. Some had been broken, and the shapes of bones and rags could be made out as the lantern cast its dim glow around the chamber.

'Come,' said Armand. 'This is where they were kept.' He pulled an electric torch from his pocket and gestured Duchene away from Madame Noirot and Lucien towards an open tomb. It was narrow but just wide and high enough to fit an ammunition crate.

'This is where they were stored,' said Duchene, 'with the capstones closed?'

'Yes,' said Armand. 'These three tombs along this wall, three on the wall opposite.'

As Duchene's eyes had adjusted to the gloom, he'd begun to appreciate that there were shades of darkness. He could see the six empty tombs, black squares cut into black, narrow but deep – the perfect size and shape for a body to be interred or an ammunition crate to be hidden. The capstones had been pulled off the tombs and lay on the ground. 'This happened recently,' he said to Armand. 'You resealed them when you first placed the guns inside?'

'We did.'

'And the bodies?'

'You're not looking for them. You're after the priest.'

Duchene remained silent and stared at Armand.

'I'm not a heathen. We reinterred them with the priest's

help, and he gave them a blessing. They're over there.' Armand nodded ahead to the left.

'Did you mark these tombs?'

'No. We memorised their names.'

'Who memorised them?'

'Father Ramelle, Philippe, me. No one else knew about the cache.'

Duchene lowered his voice. 'Madame Noirot?'

'No. The first time we brought her down here was after the priest disappeared.'

'What have you told her since?'

'Only that he was keeping something here for us. We needed her to let us in with the key – we didn't know where the priest hid it.'

Madame Noirot was still standing in the centre of the crypt, watching them closely.

Duchene moved to the open tombs on the other side of the chamber. This row was set a little higher from the ground, and the capstones were completely shattered. He waved a hand for Armand's torch and shone it into each hollow. The first two contained only dust, stone and the scraps of ancient shrouds. But at the back of the third, a box was pushed deep. 'There's something here.'

'It's nothing,' Armand said. 'Trust me.'

Duchene leant into the tomb, reaching as far as he could. As he pressed his head to the cold stone, he extended his arm and shoulder, his fingertips gripping the edge of the heavy box. With slow movements, he finally managed to get it close enough to tug out.

It was an old leather document box. Pulling open the lid, Duchene found it full of flyers printed on a lithograph. There were at least twenty variations, each detailing the injustices of the occupation and calling for acts of resistance. The oldest flyer was dated November 1940, five months after the occupation; the most recent had been printed a month ago.

'See, nothing of use to you,' Armand said.

Duchene closed the box and carefully returned it to the tomb. 'Ramelle wrote these?'

Armand nodded. 'It's how Philippe found him. He wanted to meet the man who wrote so passionately against the Germans, or so the story goes. I wasn't there when they first met.'

Getting to his feet, Duchene dusted his hands against his trousers. 'Let's go outside.'

Armand stepped towards him. 'Why?'

'I want to look at something.'

The grey haze that had covered Paris was lifting, just in time for the last rays of the sun to enter the city. The sunset cast an amber glow over the apartment houses that lined the narrow Rue Blomet. This same light passed through the trees behind the church and fell on Duchene, Armand and Lucien as they smoked Lucien's American cigarettes. Madame Noirot accepted one but tucked it behind her ear.

Duchene exhaled smoke as he gestured across the small church garden with the tip of his Lucky Strike. 'Where did you deliver the crates?'

Lucien scanned the ground to get his bearings. 'We parked just on the street. Armand and I moved them into the bushes, there, while Philippe kept watch. Once we had them concealed, we moved them again, back through those doors we just came through.'

'And it took two men to move each crate?'

'Philippe moved the last one by himself – he could see a patrol at the end of the street. But only a short distance from the garden into the church. It's a two-man job.'

'And the only other way into the church is through the front doors?'

'Yes,' Armand said.

'Madame?' Duchene asked.

She had maintained her benign expression since leaving the crypt. 'Correct,' she said in a measured voice. Duchene looked at Armand and Lucien, but they were preoccupied with a critique of their American tobacco.

He glanced at his watch: just past six. 'Gentlemen, Madame, I must go.'

Armand frowned. 'Wait. Do you know where to go next, to find the priest?'

'No.'

'You've only spoken to the old woman. What about the parishioners? You need other names.'

'Who's to say they'd know anything?'

'I have no idea. That's not my job.'

Walking towards him, Duchene lowered his voice. 'Neither do I. Yet. But I have a few theories I'd like to test. Nothing that can be done with you present.'

'What do you mean?'

Duchene cast his eyes around; the trees were good cover for their little meeting, but not so much that he'd like to prolong it. 'I will ask just before curfew when people are in their homes. And later when you aren't around.' Armand moved to speak, but Duchene cut him off. 'A member of the Resistance will raise suspicions, make people afraid to speak. Surely that must be obvious to you? They don't want the Gestapo visiting, don't want to be branded as political adversaries. Each time you assassinate a German officer or roll a grenade into a group of soldiers, the reprisals become worse.'

'Reprisals are worth the price of resistance. Surely even you can see that.'

'Let's try not to cause any before I find your weapons, all right?'

Armand shrugged for a reply – agreement, non-committal, unconcerned by the death he left in his wake – none of it made Duchene feel comfortable.

SEVEN

As the apartment door opened, the fragrance of roasting meat and the sound of good-natured conversation greeted Duchene. He had expected admonishments from Marienne – he was fifteen minutes late – but she smiled and kissed his cheeks.

One glance at her told him he was underdressed. She wore a blue evening dress with large accordion pleats and embroidered straps; it was new and, Duchene assumed, the latest fashion. Her dark lipstick accentuated her fair skin, which had never had a summer hue, even in childhood.

'I'm glad you're here,' she said, taking his coat.

Duchene opened his valise and brought out a bottle of cognac. He gave it to her as she guided him down the short corridor to the open-plan living and dining room. While her back was turned, he slipped a novel from his bag: Alain-Fournier's *Le Grand Meaulnes*. He quickly scanned her shelves for its spine; if it was already there, he'd brought something by Raymond Chandler. Satisfied that she didn't have it, he placed it on the shelf in the corridor for her to discover – a recommendation, a secret, a surprise, a kindness.

She glanced back at him, and he nodded to her as he passed through the sliding doors towards the three people gathered around the dinner table. Their laughter quieted as he approached, and a young Luftwaffe officer leapt to his feet. He was tall with a tight blond haircut and the trimmed pencil moustache of an airman. 'Good evening, Monsieur Duchene, I'm Maximilian, Max,' he said in raw French and thrust a hand at Duchene. His grip was firm but moist. *He's nervous*.

Another German, dressed in an elaborate tunic complete with ornamental braids and piping, sat beside Camille. Duchene didn't recognise the uniform: army but not infantry. A medical officer, perhaps? Regardless, it was clear he was very senior and, from the Honour Cross on his lapel, had served in the Great War.

All this finery magnified Duchene's sense of inadequacy – he was wearing his best suit, but it was worn around the cuffs and frayed at the pockets. If he'd been given a sense of the formality of the evening, he could have arranged something better through Lucien.

'Monsieur Duchene,' the senior officer said, remaining seated as he gestured towards Duchene. 'Come and join me at the far end of the table, where it would seem we elders have been relegated.' His French was impeccable. Unlike Max, he glided through his sentences without hesitation. His German accent was so slight, he could have easily passed for Swiss.

'This is Major Faber,' Marienne said.

'Thomas, please,' said Faber as he poured wine into Duchene's empty glass.

'Auguste,' Duchene replied, sitting beside him.

'Best to keep us old military men together.'

'Marienne was just telling the major how you served in the last war,' Camille said.

'It feels like a lifetime ago.'

'Doesn't it,' said Faber. 'Which is a blessing. There's much from that time I'd rather forget. What rank?'

'Sergeant.'

'An enlisted man. Very good. And promoted to a leader.'

'Not really, just the last man left who could do the job.'

'Yes, a terrible war. I won't disagree with you there.'

Duchene couldn't imagine the distinction between a terrible war and some other kind. Perhaps Faber was referring to being on the wrong side.

'But you are both here now,' Max said. 'Ready to enjoy this fine meal of both German and French food. It's the way of the future.'

Although Faber smiled, Duchene could see his eyes had hardened. He raised his wineglass. 'Now that we are all here, a toast perhaps? To the meal that Mademoiselle Duchene has spent so much time preparing. A beauty, an intellectual, a wonderful cook. To your health!'

Glasses chimed. Marienne swept back into the kitchen.

Duchene found himself assessing Faber. Although they were about the same age, nearing fifty, Duchene was very aware that to the casual observer, he would have appeared the older of the two. The major was a testament to the Teutonic emphasis on robust living and physical health. His blond hair was slicked back from a receding hairline freckled from days spent in the sun. His hooked nose was unmarred by drinking, and his strong frame was still firm and without a spilling gut.

None of this was made any easier by Duchene's growing sense that Faber was the focus of everyone's attention, the motivator of their desire to be both erudite and entertaining.

'I hear you speak excellent German,' Faber said to Duchene as Max struggled to describe to Camille the summer house his family owned.

Perhaps Faber was looking for a compliment on his French. 'I do my best,' Duchene replied.

'Anything else?'

'English.'

'Ah yes, I've caught that affliction too. Although, very useful in this war. I do enjoy being back here in Paris and speaking the language, walking the streets. I was disappointed by what you did with the Louvre, but I dare say the Führer would have shipped it all back to Berlin. Probably better that your government had it removed. That's sedition, I know, but there you have it. I'd like this city to remain as it is. Too beautiful to bomb. Too much history and culture to let it burn. You must at least give us that.'

'I can do that. You didn't bomb us.'

'No. But the English … Well, that can't be said for them. I heard about your school. So much for your allies, eh?'

Duchene carefully set his wineglass back on the table.

'You don't like my directness?' Faber asked.

I don't like anything about you.

'It's not something I like to discuss.'

'I apologise. I forget how important decorum is in Paris. Max warned me. As you've already seen, he says far too much. How are you with Latin? As a linguist, I take it you share a passion for the classical world?'

'A little. I'm a modernist, really.'

'Oh, dear. That won't do. You've read Ovid?'

'None.'

'Homer?'

'No.'

'This is a major setback. I'd hoped we would find a kinship there.' Faber held out his left hand. He wore a ring with a small cameo; on a lapis-blue background was the ivory profile of a Roman centurion. 'I bought this here, when I visited with the delegation in thirty-seven. A street vendor was selling a pair of them. I had to have them both. In Rome, a man needed to fight before he could vote, before he could assume a role in determining the future of his civilisation. There's an honest simplicity to that, don't you think? You must sacrifice something of yourself for the state before determining its future. That's the problem with Jewish Bolshevism – every man is equal, regardless of service or status. But how can we be? You must earn your right to participate, because to be given it for nothing makes it worthless.'

Faber was testing him, that much was clear. Duchene paused while he considered his response. 'I don't think I understand the world any more now than I did before I fought in a war. If anything, it makes less sense.'

'Ha!' Faber clapped him on the back. 'Well, that's the challenge of having lived and travelled. The more you see, the more you realise how little you know. But the essence of men, this never changes. Is this uncertainty why you left the army? A sergeant's salary would have been difficult to turn away from.'

'I didn't have the passion for it.'

'So you turned to teaching . . . I suppose it's an admirable profession?'

Marienne came back to the room holding a large roast ready to be carved. Beside this she placed a kaiserfleisch tartiflette and mushroom tournedos. She held out the handle of a carving knife to the older German. 'Major Faber, would you like to do the honours?'

'Oh, I couldn't. Monsieur Duchene should do it. He is the guest of honour, after all.'

He was? To what end? Perhaps it was no accident that Lucien had brought him to the Rue de Castellane that morning.

'Come now,' Faber said, taking the knife from Marienne and passing it to him, 'you're among friends. We won't judge your skill.'

Among friends . . . He felt conspicuous. Complicit. Held captive by Faber's social decorum.

Duchene did his best to bring a casual smile to his face. There were a great many Germans in the city, whom he had learnt to tolerate while he kept his head down and survived. Now he found himself considering if he should actively offend one. He had the knife in his hand and a German officer a few inches away.

Duchene carved the roast, and Faber beamed from ear to ear. Once everyone had been served, Duchene took his seat.

'You say a Frenchman produced this kaiserfleisch?' Max asked as he raised more tartiflette to his mouth.

'From Guillaume's,' replied Marienne.

'Amazing.'

'A master charcutier,' Camille said. 'Accepts only a few apprentices on the agreement they'll never work anywhere else in Paris once they learn the secrets to his technique.'

'The skill of the French as cooks was never in doubt,' said Faber.

'Or as romantics,' Max said in German, taking Marienne

by the hand. 'Which brings me to an announcement.'

Duchene's stomach clenched.

'Marienne and I are engaged. Monsieur Duchene, you must forgive me for not asking your permission first. I had meant to do so at the start of the evening, before everyone had arrived. But it seems that the moment is now. I wanted the major here too – as close to family as I have in this foreign land.'

'I understood only a little of that,' Camille said in French. 'Is this word *verlobt* what I think it is?'

'Yes,' said Marienne. 'We're engaged.'

'Congratulations,' Camille said as she hugged Marienne and kissed her cheek.

'Yes, wonderful news,' Faber said, standing to reach for Max's hand before kissing Marienne. 'Takes me back to when I first proposed to my wife.'

Duchene gripped the sides of the table as he pulled himself up. His mind was numb with disappointment. Disappointment with France, that it could let itself be taken by enemies who would ingratiate themselves with his daughter. Disappointment with Marienne, that she had fallen – not so much for a German, but for a man who was so far from her equal, this grinning imbecile in a uniform. But most of all, disappointment with himself, that he hadn't done more to guide Marienne, to fight for a larger role in her life. If he had done that, she might have confided in him about Max's plans, and he could have counselled her otherwise.

'A toast, then you must tell us how you met,' Faber said.

'I'll fill our glasses,' Camille said, and distributed them from the sideboard. As she poured the Hennessy, she looked at Duchene, a subtle narrowing of her eyes. In less than a second, she had turned away and was filling Faber's glass.

Their glasses charged, Faber gestured towards Duchene. 'Please. I spoke at my daughter's engagement and her wedding, and whenever my wife would let me. Please, from the father of the bride-to-be.'

Duchene felt as if he was looking at the smiling faces from a great distance rather than mere centimetres. Marienne was watching him with a slight frown, her hand gripping her glass too tightly. There was a pinching below his eyes as he forced his lips into a smile. 'A happy day. To my remarkable daughter and this young man whom I hope to one day know better. Cheers!'

'Prost!' shouted Max before downing the cognac.

'A remarkable find in a city of scarcity,' Faber said, examining the amber liquid.

'It was a gift,' said Duchene.

'Recently?'

Duchene stared at Faber. He refused to let an expression pass across his face.

'No need to fear. I've heard about your good deeds, about how you assisted the Verniers. An impressive feat, finding a child in the midst of a war. My congratulations to you.' Faber held up his glass to Duchene.

'It comes as no surprise to anyone here that we Germans haven't had the warmest welcome in Paris,' Max announced to the room in German. 'I understand. I would feel the same if France had come to Germany. I think of Napoleon marching into Berlin, when he paid his respects to Frederick the Great. We should act with honour, even in war.'

'We don't need to get into that now, Max,' said Faber. 'Tell us the story of how you met – and in that terrible

French of yours, so Madame here can appreciate it.' He nodded in the direction of Camille.

'This is part of the story,' Max said, switching to French. 'I come to Paris, and I am ignored. A woman loses the umbrella from her hand. I chase it down the street. Bring it back. I am ignored. I ask for directions. Parisians don't know where anything is. I ask again, more slowly. They shrug. Perhaps they have forgotten their French too?'

Marienne laughed.

Max continued, 'I can see what is happening. I am not alone. The Luftwaffe all agree. But one day, I am in the Métro, and we are boarding the train. I drop a parcel in the rush. I think it will be crushed. But it is lifted from the ground and passed to me. A woman says in German, "Is this yours?" Not any woman. A beautiful woman with a smile and fire in her eyes – my angel of the Métro. Everyone is looking at us. I say back to her in French, "Thank you." And then in German, "Let me buy you a coffee. Let me return the favour." She doesn't say yes. She says, "Of course," as though it the most natural thing to do. She is brave, and she is, as Monsieur here says, "remarkable".'

Marienne beamed and placed both hands on Max's face as she drew him forward to kiss her. Duchene looked down at the table.

'I'm happy to be called "remarkable", but I am tired from cooking for all of you.' Marienne smiled. 'Enough of your stories. Go and get the tart,' she said playfully, pushing Max out of his chair.

'Of course,' he said as he left the room.

Almost immediately, Marienne leant close to Camille and started to talk to her. They laughed and whispered, and Duchene turned his head so that he didn't hear anything he might otherwise regret. This brought him back to face Faber, who was picking the cognac up from the table and pouring them both another round.

'Of course, it's an awful idea,' he said in hushed tones to Duchene.

'It is?'

'Come now. Don't pretend you don't know it too. What is to happen here? What is their next step to be? We're at war. He'll be recalled soon. She'll be without his protection. Or worse, the Americans will get here, and we'll have no choice but to shell the city to drive them out. He's Wehrmacht – if he's recalled, she won't get to go with him. That's just the way it is.'

Another moment of frankness. Duchene was unsure if Faber was trying to test him or draw him into a compromise.

'On that we agree.' Duchene took a slow sip from the glass. The cognac no longer caused him to wince. He wondered how much he'd drunk in the past two days. 'She says he has a powerful family?'

'Max? Yes. If we weren't at war, they could probably do what they want. His father is an old friend, a captain of industry. But while we're at war, it's the captains, majors and generals who make the decisions. And right now, it's everyone reporting for duty – no excuses. Bolshevik dogs harassing us in the east. Americans fucking with us in the west.'

Duchene remained silent.

'Oh, you think we're not in this together? How are you not "one of us", Monsieur Duchene? I'm not sure if you've noticed, but our countries are no longer enemies. You yourself recently saved the child of German supporters. Yesterday, you drove around the countryside with papers signed by none other than von Choltitz's personal secretary. You're very squarely and firmly rooted in soil owned by Germans, metaphorically and physically.'

'I did that for the child.'

'Seems a long way to go for a stranger's child. To take such risks for – what do your insurgents call them? Collaborators.'

'I did it for the child. Not for the parents. Not for collaborators.'

'Rubbish. You did it for yourself. For your own advantage.'

Duchene picked up his drink and sipped; he could feel his resentment growing. There was little point in arguing his defence, but this did not lessen the insult. 'I'm uncertain what you want from me, Major Faber.'

'Well, there's some truth to that. I do want something from you. But I'm afraid I'm not asking you to do it.'

'And if I don't?'

Faber glanced at Marienne. 'As you say. A remarkable woman.'

Duchene sipped the liquor. Let the heat of it push back his anger. 'Go on.'

'Oh, now, Monsieur, I must say that for the first time tonight you have surprised me. I was certain you would protest. A father's indignation, his protective instincts … but this. Cold and without passion. Impressive.'

Hardly. But I've heard it all before. Four hours ago.

'What is it that you are going to tell me to do?'

'To find someone, of course. This is what you do, no?'

'That would seem to be the case.'

'I need you to find a missing soldier. Lieutenant Christian Kloke, 2nd Panzer Division.'

'Desertion?'

'I think not. He was one of my best field commanders. He enjoyed the job. And there's no sign of assassination – no body to be found. Which surely is the point of an insurgent attack, to demonstrate non-compliance through violence. It makes very little sense.'

'Does he have a hotel room, an apartment? Has someone checked his belongings?'

'They have. But perhaps you should look for yourself. He kept a room in Montmartre. Nothing has been touched. He didn't report in yesterday, and no one has seen him since Friday night.'

'Might I ask you something?'

'Of course.'

'Why me? Why not your military police? The French police?'

'You joke. French police? I should hand this to the Feldjägerkorps, our chained dogs. But they are under orders to shoot deserters. And I'd rather Kloke was not executed, even if he is a coward. Like Max, I'm a friend to his parents. And like Max's parents, they're influential. It wouldn't look good if their son was executed while I was in the same city. I'd prefer to keep it all off the record, for you to find him and for me to convince him to return to battle. Germans should be killing the enemy, not one another. But that isn't the biggest problem with the military police.'

'And that is?'

'Whatever Kloke's reason for disappearing, German soldiers are going to struggle to find him quickly. You heard Max, your city is not open to us. But to a Frenchman who excels in finding the missing, someone who's not hated by the locals … It makes perfect sense.'

'Is that why you came here tonight?'

Faber shrugged. 'A home-cooked meal, the company of beautiful women … there are many incentives. But yes, to drag myself away from the company of Germans to sit in the house of a French whore, I'd need to have a very specific goal – you.'

Duchene was clutching the glass so tightly that his hand ached.

Faber unbuttoned the front of his tunic and reached into his breast pocket. He handed Duchene a folded piece of paper. 'You are now authorised to be out after curfew. Find Kloke, and be quick about it. You have –'

'– two days.'

'Yes. Exactly. I'm glad you sense the urgency. Anything else you need to know before you begin?'

'No,' Duchene replied.

'Good.'

Faber's expression changed in an instant from the blank certainty of a killer to the smile of a long-term host, just as Max emerged from the kitchen with a tarte tatin in his hands. Plum. That hanged farmer, the stench of his death, had followed Duchene to the city.

EIGHT

Duchene's mind raced. Faber's threats had revived him. He stood and poured more cognac to go with the dessert. He could do little more than prod at the tarte.

Faber excused himself as soon as he'd finished eating. To Duchene's surprise, Max left with the senior officer, to return to their hotel headquarters.

Camille waited just long enough for the Germans to have cleared the building before making her farewells. 'My darling, such a wonderful dinner. And this news of your engagement! I am so happy for you.' As she kissed Marienne on both cheeks, she looked pointedly at Duchene. He nodded back and kissed Camille farewell. 'Curfew is soon,' she said.

'I know. I'll be back soon.'

With Camille's departure, the mood in the apartment changed. As if on cue, the lights started to flicker. Marienne was no longer smiling, no longer wrapped in the warmth of her own hospitality – that bonhomie she had worked so hard to bring into her apartment. She was without expression, like the dark before the storm, so much like her mother whom she surely did not recall being this way; she had been too young. It was uncanny and filled Duchene with dread. Was she about to leave him too?

'The lights will go out soon,' she said as she lifted a burnished candelabra from the sideboard and began lighting the candles.

'I did try, Marienne.'

'Really? I'm not sure what I was thinking by inviting you. I wasn't expecting your blessing, but it was important to me for you to be here.'

'You know that I love you.'

'In your way. But it's not the love I need.'

He paused, confused.

A candle was refusing to take, and the flame of the match crept closer to her fingers. 'What happened to the love of a father to a daughter, no matter what comes?'

'He's a German soldier. With any luck, they will lose this war. They're already coming undone. What happens then? What life will you have? Or do you want them to win so you can live in wealth in Germany?'

She shook out the match and lit a new one. Moving around the last of the candles allowed her to keep her eyes from his, to speak words he suspected were difficult for her. 'After all this time and you still can't see it? It's not just Max's and my decision, a decision for which I don't need your support. I was just trying to be civilised. But I could have used your support, your love when she left.'

'This is about your mother?'

She looked at him with clinical distance. 'Where were you then?'

'With you. Right here in Paris.'

'No. You were still with her. Hoping she'd return. You could think of nothing else.'

'Marienne ... that's not true. I fretted for you every day. We had to make a life on our own. I spent so many nights thinking of how we might survive. You know, about the sacrifices. What it took.'

'But the one thing you couldn't sacrifice was her memory. You told me she'd return. You told me she still loved us. You told me she was doing a wonderful thing to help other people.'

'That's what she believed.'

Marienne lifted the match to her lips and blew it out. 'And did you?'

He watched as she positioned the candelabra in the middle of the table. 'I wanted to.'

'You really didn't think she was running away from us?'

'"Passionate" is a word we use too frequently. People think it's glamorous, that it's desirable. But there's madness to it too. She truly believed that she needed to go to Spain, that she had to fight the fascists. There was nothing I could do to convince her otherwise. Was I to lock her up? Tell her not to be the person she was deep down inside?'

'She could have done all that from France. There were communists raising money for the International Brigades.'

'Not really. Not truly. Not the way she saw it. She feared that the world would be ruled by dictators. Can we say she wasn't wrong, with the benefit of hindsight? Spain was the beginning, and she saw it. She wanted a better world for people to live in –'

'Rhetoric.'

'No. Truth.'

'If that is really true, then it makes it much worse.'

He blinked. Could Marienne think this little of her mother? Or could it be that she was right? Perhaps he had built the story like a wall, concealing the facts, obscuring his objectivity?

'I don't understand.'

'You were her husband. I was her daughter. She should have wanted a better world for us. First. Before all others.'

Duchene sighed. 'Yes. I would have liked that too.'

As he said this, as if it had been planned, the lights died. With only candles, the room seemed to grow smaller. The glow of the flames lit Marienne's face and pushed away the shadow of her frown, the rings under her tired eyes.

'Can we sit?' he said, indicating the chairs around the dining table. He led the way and sat down.

Marienne's face didn't soften, the furrow on her brow remained, but she did sit opposite him. He navigated a hand past the glasses and candelabra to lift up the cognac. She refused his offer of another drink. He poured a generous measure into his own glass.

'You're right. I shouldn't have tried to keep things from you. About her, about the reasons for her leaving. But I was trying to protect you. The time I had with her was short, and I spent most of it worried that I didn't deserve her. To live a life through her eyes … it was glorious. I spent so much time afraid I wouldn't live up to her expectations, I think I started to convince her of that truth. Maybe I didn't offer her a good enough reason to stay. Or maybe it was always going to be this way – she was younger than me, she had only ever lived in Paris. She was bound to discover ideas and places outside of her experience that would draw her to them. I wanted stability. She wanted to be excited.'

'And me? What about me, her child?'

'Marienne, she loved you very much. You were still small, and she thought she'd be back. She really, truly did. Things changed, her life changed. For a time, I thought she must be dead or captured. She fought at Ebro – it was a bloodbath.'

'But she wrote to you.'

'To us. She was fleeing with a Polish general and had crossed the French border. I don't know why she never made it back to Paris.'

'Can you see that you are now doing the same thing, with me?'

'What's that?'

'You want stability for us. I want something more – possibility. A compelling life.'

'It's not stability I want for us. Although wouldn't that be glorious right now – the war over, life returned? No, I want something more straightforward and seemingly impossible.'

'Peace?'

'No. Survival. I want us to survive, Marienne. I can see no further than that goal. And with every day it seems further and further away.'

Duchene paused in front of his apartment. Earlier today, men had been waiting for him on the other side of the door. Earlier today, he had been threatened by both Partisans and Germans.

He surprised himself by smiling. Less than an hour ago, Marienne had accused him of seeking a dull life. And yet he couldn't even succeed at that. Threats, deadlines, lives on the line – perhaps that might impress her.

A soft glow underlined Camille's door, through which he would find candles, conversation, a patient ear and a sympathetic voice to soothe his troubled mind.

A note was pinned to his door: *I'm here if you want to talk*.

He could use an ally, someone to help him try to fathom Marienne, her motivations, her mind. Camille always understood her better than him. She had been Marienne's confidante at the table, and long before that. She was smart enough to guide him, without revealing a confidence, through the complicated emotional terrain of his daughter's mind. But such deeper understandings would be pointless if he or Marienne ended up dead. He had only a limited time to make sure that wouldn't happen and as much as Camille was the only one who could soothe his troubled mind, he couldn't spare a minute.

He took the note from his door as he opened it. Inside, his apartment was dark. He reached for the trench torch he kept by the door and squeezed the lever that ran down the length of its handle. Slowly its motor whirred into action, and its small bulb started to glow.

He staggered a little, the cognac catching up with him, and knocked over a pile of books on his way from the living room to the kitchen. Here he found the nub of a candle and lit it with a match from above the stove. With the breadboard beside him, he spread out the papers Faber had given him. The German was to the point in granting him an exception from the curfew. The signature at the bottom was unrecognisable, but the stamp beside it was clear: Dietrich von Choltitz, their chief warden and the administrator of their fates. While Duchene had no sympathy for the man, he didn't envy his position – deployed to a city that despises your presence, its Resistance plotting your assassination, while enemies approach from east and west.

He re-read the dates, hoping he'd misheard Faber and that he'd find he had more time to complete the task. No, it hadn't changed. He had less than forty-eight hours to find this missing soldier, Kloke. Less than forty-eight hours to find the missing priest. Each task was almost insurmountable on its own, and impossible when performed simultaneously. He would have to find more hours in the day. To do that, he'd need to look to the night.

He tucked the papers back into his jacket pocket and blew out the candle. Using the trench torch to guide him, he made his way to the front door and out into the darkness.

Wednesday, 16 August 1944

NINE

Madame Noirot stood in the doorway to the rectory dressed in a faded floral house coat. In the light of her torch, he could see that she had maintained the robe with stitches and fabric patches. Her grey hair was concealed under a crocheted boudoir cap. He removed his hat and nodded at her. 'Sorry to disturb, Madame.'

'Are you mad? There is a curfew.'

'I have papers. I wouldn't have come if it wasn't important.'

'What is so important that you need to disturb a woman at one in the morning?'

'Father Ramelle. Can we talk inside? There's no telling when the power will come back on and your neighbours catch sight of us. Papers might be good for the Germans, but I'd rather the Resistance didn't know of our meeting.'

The concern dropped from her face, the hint of a smile appearing at the edge of her mouth. 'Come in, then,' she said, holding the door open for him until he was across its threshold. She pulled it closed with caution, making very little noise. 'Come to the office. Let us talk there.' He followed her. Once the curtains were closed, she reopened the drawer in Ramelle's desk where he kept his keys, removed one and approached the liquor cabinet. 'Whisky?'

'Perhaps I'd better not. I've only just walked off the wine from dinner.'

'Lucky you. Wine and dinner.'

'My daughter announced her engagement.'

'Then there is still hope in these troubled times.'

'You might not agree if you met her fiancé. Sorry to be so indiscreet, Madame, but I'd like to ask you some questions.'

Madame Noirot held up a finger until she finished pouring herself a measure. 'Proceed.'

'Madame, I sensed there were things you weren't saying when we visited this afternoon.'

She sipped the drink. She didn't flinch. 'Monsieur, I don't know you. But you work with those men.'

'*For* those men. And not by choice. But I suspect you've figured that out already.'

'Words are dangerous things these days. If they were said, I too might disappear.'

'Then let me offer you something. We were talking about my daughter before – she's betrothed to a German. Luftwaffe, an airman. Armand, Philippe, they're threatening to kill her as a collaborator if I don't find your missing priest for them.'

'And she isn't a collaborator?'

'She's young. Looking for a way out of Paris. I don't know. You have children of your own?'

'No, but I'm close to my niece.'

'Then you know. My point is, I'm not going to betray you to the Resistance. I'm compromised. And now you know why.' *Well, half of it, anyway.*

She took another sip of the whisky. 'It wasn't your presence that bothered me. It was theirs.'

'But you must have known Father Ramelle was working with the Resistance?'

'I knew. I'm not troubled by that. I hate the Germans. And although I'm concerned that Father Ramelle has disappeared, I can't say it's a surprise. Those were the risks he took. It's those men, specifically – *they* bother me.'

'Armand and Philippe?'

'And the other.'

'Lucien?'

'They brought guns into a place of worship. I have no idea why Father agreed. He was not a violent man. Perhaps he thought it was a necessary evil. War does things to people, and he lost many parishioners to it. "Lives spent for the vanity of dictators and fools," he used to say.'

'You don't think he's alive, do you?'

'I do not. And I suspect those men don't think he is either. It's the guns they want. They care nothing for his safety.'

Duchene shifted, and the housekeeper raised an eyebrow.

'Why have you come tonight?' she asked.

'When I was here earlier – when Armand and Lucien were showing us where they had parked when they unloaded the weapons –'

'Yes. I recall that.'

'I asked if there was any other way in and out of the church.'

'Your exact words were, "And the only other way into the church is through the front doors?"'

'So?'

'Other.'

'Yes. There is another way.'

'Could you take me there?'

'For that, you'll need to come downstairs again.'

Soon they were standing before wood and iron, four hundred years old. Duchene waited as she inserted the key. Within moments the door was open, and the damp cold of the room drifted across them.

'There's another entrance, down here,' he said.

Madame Noirot said nothing as she crossed to the tombs on the far side of the room. With the base of her torch, she tapped along the capstones until one came back with a dull thud. She waved Duchene over and shone her light onto two narrow crevices cut into either side of the capstone.

He approached and indicated with both hands. 'Here?'

'Yes, please. Pull it.' She trained the torch between the edges of the capstone.

Even though he had anticipated what would happen next, Duchene was still surprised when he heard a grinding noise and felt three capstones move forward simultaneously. These tombs were only a façade, and a hidden door opened on a hinge.

'Where does it go?' he asked.

'Deeper, into the Catacombs. Down to the old mines. Who knows?'

'Do you think someone could find their way into this room, through those Catacombs?'

'Maybe. If they knew what they were doing.'

'I need to follow it.'

'That's not a good idea – the tunnels go for hundreds of miles.'

'I'll just follow it a short way.'

'Take this,' Madame Noirot said, offering him her

electric torch. 'Better than that relic.' She nodded at his trench torch.

'Madame, I won't have you wait here for me in the dark. Please return upstairs. I won't be long.' She shook her head, and he insisted again, 'Madame, it is cold down here. If it helps, perhaps pour us each one of Father Ramelle's whiskies, and I'll return soon to join you in drinking it. I won't go far.'

This seemed to sit better with her, and Duchene watched as she left.

The floor was covered in dust and dirt. A long-dead rat lay part way down the tunnel. There were no clear footprints. After a few paces, he stopped and shone the torch back over his steps. He had disturbed some of the dust, but he didn't see anything so obvious as a tread mark.

It might have been the silence, or that his vision was limited only to what he could see by torchlight, but his senses came alive. He could feel the air moving across his face, and smell the dust and the musk of vermin in their nests. He was suddenly aware of how alone he was. Just him and the dead.

Soon he had to turn his body sideways to fit through the narrow corridor. The further he went, the more he had to bring his mind back to the moment and away from speculation about a collapse from above or a sudden pitfall. Shining the torch behind him to see the open door of the crypt gave him some comfort. But the fears remained close by.

He pulled up his collar against the chill and continued. The tunnel intersected with a wider corridor, more recognisable as part of the Catacombs for which the city was known. But it was less maintained than those tunnels, which were frequented by tourists and visitors. Here, the orderly shelves of skulls and bones had collapsed onto one another or tumbled out into the corridor itself. Perhaps some of his fears were better founded than others, as there was movement in the earth here, a good reason for the catacomb to remain sealed.

Duchene unwrapped his scarf and tied it to a femur near the edge of the tunnel that led back to the church crypt. He took the corridor to his left, stepping over broken bones, afraid to offend the dead, while he looked for signs of recent disturbance. Around him were sounds of quiet movement – small paws scratching over cloth and stone, a persistent drip and echo from somewhere above him. He passed many thousands of bones of the ancient dead, brushing cobwebs and brittle roots aside. The faint smell of something rotten rose up at him as his coat stirred still air from the ground. Perhaps another rat that had fallen prey to something larger.

Ahead was a wall of rubble – another collapse. Stone and bone blocked the corridor. It would have been impossible for someone to squeeze through, much less six large weapon crates.

He checked his watch. He'd followed this corridor for ten minutes. It had felt like more. Turning, he retraced his steps and soon found his scarf like a waypoint in the darkness.

After a quick check back down the tunnel to see that the crypt door was still open, he continued along the other pathway. He wasn't sure what he was looking for: a blood spatter, a torn piece of cassock, or an indication that the crypt had been breached via its hidden door, the crates dragged – some sure sign that this was the answer to the question of the stolen cache.

It became clear that there was no easy answer.

Within a few minutes, he found himself tracking through a heavy layer of silt. Looking at the ground behind him, he could easily see the tread of his brogues. He walked a few more steps, trying to travel light and leave no disturbance. Impossible: each step scraped the dirt to the stone.

He crouched low and shone the torch on the ground ahead of him. The light revealed the tracks of a small cat; nothing else had come this way.

'No one has been down that corridor in a very long time,' Duchene said to Madame Noirot as he arrived back in Father Ramelle's study.

She was sitting at the desk, two glasses of whisky already poured. She had brought up the old oil lantern and had set its wick low. The smell of it filled the air. It reminded Duchene of dinners in the trenches, with sandbag cloth soaked in candle wax to create a fire barely hot enough to warm a canned vegetable stew.

He sat across from her, and she passed him a whisky. She pulled a packet of cigarettes out of her pocket and offered him one. Lucky Strikes. 'Your friend gave me his packet. There are still quite a few left.'

Duchene nodded and let her light it for him. He sat back in the chair and peered through the gloom at an icon on the wall. Framed in gold leaf, it was a portrait of Jesus, his robes red, his beard symmetrical. It was strange to see a Russian Orthodox symbol in a Catholic church.

'What will you do next?' Madame Noirot asked, letting the smoke roll from her mouth before drawing it back into her nostrils.

'I have to think. Are you certain there's no other key to the crypt?'

'Just the one that's kept in here,' she said, patting the drawer.

'And only Father Ramelle and yourself have keys to open it?'

'Yes.'

Duchene sipped the whisky. It was strong, tasted like smoke and iodine, filled him with warmth. He winced as it went down. Madame Noirot smiled.

'Has the key to the crypt always been locked away?'

'Ever since Father Ramelle hid the guns down there.'

He placed the cigarette to his lips, drew the smoke deep into his lungs, held it there before exhaling, let the buzz of the tobacco tingle to his fingers.

'What are you going to do?' she asked.

'Probably look at that key next. Have a look at the drawer.'

'Not that. About your daughter?'

'What can I do? She's made her decision. She's no longer my responsibility.'

'This is what you are telling yourself. But it's not really how you feel.'

He sighed. 'You're probably right. But I need to take care of the other work first.'

'Perhaps it's too late, then. You don't want to regret speaking sooner.'

'You know this from experience?'

She nodded. 'I do.'

Taking another sip, Duchene let the heat from it stir his mind. 'Did you hear anything the night he went missing? That was Friday, yes?'

'Nothing.'

'No sound at all? Something mundane, normal, that might make sense now that you think back on it?'

'No. It's a big building. I sleep at the back, and the walls are thick. You were beating a storm on my door this evening, and I could hardly hear you.'

He drew back on the cigarette.

'You should acknowledge your own sins,' Madame Noirot said. 'Seek her counsel. Show her that you too make mistakes. Not even Christ was perfect.'

'I seem to recall being told he was.'

'He was without sin. But he made mistakes. He chose Judas as his friend.'

'Well, that's true ... So, tell me, Madame, what is it you would like to confess?'

'Pardon?'

'Come now, we're both too old for this. I think you knew the moment I walked into the room, I was going to think about your involvement in the priest's disappearance.'

'My involvement? I have helped you. What do I have to hide?'

'Something. Two people have access to the crypt key. It is well hidden. We can surmise that Father Ramelle didn't have it on him or else it would have disappeared with him.'

'I –'

'And this discussion about my daughter ... it was a valiant but failed attempt to draw me away from my questions.'

'It's still good advice.'

'It is. But now I'd like to know everything. The truth. I promise none of this will be revealed to Philippe and his men.'

Madame Noirot poured herself another whisky and lit another cigarette. 'I lent the key to my niece.'

'When?'

'Last Thursday night. She swore she'd have it back to me by Friday morning.'

'And did she?'

'Yes.'

'But you don't know what she did with it. How long did she have it for?'

'She borrowed it around seven in the evening. She returned it by eight the following morning.'

'Thirteen hours . . . What did she say she needed it for?'

'Money.' She refilled her glass. 'I'm no idiot, Monsieur. I suspected it was to do with the guns. I hoped they'd be taken – but I just never anticipated Father Ramelle would go missing as well.'

'How could you be sure it wasn't the Germans who were paying her?'

'Since when do they behave like that? That is not their way. If they had any idea, they would have simply broken down the door. That is their way.'

'You're right. The one thing we can be sure of is that the Germans didn't take the cache.' Duchene smoked, sipped. 'Why does your niece need money?'

'She's not well off. The war is bad for her. And unlike me, she doesn't have a church to live in.'

'I'll need to speak to her.'

She took hold of Duchene's hand. Her skin was thin. Her hands cold. 'I didn't expect that Father Ramelle would disappear. You must believe me.'

He looked back into her eyes, and while there were no tears forming, she held his gaze with sadness, an unmoving stare.

'I do. But you must understand, my daughter, my life, it all depends on knowing what happened to him and where the weapons went. Your niece – I need her name.'

Madame Noirot moved to pour him another whisky. He held his hand over the glass.

She returned the bottle to the table. And looked at him, her eyes fixed on his.

'Madame?'

'Her name is Eliane. Eliane Payet.'

'And where will I find her?'

'I can give you her address, but she's rarely home.'

'After curfew, surely.'

'I'm afraid to say that's when she's usually at work.'

'Work?'

'Monsieur, I'd rather you didn't make me say it. These past four years have been difficult for her.'

'I understand.'

It was a ridiculous extravagance to drink more of the cognac. Just one, he thought, before trying to sleep. A few hours, he needed a few hours of rest before heading out into the city again to race the clock and search for the missing men.

His arrival home had stirred Ernest. Or perhaps the creature was also struggling with sleep. The sound of it stirring up the gravel of its tank was the only noise in the room. Duchene chided himself for not grabbing some of the lettuce from the salad Marienne had served. 'Forgive me,' he said in the direction of the tank. Tomorrow he would make amends.

He sniffed the cognac – dried fruit. Floral sweetness.

Marienne's mother.

They had been drinking Hennessy on the day she left. In a small apartment not unlike this one, in a room that had much the same view. They were in Boulogne, on the outskirts of the city, its beige stone residential buildings interspersed with factories and smokestacks.

They had argued, so many times, about her leaving. So often that the patterns were the same, the debate already mapped, their words drawn from a limited vocabulary. The more he insisted she should stay, the more she seemed determined to do the opposite.

Perhaps it was the difference in their years. He was forty, she twenty-eight. She still had passion, energy to give, to find meaning, to change. Work on a factory floor was not what she'd intended for her life. She couldn't stand to one side and watch the world burn.

Funny how the passion that had drawn him to her, the vitality for life that buoyed him up from his growing sense of the futility of it all, had become his greatest enemy.

The International Brigades were fighting the fascists in Spain, she said. He had fought for what he believed. How could he not understand?

So, there he stood, a hypocrite, while he presented one last case for her remaining: it would change her. Like it had changed him. If it did not take your life, the war took your spirit.

She smiled, sad and disappointed in him. If she had spirit to give, to make a better world for their daughter, then that was a sacrifice worth making. She reassured him of his worth – his place as a good father – that she would always love him. And then she made love to him, and left.

TEN

A convoy of German trucks, laden with supplies and men, rattled past Duchene as he waited to cross the street. The sun had risen, although it hadn't been seen all morning, hidden as it was behind the grey clouds that loomed over Paris. The trucks were heading north, out of the city – to fight the Americans, to fight the Free French. The tarpaulins had been lowered onto the trucks to limit sniper fire from the roofs above. Duchene had heard the stories – grenades rolled into clusters of soldiers staring at the sex shops on the Place de Clichy, pistol fire in the Soldaten Kino – but these were rare. The coverings were as much a precaution as an instruction to the men beneath them: 'Remember who your enemy is.'

At the back of the trucks, through the canvas doorways, the soldiers peered out, their faces set with a grim determination as they pondered their future. They were dressed in rain smocks patterned with oak leaves. The dark grey helmets had been repainted with daubs of camouflage green. The Germans were now concealing their men, giving them equipment to help them hide. To them, their victory was no longer certain.

Fear. It makes men more dangerous.

He'd already visited the home of Eliane Payet on the outskirts of Montparnasse. It was an old terrace house, clad in silver timber and not much to look at. As her aunt had predicted, she wasn't home. He'd been let inside by another woman who wore only a shift and he passed three grubby children on his way to her door, where he left a note. The letter had made him uncomfortable, but he was desperate and couldn't take his time getting a response.

Mademoiselle Payet,

I'd like to meet with you to discuss some advice your aunt gave me – a key lent and returned. I'm looking for Father Ramelle. The priest is missing, and I believe you might be able to help. These are troubled times and I try to make a difference. You may have heard of my few successes. Perhaps you can help me with one more.

Kindest regards,
Auguste Duchene

He would have preferred to call and speak to her in person. But it was clear that the house had no running water, let alone a phone.

The convoy passed on the road ahead of him. He crossed in a break in the traffic and turned onto Rue du Mont-Cenis.

Major Faber's missing soldier had kept a room in the Hotel Saint Clair. As Duchene walked up the hill towards it, he could see the basilica itself. This was a good location, a popular tourist destination. In the attics and apartments around him, the artists and performers of Paris had congregated. Who knew how many remained? It was rumoured that Picasso had holed up somewhere, painting while the Germans marched into the city. Perhaps he was still here.

Duchene had taken Marienne to see *Guernica* when it was exhibited at the World Fair. They'd waited for an hour to reach the front of the line. He'd expected something different, perhaps. Something more overt. It wasn't a painting of any war he'd ever seen. Cubism left a lot to the imagination, which was probably the point. But Marienne found it gripping; she spoke about it all afternoon and into their dinner in a small brasserie by the Bateau-Lavoir. Had that been its purpose? Not to document, from the view of someone who'd seen war's devastation firsthand, but to provoke emotions in someone who'd never been to war? There was definitely a value in that.

The Hotel Saint Clair was narrow and tall. It sat between a café and a gallery, the walls of which bulged under their age on uncertain foundations.

Something green caught his eye at the base of the gallery, between a downpipe and a cobblestone. He hunched down and teased out its leaves. Sorrel was growing wild in the city. He looked above him, searching for its origin, and saw the remnants of a shattered window box. Perhaps this small plant was the lone survivor, coaxed into growing on a windswept ledge. He plucked the sorrel from its mooring and wrapped it in his handkerchief.

He pushed the hotel door open and walked into the foyer. Dark-red, tasselled curtains framed the windows that looked out onto the street; although dusty, they were free from holes and fraying. They complemented the rich timber that lined the walls and made up the balustrade of the staircase that led to the upper levels of the building. The reception desk was unattended. By the number of keys hanging in their pigeonholes, it was clear that almost every room was vacant. On the wall opposite were over two dozen oil paintings and watercolours of the hotel and its neighbouring businesses at various seasons by various hands. These had been painted from the street outside, and the dates and signatures of the artists told a story of visitors from around Europe. The most recent of which marked history too: *Mahler, Lietz, Falsch.*

Duchene rang the bell on the counter, and a ruddy-faced concierge emerged from the office door behind it. His waistcoat was too large and billowed in front of him as he walked up to Duchene. 'You are looking for a room?' he asked. There was no pleasure or interest in his tone.

'I'm wondering if you can help me?'

'I can help you with a room.'

'Monsieur, I need to visit the room of one of your guests. He's been missing now for some days.'

'Christian Kloke?'

'Yes. Others have come looking for him?'

'His commander, I think. You're the first Frenchman to visit. So a risk for me, do you understand?'

'Would this help?' Duchene said, sliding across the two packets of cigarettes he'd been given by Lucien.

The man took them back into his office. Within a few moments, he returned holding a master key and gestured towards the stairs. 'It's at the top.'

The stairs bowed and creaked as they walked up them, a testimony to the age of the hotel and the frequency with which it had once been used. Their footsteps stirred up motes of dust that fell past them, lit by a skylight above.

'Do you live here?' Duchene asked the concierge.

'I do.'

'Did you hear anything strange coming from this room, over the weekend or on Monday morning?'

'Strange?'

'Anything that might make you suspicious?'

'He was German. His visitors were German. Everything about them is suspicious.'

On the fourth floor, there were six doors arranged in the same sequence as on the floors below them. The lifting and puffed wallpaper was the same too, a burgundy fleur-de-lis.

'Four zero one,' the concierge said, making the short journey from stair to door.

Within moments the room was opened, and Duchene was standing at its threshold. The curtains were open, letting the grey day in and showing a view up the hill to the stairs and entrance to Sacré-Cœur. The room itself was unkempt. The bed, which faced the window, was a mess of sheets and pillows. A small pile of books, all German, sat on the nightstand, on top of which rested a *Baedeker Guide to Paris*. This was well-thumbed and dog-eared. Duchene picked it up.

'I offered to clean the room for him, but he refused,' the concierge said. 'Most of the Germans did. They treated it more like an apartment than a hotel. They even cooked in the rooms on camp stoves, made the place smell like a hostel.'

Duchene opened the book. The folded corners of pages marked all the main tourist sites. A black-and-white photo had been tucked into the entry for the Eiffel Tower: three young German officers smiled beneath the monument. Kloke stood in the centre. He was taller than the others, with dark hair and a strong frame. His eyes were a piercing dark-blue or brown, and his smile was off-centre. It suggested he was smirking at the absurdity of his situation, or perhaps he was reacting to a joke that had just been said. While the others posed, he was relaxed, leaning on a rail, arms spread wide to grip it. He even had the top buttons of his jacket open. From Duchene's experience in the French Army, this would have risked a citation, but for a German soldier ... it was almost unthinkable.

In the back of the guide were ticket stubs from cabarets, dance halls, galleries and tourist sites. Kloke had kept himself busy.

'What's that?' asked the concierge.

'How much to go through the room in private?' Duchene asked.

'It's not really how things are done.'

'But, as you said, Germans frying up Spätzle in your rooms isn't how things are done either.' Duchene held out the last of Lucien's cigarette packets. 'How's this to leave me to go through this place alone? I won't be long.'

The concierge took the packet and pulled the door shut behind him. 'Don't steal anything. I don't want any trouble.'

'Neither do I.'

The door shut, and Duchene sat on the edge of the bed as he continued to work through the guide.

The front of the book had an inscription in French: *Welcome to Paris, my love*. The hand was neat, the words tucked in between title and credits.

Perhaps this was from a lover, a woman not unlike his daughter who had found herself drawn to the handsome young soldier. Duchene sniffed at the pages. Cologne and cigarettes. Nothing on which to form an opinion. A German book that might have been bought by a

Frenchwoman – not a difficult task. There were Baedekers on sale throughout the city. Less so these days, but in the early years of the occupation Paris was rife with them. It had seemed that every German had a copy in their hand.

The last pages of the guide were given over to maps. These grids tried to contain the city's winding medieval streets and the wide flow of the Seine. Pencilled circles marked out the sites. A quick audit suggested each of these corresponded to the dog-eared pages.

Duchene paused for a moment. Weighed the book and its spilling contents in his hand. Then tucked it into the inside pocket of his overcoat.

As noted by the concierge, the room wasn't intended for a long-term stay. The small closet that stood against one wall was overflowing. The clothes had been left where they fell: uniforms, civilian suits, some still on the hook. Duchene felt along the top of the closet: dust, dead flies – nothing else. He wiped his fingertips on the lapels of Kloke's dress uniform.

The story was the same for a chest of drawers. Nothing was hidden behind it. Inside its drawers were undergarments and socks, most of them dumped, the socks not even partnered. This was not the usual behaviour of a soldier during active service. But thus far, nothing about Kloke was usual.

Under the bed, Duchene found an old hatbox. Its cream fabric was stained brown around the edges of the lid. Parisian, and from the 1800s given the stamps on the side. It was the type sold at flea markets throughout the city. He pulled it out and placed it on the bed, then crouched in front of it – before reconsidering. Knees cracking, he repositioned himself beside the box on the bed.

As the lid lifted, it sucked air. Duchene blinked at the contents.

A Webley revolver lay on top. He carefully took it out and scanned for the safety latch. It was in position. He sniffed at the gun. It hadn't been fired recently. He pushed out the chamber – it was full. There was no spare ammunition in the box.

Under the pistol was a smaller tin that rattled when Duchene picked it up. Popping it open revealed medals and pins, a collection documenting some of the men Kloke had fought. A British epaulette. Several Red Army Patriotic War medals. Half a dozen French uniform buttons.

War trophies. It was what young men did. Like the British Webley, collected and stored.

To one side of the box was a Risinetten medicine tin. Inside this were several pieces of wax paper folded into neat rectangles. Duchene opened one and found a white powder. He dabbed his finger against his tongue, into the powder and back again.

A chemical taste. Methamphetamines.

He took one of the packets then returned the tin to the hatbox. He replaced its lid and slid it back under the bed. Lifting the mattress, he felt under it, checked both sides. Nothing.

He left the room and started back down the stairs.

The concierge was waiting for him in the hotel foyer. He had one of the cigarettes in his mouth, and he let it hang at its edge as he spoke. 'Is he coming back?'

'I have no idea.'

'What do I do with his room?'

'That's probably a question for the Germans.'

'I asked. That commander of his, he said leave it untouched. There would be an investigation. Now that you've been –'

'When was this?'

'Yesterday morning.'

'I'm not sure he's referring to me specifically. Probably best that you leave it alone. You don't happen to remember this commander's name?'

The concierge shrugged.

'Was it Faber?'

Another shrug.

'Did he speak French – very well, with a Swiss accent?'

'He did.'

Faber. It made sense.

Tipping his hat to the concierge, Duchene walked out onto the Rue du Mont-Cenis. The dark clouds had made good on their promise, and a light rain was falling, just enough to force a decision on those pedestrians who'd come prepared. Was it worth the effort to open an umbrella? A wind moved up through Montmartre – turning its windmills, blowing loose petals from window boxes and ruffling the paperbacks on the stands outside its bookshops.

Duchene let a car pass, timing his exit from under the hotel's awning, and started across the street. The car, a black Citroën sedan, came to a sudden stop, and two men stepped from it. They were dressed in dark coats, dark hats. Their eyes locked on Duchene. He moved his hand to the guidebook in his pocket. But they were coming too fast. His actions were in their full view.

On the street around him, both Germans and Parisians had stopped what they were doing. The bookseller stood watching Duchene as two magazines were pulled away by the wind. All eyes were on him.

Duchene turned and started to walk away from the men. They were built like apes and committed; there was no way he could outrun them. But better to show some resistance than be observed acquiescing without any national pride. A young soldier ahead of Duchene started to spread his arms, sensing the moment and a similar need for symbolic action.

Holding their hats, the men ran, their dark coats blowing about their legs. Duchene gave it a token effort. He made a quick right step around the young soldier before accelerating left to avoid his open arms. Cheers and whistles rose up from a few of the bystanders.

This spurred his two pursuers into greater speed, and they closed in quickly. One swept a leg sideways, kicking into Duchene's feet and causing him to trip over and sprawl onto the cobblestones.

Seconds later, a knee was in his back, and he was being dragged up onto his feet. Their iron grip held each of his arms as they lifted him into an unstable balance.

'Geheime Staatspolizei,' said one of the men. 'Walk!'

Duchene replied in French. 'Sorry, I don't speak German.'

'Sure you do,' the other one said in German, and they marched him back to the car.

ELEVEN

As they drove, the storm grew. From the peak of Montmartre, they could see back down into Paris, a grey city divided by the black waters of the Seine. They were heading west, towards the 8th arrondissement.

Duchene was flanked by his captors, their wide shoulders pressing in at him. They hadn't removed their hats, and he glanced up at each of them in turn, making a note of their faces. They studiously ignored him, keeping their eyes to the front. The driver, on the other hand, did not wear a hat; his lay on the passenger seat. He would occasionally glance at the rear-view mirror to assess traffic and watch Duchene. His eyes were an intense ice-blue, instantly recognisable and quite memorable. *Strange choice for a secret policeman*.

A haze of cigarette smoke had gathered in the back of the car as all three men smoked. Duchene found himself breathing it second hand, letting it fill up his lungs to try to calm himself.

They passed the Arc de Triomphe and the giant swastika flags that hung from its centre.

From the roundabout, they turned into Montaigne before winding their way down side streets to arrive at Rue des Saussaies. Before the occupation, this had been a sought-after neighbourhood. The residences and townhouses were home to doctors and bankers. The broad gardens that ran down the Champs-Élysées were at its heart and the apartments overlooking them were spacious. Now they were occupied by a very specific mechanism of the German state. Duchene knew all too well the whispered rumours among Parisians and German soldiers alike: the street was also home to the Nazis' secret police.

The Citroën pulled up outside a building unremarkable but for its finery. Wrought-iron filigree framed its many windows, which filled the width of each of its six floors. Embellished stonework and a gently rising roof placed it in an artful consistency with its neighbours.

The driver put on his hat and stepped out into the rain. He pulled open a passenger door, and the men on either side of Duchene pushed him into the street. He was manhandled through an iron gate and past a lush garden before being hauled into the foyer. The door slammed behind him, and he was released with a violent shove.

'Arms *up*,' the driver with ice-blue eyes said in German.

Duchene gave him a confused look.

'Herr Duchene, we know who you are. We know you understand us.'

Duchene raised his arms, holding them out to the side. One of the apes behind him wrenched his coat from his shoulders; the other pulled the hat from his head. They prodded and felt his clothes. Sliding fingers around hatbands, turning out the pockets of the coat. Rough hands pressed along his suit and pulled everything from his pockets, no matter how trivial. Into Duchene's upturned hat were tossed the keys to his apartment, his trench torch, his lighter, the square of waxed paper, Kloke's guidebook, the folded handkerchief, his wallet, a broken cigarette and the letter exempting him from the curfew.

With this offering in tow, he was walked up a flight of stairs to the second floor. Many closed doors lined its opulent corridor. Only one was open. His handlers slowed as they passed it.

The room had been stripped of its carpet and wallpaper. In its centre was a heavy wooden chair beside a basic table. These furnishings were nicked and damaged, while dark stains made an irregular pattern across the exposed floorboards. On the walls were the water stains of where a sponge had been used. Of all the things in the room, only a woodworking kit on the table was in good order. Its doors stood open to display woodworking tools polished to a high gleam.

Duchene was hauled past this room and into its neighbour, a large chamber that had been converted into an office. He was made to sit opposite a white baroque dining table that had been repurposed as a desk. Dark-brown folders had been precisely stacked to one side of the table; on the other was a heavy mantel clock that featured a stag rearing over an outcrop.

Duchene's hat was deposited, incongruous and dripping, in the centre of the desk. The men stood behind him and waited.

The door eventually opened, and a man entered. He wore a pair of black-rimmed half-glasses through which he looked carefully at Duchene.

Their eyes met.

It struck Duchene that this man was nothing like the other three. His face had a jowly softness to it. His jaw was weak, his hair parted to flop over one side of his face. Although his age was hard to determine, the lines across his features showed he was certainly advanced in years. But his eyes were focused, exacting. They scanned Duchene and seemed to draw conclusions, mirroring his inspection of the Gestapo boss.

'Auguste,' the man said.

'And you are?' asked Duchene.

'That's no concern of yours,' he said in a thick Bavarian accent. 'Feel free to address me by my rank – Oberführer.' A colonel. He reached forward and pulled Duchene's hat towards him. 'Do you know where you are?'

'The headquarters of the Gestapo.'

'That is correct,' he said without looking up as he picked through the contents of the hat. 'Do you know why you are here?'

Duchene gave the answer he hoped was true. 'This could have something to do with a missing German soldier.'

'Correct. And do you know how your name came to us?'

'I'm assuming you're aware of the letter that is in my hat. It would have raised some suspicions.'

'Very astute. Your reputation would seem to do you justice.'

'And what's that?'

'As a good investigator. A keen observer of detail. Someone who unpicks a knot of information then assembles it into the correct facts.'

'I'm just a retired schoolteacher.'

'To the Verniers, you are the saviour of their child. And I hear tell that there have been other incidents. Other missing children, found and returned. Some of the details are not so pleasant.'

'People see a war and take advantage of it.'

'So it would seem.' The Oberführer turned the contents

of the hat onto the desk. He pushed the letter to his right-hand side. 'We'll come back to this.' He dragged the house keys, cigarette, lighter, trench torch and wallet to his left-hand side, then paused with his finger on the small folded paper. 'Amphetamines? Methamphetamines?'

'Yes.'

He looked at Duchene. 'A man your age ... if it helps.' He unwrapped the handkerchief. 'And this?'

'Sorrel.'

'Times must be lean.'

'Less so if you're a tortoise.'

The Oberführer let the comment pass, sliding the handkerchief into the items on the left.

All that remained was the Baedeker guidebook. The Oberführer picked it up. He first turned to the bulging press of tickets in the back, then held the book spine down and fanned the pages with his thumb. He soon found the photograph of Kloke and the two other soldiers at the Eiffel Tower. 'Not yours, obviously.'

'No.'

'Who?'

'Lieutenant Christian Kloke.'

'Ah. Which brings us back to this.' He slid the letter from his right-hand side back to the centre. 'Did Major Faber tell you why he's so keen to find this man?'

Faber. The Oberführer clearly knew more than he was revealing. Duchene carefully considered his response.

'Do I need to explain the purpose of my organisation to you?' asked the Oberführer.

'The Gestapo? No.'

'Let me do it anyway. I investigate crimes on behalf of the Reich. Crimes committed by our enemies, and even our own. And while I outrank Major Faber, it would also be in the power of my men to question him.'

'He said he wanted to stop Kloke from making a bad decision.'

'And that was?'

'Deserting the army.'

'If that is what has happened.'

'It would seem the obvious conclusion.'

'And yet you've been to his room. Tell me, did it look like he'd deserted?'

'Hard to say.'

'Please, Herr Duchene. You're insulting us both with an answer like that.'

'No. I don't believe he did. There were things he would have taken with him. Keepsakes. Money.'

'And you didn't take these things yourself. Why not?'

'Because the military police would have got there eventually. It was too risky, stealing from a German.'

'Nevertheless, you did steal,' he said, tapping the guidebook.

'That was necessary. In order to find him.'

'Why?'

'To work out where he's been, those places he frequents. There will be people I can ask. The knot to unpick.'

The Oberführer leant back in his chair and pushed his glasses onto the bridge of his nose. He folded hands across his lap and looked at Duchene.

He sat like this for some time. Duchene counted the ticking of the mantel clock at the edge of the desk. It was the only thing to make any sound in the room.

Seventy seconds later, the Oberführer spoke again. 'There is something that you will do for me. Let's not even address the consequences if you don't. You know who we are. You know what we do. Is that understood?'

'It is.'

'You will make no mention to Major Faber that we have met. Not a word. Whatever you learn about Lieutenant Kloke, you tell me first. Then I will advise as to what you shall pass on to Major Faber.'

'He's expecting me to find Kloke. What if I do?'

'We will address that outcome if and when it happens.'

Duchene could feel the Oberführer watching him, waiting for his next response – a viper, coiled.

'That is very clear,' Duchene said. 'Anything about Kloke, I will bring to you.'

'Good.'

'Do you have any idea what might have happened to him? Something that might help me find him?'

'I can tell you that it is an unsafe time to be a German in Paris.'

It's an unsafe time to be a Parisian in Paris.

The Oberführer continued, 'Kloke is one of four soldiers who have gone missing. No signs of desertion, their rooms left abandoned.'

'Do you think these disappearances are connected?'

'Maybe.'

'Do you think it's the Resistance?'

'Of course, it's a possibility. But your insurgents tend to be more overt in their actions. Suicidal, at times. Only today we trapped some of them as they tried to smuggle guns into the city. It's an insult to us that they'd think we wouldn't catch them. So many of them – thirty-five – so rash. But it's always the young men, isn't it? They believe they are invulnerable, that death will never come to them.

But you know better, don't you? Going by that relic you use for a torch, I can see you served in the Great War, so I know you've seen death firsthand. I know you understand that some of us have the power to trade death like a currency. The significance is in numbers and not names. That's how we can show the strength of our convictions. We executed them today, in the Bois de Boulogne. Do you know what they called themselves at the moment of their deaths, these thirty-five men?'

Duchene was unsure if it was a test. He gave the answer anyway. 'Martyrs.'

'Yes. Like a saint. Like your Jeanne d'Arc. What miracles have they performed? How did they die in Christ's name? *Martyrs*. It's an insult to God.' The Oberführer dropped the Baedeker back into Duchene's hat. 'Do you support the Resistance, Herr Duchene?' he asked without looking up.

Duchene blinked. Another test, perhaps. He remained silent.

'I only ask because you seem to spend a lot of time working for us. In their eyes, you're already a collaborator.' He held the hat, now full, towards Duchene.

'This has been suggested.'

'Well, if you're damned already you might as well get something for it. Wouldn't you agree?'

'And that is?'

'They're just names. You give them to us, we do the rest. Perhaps in return we can help you with Major Faber. Lift you out of your predicament.'

'Names of Resistance members?'

'That's right. You're observant. Observe and report. Stahl?'

The driver stepped forward and held out a card.

'This is our number,' said the Oberführer.

Duchene took the card.

'Do call. Update us on Kloke. And should the thought strike you, pass on a few names.'

TWELVE

The Métro train rattled at speed through the tunnel, the frosted bulbs that lined the carriage flickering as the train glanced across the powerlines suspended above. The train was crowded, and Duchene had stood so a young woman could take his seat.

She'd thanked him with a noticeable German accent. A faux pas.

Now, even though there was little room on the train, a small circle had formed around him. Parisians turning their backs, their sides to him. Making a note of even this minor indiscretion.

Perhaps he'd spent so much time with Germans, he was forgetting the basic rule of an occupied city: give no support to the enemy. This seemed to include acts of kindness on the Métro.

How could he have known the girl was German? Had anyone known until the moment she thanked him?

She smiled at him from the seat beneath a Noilly Prat advertisement, which only made things worse. An audible hiss came from somewhere in the carriage.

He had first seen her, two suitcases at her feet, standing at the entrance to the Porte Dauphine Métro. A man in civilian clothes was taking a photo of her positioned directly below the ornate art nouveau archway, its stylised lettering made famous all around the world.

That should have been Duchene's clue. But in the rush to get away from the Gestapo, he'd let his attention slide. The suitcases, the photo, this should have suggested a tourist. And other than the occasional Italian, who were mostly absent from the city now, there were no tourists – only the occupiers.

In his defence, she was a woman. As far as he knew, all female German workers – secretaries and nurses – had been recalled, withdrawn from being so close to the front.

She had a nice smile, her blonde hair was recently curled, and her large eyes stayed fixed on him. He hadn't noticed himself growing older; from time to time, he even forgot. The gaze of an attractive woman remained the same reward it had been when he was twenty.

All too easy to fall for the enemy.

He pulled out the Baedeker guide and started to thumb the pages. Consulting the map at the back, he worked through the guide systematically, looking at each circle on the grid and tracking it to the entry in the book. Each was marked with a dog-eared page, each a notable destination. All but one.

On a map of the Right Bank, a circle had been drawn a block from Square Léon Serpollet, but it didn't highlight any monument or destination.

Turning to the back of the book, being careful not to spill its contents in the rattle of the train, Duchene leafed through the ticket stubs and clippings. Kloke had visited the Eiffel Tower three times, or perhaps the other two tickets had been purchased for his friends. Many of the cabarets in Montmartre were here: Lapin Agile, Moulin Rouge, The Elysee. The Louvre, of course. Napoleon's

Tomb, and five stubs from the music hall Café de l'Olympia.

On the back of one of these was written: 5 *Rue des Cloys*.

The narrow, cobbled street was unremarkable, which immediately caught his attention. Rue des Cloys was lined with storehouses and the occasional shopfront. Most of these were closed up, and there was little foot traffic.

He stopped outside number five. It was a grey building two storeys high, its render falling free in places, exposing the brick beneath. *Molyneux Textiles* was written in fading paint over the door. Duchene peered through its window. He could see very little, as rolls of fabric had been stacked up against the glass. Dust and cobwebs covered the cloth, and some of the lighter rolls were marked with mildew.

Pushing open the letter hatch, Duchene could see a pile of curling envelopes beneath it. These had fallen into the only clear space on the other side of the door. Heavy rolls of bunting had been pushed up against the door, barring access and confirming that Molyneux Textiles was long since closed to business.

He walked around the corner of Impasse des Cloys. The storehouse ran most of the length of the short alleyway that it shared with the backs of other stores. Old wooden winches hung above him, outlined against the grey sky. There was no other entrance.

He moved along the alleyway, scanning the ground and looking for signs of activity. About halfway down, he stopped.

An empty beer bottle had been placed against the wall. He hunched down beside it. Its label was damp, the letters and brand mark puckered from the damp: Kronenbourg. Not normally uncommon, but with the recent bombings and ensuing food shortages, a scarce commodity. Something was in the bottom of the bottle.

Duchene upended it and let the dripping contents slide onto the cobblestones. Two cigarettes, both with lipstick, and a tiny, balled piece of paper. He plucked this up and slowly unravelled it. It had refused the water, being waxed on one side, and soon he had spread it out into a small brown rectangle. From his pocket he drew out the methamphetamines he'd taken from Kloke's room. Careful not to lose any of the powder to the wind, he spread out the paper. He didn't risk placing them side by side for comparison; it was enough to eyeball them. They were cut from the same paper. Across the wax, fine lines like a spider's web had appeared when the slip had been crumpled. But beneath these, thicker score lines marked out the original folds.

These matched the paper in Duchene's hand. He refolded his piece and slipped it back into his pocket.

THIRTEEN

Duchene placed the telephone receiver back in its hook. A coin clanked through the machine and fell into the return tray. He took it and sat for a moment on the narrow bench inside the phone booth. He fished out his half cigarette and lit it. The rain had resumed; he knew no one would come out to make a call in this weather, not unless they were desperate.

Lucien had not been at home. The housekeeper who lived in the small apartment on the ground floor of his building had been brisk when taking Duchene's message. No doubt Lucien kept her in chocolate for agreeing to take his messages, but the task was obviously wearing thin.

Duchene had made sure to express his appreciation to the housekeeper. If it weren't for her, he'd have next to no chance of contacting the smuggler.

He checked his watch. Six p.m. Still too early for the brothels and clubs to open. He could eat and then make his journey out into the night.

Pulling up his collar and firmly securing his hat, he stepped out into the rain. Few people were on the street, and he cursed himself for leaving his umbrella back at the apartment. Splashing through the downpour, he reached a nearby café, Adelelmus, and huddled at the edge of its awning beside a large group. He knew the owner, Marcel. Before the occupation, Marcel would have joined the rest outside on a day like this, pouring coffee into cups held by cold, damp hands and offering the women dry towels. That ruddy-cheeked host had always been quick to refuse payment and keen to offer a moment of respite. Looking over the heads of the crowd, Duchene could see him now, a different man, sitting at the back of the empty café in front of an empty patisserie counter, sipping water and staring at the ceiling.

On the opposite side of the street was a man who had remembered his trench coat – the only person standing still in the rain.

Duchene left the shelter of the café awning and hurried down the street towards the nearest Métro. Moving from awning to awning, he glanced over his shoulder. He must be spooked by his time in the Gestapo headquarters.

But the man in the trench coat was still on the street behind him. He was being followed.

There was only one place in all of Paris he could go without revealing another source for the Gestapo to arrest: home. A place that was no secret to anyone with access to a phone book.

Returning to his apartment, he found the hot water was not working in his meagre shower. A visit to the basement revealed the boiler was out of fuel. It seemed unwise to try to restock it, with supplies in question and winter still some months away.

After a quick cold shower, he rewarded himself with the last of his tea. He eyed the last bottle of cognac but rebuked himself. It was there for trade; it would be worth more in meals than as a drink.

His larder hadn't changed, and he took out the can of compressed meat and two small potatoes. He diced them and used them to cook up a stew, adding a little dried stock and some stale bread to thicken it. It sufficed.

He held back on eating all the tinned beef, reserving some to add to his egg for breakfast. Besides, he knew too well from his time in the trenches the perils of eating too much canned meat on an empty stomach.

After washing his plate, he left his apartment and crossed the hallway to Camille's door. She answered within a few taps. 'Auguste.'

She was wearing her silk robe. The collar was loose around her shoulder, and he could see a dark-green corselette contrasting with her pale skin. She smelt of musky perfume and face powder.

As she stood on her toes to kiss his cheek, he found himself remaining there, her face against his. 'I saw your note last night,' he said.

'I heard you come and go, during the curfew. I was worried.'

He held her against him. She remained there, pressing her warmth into him. 'It was important.'

'So important to risk being sent to a work camp?' she whispered. 'That's what they're doing now. No reprimand, no lock-up overnight. For breaking the curfew.'

'I'll be all right. Faber gave me a letter – he's asked me to find someone.'

'Oh.' Camille stepped away. The concern on her face became something else. Sadness? No, disappointment.

'I was wondering if I could use your phone? I can't use the one downstairs. It's complicated. I can pay?'

She stepped back from the door. 'Then come in.'

'I need to make the call in private. Would you mind waiting in my apartment while I do it?'

She frowned.

'I wouldn't ask if it wasn't important. I'm sorry.'

Without another word, she crossed the hallway.

He walked into her living room and sat on her settee. Looking over to her bedroom, he could see that he'd interrupted her preparations for the night ahead. A green evening dress had been carefully laid out on the edge of her bed, and on her nightstand was the last of her makeup and perfumes.

Picking up her phone, he dialled Lucien. He planned the brief note he'd ask the housekeeper to take, but to his surprise, Lucien answered.

'It's me, Auguste,' Duchene said.

Lucien laughed. 'Are you checking up on me? I saw your message. I'll be there. On time.'

'We'll need to meet another way. Can you get a car, come and get me from my place at eight tonight?'

'I'm flattered you think I have access to these resources.'

'I can pay with trade. I need the car.'

'Auguste –'

'Two cartons of Ecksteins. Twenty packets. They're all I have left.'

'It's not that I don't want to. But at this short notice it's going to be hard for me to convince the owner to let me borrow it.'

'I also have one last bottle of cognac. Would that do it?'

'That could get you food for a week. What are you going to do? Put aside your dislike for Max and have all your meals at Marienne's? Are you sure it's that important?'

'I might not have a week. Can you get the car for the cognac?'

'Yes, that and the cigarettes will do it. Honestly, you need to make better deals. That was their only child, Auguste, almost lost to them forever. You could have taken a car as payment – you could have taken two. Then you wouldn't be in this predicament. In fact, because we split it all fifty-fifty, we'd both be better off.'

Duchene patted his jacket pockets, then trousers, for a cigarette. Nothing. 'See you at eight. On the dot. And keep the engine running.' He hung up and placed a franc beside the phone.

He tapped on the door to his apartment before pushing it open. Camille was sitting on the edge of his couch between a pile of English poets and a complete collection of Victor Hugo. 'When this thing is over,' she said, 'you need to buy some new bookshelves.'

'I know.'

'Not that I didn't appreciate you burning some of these as fuel last winter.'

'I'm sorry about before. I'm caught up in something. Three things, really, and I don't want to drag you into them.'

'Oh, please. I play piano for Germans. Drunk Germans. What I already know could have me executed. That's the thing about being a woman over a certain age. They assume I'm harmless – too old to be a honey trap – and so the talk flows freely.'

'They don't appreciate you.'

'Not in that way – not as a threat. It's a relief. I'd feel better away from their attention entirely.'

'If you want to stay away from German attention, the less you know the better.'

She nodded, her face softening, and reached into her pocket for a cigarette. 'You can't protect everyone,' she said as she lit it.

'May I?' he asked as she was putting the packet away.

She passed him her lit cigarette and started a new one for herself.

Sitting on the edge of the couch beside her, he said, 'I know I can't protect everyone. But I can try to protect Marienne and you.'

Camille placed a hand on his face.

'I'm sorry I didn't visit you last night,' he said, keeping his eyes on hers.

'Your mistake. I was drunk. Lonely.'

'I'm here now.'

'I'm not your lover,' she said.

'I know.' He moved to take his hand away.

She kept it held to the side of her face. 'Not your wife.'

'I know.'

She leant forward, and guided him slowly backward to lie on the couch. Books fell from the chair to the floor; others she brushed aside as she moved to straddle his hips. She took one last drag on the cigarette before dropping it into an empty wineglass on the ground beside him. He did the same, and as he brought his gaze back to her face, he found she was close to him now. Her blue eyes were looking down into his. 'Open your mouth,' she said.

When he parted his lips, she kissed him, her tongue pushing its way into his mouth. In a moment, her hand was behind his head, pulling him towards her. He found himself doing the same, his hands at her back, holding her down against him, her breasts soft on his chest.

He said, 'It's been …'

Placing her hands over his lips, she smiled and shook her head. She unbuttoned his trousers, positioned herself on top of him and started to grind against him, her eyes bright as she looked at him. She let out a soft groan when he felt her clitoris rubbing against him, and her head fell back. The robe slipped around her waist. Her corselette exposed, she looked down to readjust – but, seeing something in his face, instead reached in and cupped out a breast.

At this, he started to swell. She squeezed her nipple. As he sat up and sucked on her breast, she laughed and moaned. He had done as he was bidden.

Adjusting again, she brought him inside her, moving without losing the rhythm of her rocking. He rocked as well, his hands on her lower back, mirroring her. She placed her hands on his chest, her movements becoming more urgent. The blood started to fall from his erection; sliding his hand between them, he gripped its base. This provided her with something further to grind against, and soon her face was flushed red. It took only moments before she convulsed and shook, pressing herself hard against him. She kissed him again as he moved his hand from his now flaccid penis. She lay there with him in her.

'Camille …'

'I enjoyed that. Shall we try something more? For you?'

He was tempted. But her satisfaction had been achieved, and it lingered around them, warm and complete.

'I'm happy where I am. But thank you.'

They remained on the couch, holding one another, as the daylight faded in the apartment around them, shadows growing. As if by some primal instinct, Camille relit her cigarette. Bringing the wineglass with her to tap ash into, she snuggled against him. 'Are you in danger, Auguste?'

'Danger?'

'Is Faber part of this? I saw the way he was talking to you at Marienne's dinner party.'

Duchene took the cigarette from her hand, inhaled and let the smoke remain in his lungs. He spoke as he exhaled. 'He is involved. Am I in danger? Maybe. All I know is that if he'd never entered our lives, we'd be a lot safer.'

'I don't like him.'

'You're right not to. The charm, the eloquence, it's all artifice. He's savage.'

'And Marienne – is that why you're helping him?'

'Yes. She can hate me all she wants, but she's not safe until I do this.'

FOURTEEN

The rain had stopped, and now the road glistened under the street lamps. Duchene stood in the dark lobby of his apartment building. In his pocket was the fuse for the downstairs lights; he didn't want a passing neighbour turning on the switch and giving away his position.

On the other side of the street, tucked behind a wrought-iron fence that bordered a thick hedge, he could see the cuff of a tan trench coat.

A dark-blue Renault paused outside his door. The driver flicked the cabin light on and off. With his head low, Duchene pushed open the door and unfolded his umbrella. He ran to the passenger's side. The door was open when he got there, and he slid in. His foot had barely left the ground as the car pulled away, its wheels briefly spinning on the slick.

Lucien smiled across at him. 'Not the first time I've done this. But I'm guessing it is for you. Who's following you?'

'How do you know my daughter's fiancé is called Max?'

'Pardon?'

'Marienne's never used his name in front of you. You called him Max on the phone before.'

'Marienne and I talk.'

'Did she put you up to it? The other morning, that random encounter?'

'Of course. A daughter wants to see her father – who am I to say no?' Lucien didn't seem bothered. He turned a corner and cut in front of a bus that beeped its horn and flashed blue headlights at them. 'Are we being followed on foot or by car?'

'On foot. I think.'

'Well, let's not chance it,' Lucien said, cutting through a red light.

'What do you mean, you and Marienne talk?'

'You know what I do. She likes to keep herself in stockings. It's not a thing to trouble yourself over.'

'Stockings? And what does Max think of all this?'

'Nothing. He pays what I ask. Some of my best clients are Germans. Their quartermaster is one of the best buyers in Paris – he's been stockpiling for weeks. You can see it all around you. They're getting ready for a battle.'

'All right.'

'What's made you so suspicious all of a sudden? This tail, is it Armand? The Resistance?'

'Probably. I have no idea.'

Lucien laughed. 'For someone so good at reading people, you're a terrible liar.'

'Perhaps that's why we complement one another.'

'True.' Lucien gave the wheel one last sharp turn, sending a young couple running, and slowed the car as he turned onto Rue Custine. 'So where to now?'

'Do you know anything about 5 Rue des Cloys?'

'Never heard of it.'

'Drive there and see what you make of it.'

Duchene kept a constant watch through the rear windscreen. There were many dark cars, many Citroëns, many times when a car would follow them before turning at an intersection. This vigilance irritated Lucien, who was convinced no one was following them. 'I spend every waking hour watching for trouble. I know when I'm being followed.'

Duchene didn't put much faith in his confidence. The Gestapo spent their waking hours ensuring their targets weren't aware they were being tracked. But Duchene's concerns became moot as Lucien brought the Renault on to Rue des Cloys.

The street was almost empty. A couple were walking up the left-hand side, while a young man approached them on the right. Lucien slowed the car to a stop at number five. The young man kept walking. Even though he wore a coat, he must have been feeling the cold; his face was pale, lips flushed with blood.

Lucien looked up at the building. 'Abandoned?'

'I don't know. It was marked on a map. One of the few places I know he visited.'

'The priest, Father Ramelle?'

'No. Someone else.'

Lucien took Duchene by the arm. 'We're not looking for the guns?'

'Not right now.'

'But you are looking for them, right? And the priest? It won't be good for either of us if you can't find them.'

'Yes, I'm looking for them.'

'So it wasn't the Resistance following you?'

Duchene tugged his arm free from Lucien's grip. 'I don't know. Probably. What do they have over you?'

'Philippe and Armand? Nothing.' Lucien pulled out a cigarette and offered the packet to Duchene. 'I know you've already figured out my part in this. I helped them get the guns in.'

'So why did they come to me, specifically?'

'The Verniers. You're famous.'

'Lucien, did you bring them to me? Put Marienne in danger?'

'Of course not.'

'You seemed nervous as hell when they were in my room.'

'They make me nervous. Philippe is a zealot, pushed to violence, ever since he and his students were taken by the Germans. He was tortured in the grounds of the Sorbonne, right below his office window – or so I'm told. And Armand ... obviously he's unhinged. He lost his family at Oradour-sur-Glane, a couple of months ago. The SS executed the entire village as revenge for the capture of an SS commander by Maquis fighters. I didn't want you to get hurt.'

'Or you.'

'Of course, sure. I didn't want to get hurt either. I've seen Armand stab a man in the neck just for being slow to answer.'

'Spent a lot of time with them?'

'More time than I would like. They're dangerous and dangerous to be around. That much is as clear as day. Auguste, I'm struggling to understand why we're here. They will kill you.'

'I can't tell you. It's safer that way.'

'Fine. I'm just trying to give you some good advice, for the girl's sake and yours.'

Duchene glanced over his shoulder. The young man who'd passed them was now standing at the end of the street, watching them.

'Those windows are covered,' Lucien said. 'Really covered.'

'What do you mean?

'The street lamp. It's reflecting in the window.'

'So? Lights reflect in dark windows.'

'The reflection is too crisp. Normally the light is blurred. Someone has placed a blackout cover close to that window, it's made it like a mirror. I know stash houses. I've been at this game a long time.'

'Is that what this is?'

Lucien paused. 'Actually, no ... I don't think so. Too little foot traffic, not enough to conceal the entrance. You want just enough so your comings and goings aren't strange, but not so much that there are too many eyes on the place.'

'The front door's all locked up. Old mail on the floor below the letterbox. No one's been through there in years.'

'Who says that's the front door?' Lucien said as he stepped from the car and started to walk up the street.

Duchene hauled himself out and started after Lucien. 'The alley's behind us. No doors there either.'

Lucien smiled back at him and walked to the neighbouring building, a rundown townhouse. A dim light was coming through its flaking shutters, which were closed and locked in place with a padlock. He let his cigarette hang from his mouth as he removed a pair of driving gloves and knocked on the chipped door. Duchene came to stand beside him. They heard cautious footsteps approaching, then a pause – probably a peep through the keyhole – before the door was opened.

The bespectacled eyes of a bearded man looked back at them through the scantest of openings. The door chain was still in place. 'Can I help you?'

'Good evening,' Lucien said with a smile. 'We'd like to come in. We have money, and we're looking for a good time.' He was still smiling, clearly convinced of his course of action.

'Were you followed?' the bearded man asked.

'Well, a young man at the end of the street is watching us,' Lucien replied. 'But I suspect he's planning to return soon and knock on your door.'

'You scared him off. We don't get cars outside.'

'We can move it if you'd like. But I think one by itself is unlikely to raise suspicions.'

The man nodded. 'Come in,' he said as he closed the door and unlatched the chain.

'What's going on?' Duchene whispered to Lucien while their host was out of earshot.

'You're slipping, old man. You didn't read the signs. And here I thought you had a misspent youth back in the twenties.'

The door was opened, and they walked into a small, sparsely furnished living room. A wooden table stood across from an ancient, unused wood stove. There was nothing to sit on aside from the four chairs around it. A staircase opposite the door led up to a second storey.

The man was wearing a suit, with a fresh rose pinned to his lapel. In the light, Duchene could see that his spectacles were rimmed in purple.

'We'll have to let you out one at a time when you're done,' he said. 'I'm sure you understand. And please don't congregate on leaving – best to keep walking. Bar Alphonse is only two blocks from here, and they're open almost as late as we are. A good place to get another drink, if less sympathetic.'

'How much?' Lucien asked.

'Six francs each, drinks are upstairs. Enjoy yourselves.'

Duchene looked at Lucien, then sighed and dropped the coins into the man's hand. 'Is this a club?' he whispered to Lucien.

'Slow – yes, a pansy club,' Lucien said as they reached the top of the stairs. There was an open doorway on the landing; Lucien looked through it and returned his gaze to Duchene. 'Ingenious,' he said, beaming.

The doorway led to a small bedroom. An old single brass bed was scattered with a few hats. Five freestanding coat racks lined one wall into which had been cut a narrow doorway. Across it hung a pair of green curtains, each embroidered with a brightly coloured peacock.

'Didn't you notice that young man watching us?' Lucien asked.

'I saw him.'

'You didn't notice his makeup? Subtle, but visible. A brave choice considering the state of Paris.'

Lucien held open the curtain, and Duchene stepped through to the top floor of the storehouse. The transition from the shabby bedroom to the large and overdecorated space was almost surreal. From the ceiling beams hung swags of richly patterned fabric – dark greens and blues, ornate and luxuriant. Spread around the floor were divans and sofas, most of them reupholstered in the colour palette of the cloth above them. Palms and vases were scattered throughout the room, which also contained a limited dance floor at the far end and a bar closer to the entrance.

About fifteen people, in suits and dresses, sat in pairs or larger groupings on the couches. Not enough to fill the club, but the night was just starting. Some were truly beautiful, while others looked like Duchene often felt – worn down and rumpled.

A gramophone with an oversized horn played upbeat music: the Glenn Miller Orchestra. The sound was softer towards the front of the storehouse, and the makeshift acoustic baffles seemed to be working.

Duchene and Lucien approached the bartender, who offered a meagre selection of drinks: mostly beer, and some wine bottles that appeared to have had their labels reapplied. Duchene placed a few francs on the bar top. 'Is this enough to get us each something?'

The bartender, in a red crepe gown, smiled. 'More than enough. We try to forget the lean times here. Your drinks and change.'

Duchene sipped his beer, an Excelsior. It was sour, out of date.

'Can I ask you something?' he said to the bartender.

'You may.'

Duchene took out the photo of three Germans standing beneath the Eiffel Tower. He held his finger under Kloke. 'This man. Have you seen him here?'

'You'd better speak to Florette. The boss. She's over there.' The bartender nodded towards the far side of the warehouse. Lying on a chaise longue, next to the gramophone, was an Algerian woman. She wore a flowing gown, with a plunging neckline, and her lithe arms were bare. When a record ended, she would replace it.

'Thank you,' Duchene said to the bartender as he turned to approach Florette.

Lucien was staring at the photo with a furrowed brow. His eyes narrowed. 'You're looking for a German.'

'Yes.'

'Have to say, Auguste, that's going to rub the wrong way with Philippe.'

'Then don't tell him,' Duchene said, striding across the room.

Lucien scrambled to keep up. 'You're putting me at risk. Marienne too.'

'No, I'm working on getting us out of this nightmare. I'm knee-deep in shit, and it's steadily rising.'

'Who is he?'

'A friend of Max.'

'Bullshit.'

Duchene stopped. 'You're free to go, but leave the car.'

'Why won't you say?'

'Those men who have been following me. They're not with Philippe.'

'Another cell?'

'They're not Resistance.'

Lucien's brow furrowed again; an instant later, it smoothed out. He looked like a child, with all certainty, all confidence, stripped from him. Perhaps, if the room hadn't been lit by candles, Duchene would have seen the colour leave his face. He gripped Duchene's arm and leant so close his lips were touching his left ear. His whisper was more like a hiss. 'The fucking Gestapo?'

For the second time that night, Duchene pulled his arm free. He held a finger to his lips and continued towards the club's host.

As they drew near, Florette looked up at them with an amused expression. 'Lovers quarrel?'

'Something like that,' Duchene replied.

'Oh, well. This is a place of vanity and drama, where

lovers are made and broken. Although being a romantic, I'd always prefer it to be the former.'

'May we sit?' Duchene said, indicating the small couch opposite her.

'You're my guests. Of course. But please don't ask me to change the record – there's nothing so tedious as requests from the floor.'

'Wouldn't think of it,' Duchene replied. He sat on the couch, which seemed to draw him in.

Lucien observed this and perched on its end, avoiding a similar fate.

'I appreciate that this is a sensitive question,' said Duchene, 'but I'd like to ask you something.'

'About what?'

'A young man. He's missing.'

'One of ours?'

'Quite possibly.'

'Then, please proceed. But I make no promise you'll get answers. Without discretion, we'd run the risk of being rounded up. Times being what they are.'

Duchene offered her the photograph: Kloke with his lopsided grin, easy swagger and finger to the authority of his own uniform. 'The man in the centre,' Duchene said as Florette took it.

She examined the photo closely. 'He's German.'

'Yes.'

'Then that's easy to answer.'

'I understand, but why would he have this address in his personal effects? If he never visited?'

'You're mistaken, Monsieur …?'

'Duchene.'

'Monsieur Duchene. It's an easy answer – not because

he's a German and wouldn't come here. It's easy because he's the *only* German to spend time in this establishment.'

'You let a German in?' said Lucien.

'But of course.'

'Could you explain?' Duchene asked.

Florette held up a hand, soft and manicured, as she drew a record out of the pile beside her. This was well-worn jazz, Benny Goodman. As the previous song ended, she timed her replacement with confidence. The peal of a trumpet announced the first piece, and two older men got up to dance. Florette nodded to them. 'I always play it for them when they're in.' She took a sip of her drink, a martini. 'Now, where were we?'

'The German soldier,' said Duchene.

'So, yes, we weren't sure to start with. When he first came here, he came with a lover – one of ours. The German didn't seem like a soldier. I mean, of course he was, but he didn't have their demeanour. He was quite jolly. So, while his French was terrible, he was one of us, clearly. Besides, he was in the most danger of anyone in here.'

'Most?'

'Well, as you're probably aware, the Vichy have raised the age of consent. Many of our friends here are under twenty-one. But for the most part, the Germans have left us alone. I heard the rumours about Berlin after the Nazis got in – terrible, and in such a wonderful city. Have you ever been?'

'Yes,' said Duchene.

'In the twenties?'

'Yes.'

'Just so free-spirited.' She sighed. 'But here, in Paris, the Germans tend to turn a blind eye. You've heard, of course, about the Hyena of the Gestapo?'

'No,' he replied.

'Violette Morris, a French weightlifter working for the Germans. She handed over many Resistance fighters. Thankfully, she was assassinated earlier this year. But the fact that she was clearly a lesbian never bothered the Germans, as long as she gave them Partisans to kill.' Florette's eyes hardened. 'If worst came to worst – and I hate myself for having planned this – but if we were raided and Christian was in the club, I would hand him over. For them, that would be the greater crime. There's nothing the Germans hate more than a homosexual in their army. Not really in keeping with the Aryan ideal.'

'Thank you for telling me.' Duchene leant forward. 'I have no way of demonstrating that you should trust me further. But I am trying to find Christian. There's a fear he might be in danger.'

'Well, he is German, my love. That would be his just deserts. Homosexual he may be, but Frenchman he is not.'

'What about his lover? He could be in danger?'

She sniffed at the suggestion. '"Could be" isn't "is".'

'No chance of a name?'

'We spoke about discretion. As I said, I had plans for the German. I've forfeited him to you. But a Frenchman? That is a polite no. You don't build trust in the city by betraying your friends.'

Duchene nodded. 'But if Christian's lover returns, would you pass on my name? My number? Let him decide for himself.'

Florette waved a hand in Lucien's direction. 'A packet of those cigarettes he's smoking, and you have a deal.'

Duchene looked at Lucien.

'Jesus, Auguste, I'm not made of tobacco – this is the last of the Lucky Strikes.'

'You'll find others. You always do.'

Lucien scowled and dug into his jacket pocket. He produced an unopened packet and held it in his hand, as though weighing it. He gave it to Florette.

'Thank you,' she said and placed it on the pile of records beside her. 'Now, gentlemen, feel free to finish your drinks. After that, please leave.'

Duchene went over to stand at the bar with his stale beer and watched as Lucien talked closely with Florette, holding her hand and then farewelling her with a kiss on the cheek.

'Business?' Duchene asked, when Lucien was beside him again.

Lucien smiled. 'Of course,' he said. 'A place like this could do with a better supplier.'

Their trip back in the car was uneventful. Even so, Duchene asked Lucien to pull over a block from his apartment. Taking his umbrella from the back seat, he stepped out and walked around to the driver's window. Lucien cranked it down.

'The car,' Duchene said. 'I might need you to get me again.'

'Again?'

'A bottle of cognac is worth more than a trip out to Clignancourt and back. Tonight, you made a business contact because of me.'

'All right. But only once more, unless you can turn up

with something else worth trading.'

Duchene turned the corner and walked down his street, keeping a close eye on the time. Although he had Faber's letter exempting him from curfew, he didn't like the kind of attention created by being out when others weren't.

As he neared the apartment entrance, he increased his speed and quickly let himself inside. Monsieur Junet was balanced on a ladder, rattling at the light fitting in the darkened lobby. Light was spilling in from the open door of the Junets' downstairs apartment while Madame looked on. They wore matching slippers, old and threadbare.

'You know you shouldn't be up there,' Duchene said as he closed the door behind him.

With a glance back out to the street, he saw the point of a lit cigarette in the darkened doorway of the office block opposite. *More watchers.*

'It's the light,' Monsieur Junet said. 'It's out.'

'That is a problem,' said Duchene.

'And the boiler too,' added Madame Junet.

'I'll go down and stoke it up again when I'm done,' Duchene said as he moved over to pop open the fuse box. 'Monsieur, if you could stand back for a moment?'

Junet stared, his mind clearly needing a moment to catch up to Duchene's intention. Then the older man took two steps down the ladder.

Duchene slid the fuse back into its socket, and the light flicked into life again.

Madame Junet gave a brief clap. 'Well done, Monsieur Duchene.'

'I would have had it, eventually.' Junet slowly finished climbing down from the ladder, then crossed the lobby to shake Duchene's hand. 'Thank you.'

'It's nothing. I'll change my suit and go down to that boiler room.'

'There was a call for you,' Junet said, waving two fingers at the phone like a papal blessing.

'Oh?'

'A young woman, very polite. I left the note pinned to your door.'

Duchene put the ladder against the wall, offering to return it to the basement when he attended to the boiler. He took the stairs two at a time to his apartment, plucked the note from his door and stepped inside.

Mlle Payet called. Can meet tomorrow. 7 a.m., Le Fouquet's.
– M. Junet
PS, Foyer lights and boiler out.

Duchene crumpled the note and dropped it into the makeshift ashtray on his dining table. He took out his lighter and set it on fire.

Thursday, 17 August 1944

FIFTEEN

'God damn it, this is really pushing it,' Lucien said as he opened the Renault's door for Duchene. He pumped the pedal, and the car burst forward. Duchene was ready for it this time, his feet in and the door closed before they'd picked up too much speed.

He watched in the rear-view mirror as a man in a dark coat stepped out from a sheltered doorway – most likely the same man he saw earlier. He had his hat in his hand and swivelled on the spot – to chase would be futile. There was no denying it, the Gestapo were persistent.

'First, this is too fucking early. It's not even seven.' Lucien gave the steering wheel a sharp turn that made the tyres squeal. 'Second, my housekeeper has forbidden you from calling again. She's furious after last night.'

'Don't exaggerate. It was well before nine.'

'You could have waited until after curfew. I would have been in at least.'

'And left her to answer the phone anyway. Seemed the kinder thing to do.'

'Well, this is the last time we use this car. Owner's worried because it's getting low on petrol, and I don't want to run down my stores replacing it. The Germans are stockpiling it all.'

They were well into the flow of traffic now as they

moved towards the heart of the city. Duchene looked back to see if they were being followed, and kept watching all the way from the narrow tributary streets of the Palais-Royal to the wide flow of the Champs-Élysées.

Nothing.

He turned back to face the road.

'Anything?' asked Lucien.

'Not that I can see.'

'Well, that's something. You could look a bit more enthusiastic – you've got a chauffeur who's skilled in the art of misdirection. Things are looking up, my friend.'

Camille hadn't come home the night before. That wasn't unusual for her, especially if the German officers wanted her to play late into the night; they would give her an escort or offer her a spare room in their hotels. And yet, her not arriving had put him on edge. His sleep had been fraught, his memories ever-present. And with the Hennessy gone, he didn't even have anything to drink to quell the noise.

'Are they looking up?' he asked Lucien. 'I've got to get back to Philippe with an answer by the end of the day.' *And Faber.*

'I'm assuming this morning's rendezvous is to do with the missing priest?'

'It is. I'm meeting Madame Noirot's niece.'

Lucien raised an eyebrow.

'Apparently Madame lent the crypt key to her niece, who returned it before the cache was stolen. I'm hoping she knows who the thieves were. And how they got access to the crypt.'

Ahead was a convoy of German tanks, steel fortresses that shook the boulevard and everything on it. Their engines grunted under their tonnage and blasted thick smoke into the morning air. Lucien brought the car around them and detoured down a side street.

'If the niece knows something, anything, it's a start,' Duchene said to fill the silence. 'I'm hoping this will give me some names or faces.'

Lucien nodded. 'I'm keeping us clear of any convoys. There's a lot of movement on the roads today – at a guess, armour moving to the edges of the city. The Germans are twitchy. I'm not looking to give them a reason to stop us, or worse.'

'Agreed.'

Tables were set out on the pavement ahead – they sprang up each morning like mushrooms, to disappear again at curfew. They ran in a long uninterrupted row outside a line of cafés and brasseries. Although the restaurant shopfronts differed, the tables and chairs were identical, perhaps by some ancient by-law.

Lucien pulled up outside one of the restaurants. 'You're bold,' he said, peering through its windows at the glittering interior. 'Lot of Germans in there. Are you sure it's safe to talk about a missing cache of Resistance weapons?'

'We'll soon find out,' Duchene said as he opened the passenger door and slid out of his leather seat.

'Let's hope I see you later,' Lucien said.

Le Fouquet's was on a street corner. Both pedestrian and vehicle traffic was yet to pick up, but six soldiers formed a perimeter in front of the restaurant, their rifles slung, their young faces scanning the street. Several senior officers were seated at the tables on the pavement. Caps off, they ate breakfasts of pork sausage and other meats with a large beer in one hand and a cigarette in the other. Several gave Duchene cautious glances as he passed.

When he entered the restaurant, he took off his hat and scanned the room. There were more German officers and only a few civilians. The hum of the espresso machine was joined by an occasional burst of sound from the kitchen as its door opened. As they had been outside, conversations were muted. There was only one unaccompanied woman in the room; wearing a coat and hat more than a few seasons out of style, she sat in a corner, a coffee before her.

The maître d' started to approach Duchene, who waved him off just as the woman looked up. She was stunning, with high cheekbones and hazel eyes under well-defined brows. Her top lip was a true Cupid's bow. On the side of one cheek was a fine, faded scar, which seemed only to magnify her beauty.

'Eliane Payet?' Duchene asked as he arrived at her table.

'Monsieur Duchene,' she said, her voice husky and measured.

'Mademoiselle, you'll have to excuse me for being late.'

'It's no bother. I needed the coffee. The time wasn't wasted.'

He noted the black silk dress that peeked out from below the hem of her coat, the tired lines under her eyes.

The café favoured a faux-rococo style: heavy drapes, panelled walls, a crystal chandelier.

Duchene sat down and nodded towards her coffee cup. 'I'm surprised they still have some. You can't find coffee anywhere in Paris anymore.'

'Well, that's the trick, Monsieur Duchene. You have to follow the Germans.'

He smiled. 'I'm hoping you can help me with something.'

'So I understand. I got your message. I wasn't sure about

it at first, but I asked around. You're the man who finds the missing children.'

'Sometimes. If you'd let me pay for your meal, I'm hoping you'll answer some questions.'

She smirked at him. 'It would seem there is no such thing as a free breakfast after all.'

There were brass plaques on the wall behind her – the names of writers, artists and famous patrons.

Duchene waved over the waiter. Eliane seemed to know the menu; she ordered the breakfast sausage casserole and a beer. He ordered an omelette and a coffee.

'I could never get in here before the occupation,' she said. 'They wouldn't have me.'

He lowered his voice. 'I need to talk to you about your aunt. About the key she lent you.'

Eliane nodded, and the lightness left her face. 'Did you really find those children?'

'Yes.'

'I feel sick about it. The priest has gone missing.'

'Well, I'm trying to find him now. I'm trying to find him quickly.'

'You must understand that I had no idea. It seemed so … unimportant. Harmless.'

He paused. 'I guess it would have. A crypt isn't a place that people tend to go.'

'Unless they're –' she looked around the room before whispering, '– working for our side. They spoke French. I thought I was helping. I remember seeing the entrance to the Catacombs when I was a little girl. There's a secret door. I thought it was a way for them to, you know …'

Duchene nodded. 'Who approached you about the key?'

'I don't have names. There were two of them. Both tall.

One with dark hair, the other fair. They wore coats, hats – they weren't trying to make their identities known.' Eliane took out a cigarette packet: Camels. More American cigarettes, spreading like wildfire, faster than their approaching army.

Duchene reached out his lighter. While he lit the cigarette, she cradled his hands in both of hers. They were cold and shook a little. She plucked a stray piece of tobacco from the side of her lip and exhaled. 'Do you want one?'

'Please.' He regretted it immediately – the smoke was harsh. 'What else can you tell me about them?'

'They came to see me three times. The first time to ask me to get the key. They offered me forty francs – twenty in advance, twenty on delivery. The other times were to take the key and return it.'

'Where was this?'

'Near where I work.' She drew on the cigarette and exhaled. 'At Raspoutine. They took it before curfew and returned it to me the next morning when curfew broke.'

'They knew who you were?'

'Yes.'

'How do you imagine they knew about you and your aunt?'

'That's a longer story. Let's just say that I am an embarrassment to her and the congregation of Saint-Lambert. I used to go there when I was little. Then the war came, I lost my job, found other ways to make money. They learnt about it. I'm the source of much gossip.' A bittersweet smile passed across her face.

'Did these men say anything specific that might help me identify them? And was there anything strange about them, anything that didn't make sense?'

'One did most of the talking. He was stern. Blond. Frowned a lot. The other was silent most of the time – except for when I left, and he offered to escort me to the Métro. His accent wasn't French, it was German.'

'German? Are you sure?'

'I am certain. Although he didn't seem like a soldier. But what else could he have been?'

'You said he had dark hair?'

'Yes.'

'A lopsided smile, maybe?'

'Yes.'

Duchene's hands had moved faster than his thoughts; he looked down and saw he was already holding the Baedeker guidebook. He pulled out the Eiffel Tower photo and showed it to Eliane. 'Is this the man?' he said, pointing to Kloke.

She only peered at it for a moment. 'That's him.'

'You're certain?'

She nodded.

Duchene had to sit back in his chair. His mind was racing as it looked for connections, trying to unpick the knot. *How did Kloke know about the cache?*

Duchene thought of Faber. This would explain his desperation to find Kloke. And the Gestapo's interest. That made some sense, at least.

'Are you sure the other man was French?' Duchene asked. 'Perhaps he spoke with a Swiss accent, just a hint?'

'Maybe. I don't know if I've spoken to that many Swiss people in my life.'

'Not older? Not thinning across the brow?'

'They wore hats. It's possible, sure, but he didn't look that old.'

The door to the restaurant chimed as it opened. Duchene found himself looking up along with most of the customers. They must have sensed what he had: a stiffness to the movements of the new arrivals, the weight of their sizeable presence, the bristling animal intensity.

The two men in dark coats had returned.

The maître d' approached them, but one of the men shoved him aside. The other kept moving towards Duchene at the corner table.

'What's happening?' Eliane asked.

'They've come for me. It's all right.' He started to get out of his seat, but the heavyset Gestapo pushed him back into his chair.

'Fräulein,' he said to Eliane and held out his hand.

She looked at him, shocked. She looked at Duchene, her big eyes trembling.

'What's going on?' he asked in German.

The Gestapo officer ignored him. Placing a large hand around Eliane's arm, he pulled her violently from the chair. She had just enough time to grab her bag. Her eyes locked onto Duchene's as she was hauled towards the front door.

One of the officers at the table nearest the door stood up to block the path of the man with Eliane. 'What is going on? Answer immediately.'

'Move,' grunted the Gestapo officer who had remained by the door.

Two more Germans stood. The crowd at the outdoor tables had started to react. Duchene could see a senior officer talking to one of the soldiers stationed outside.

When the Gestapo officer by the door reached into his jacket pocket, several hands moved to sidearms. He took out an identification wallet and flapped it open. 'Gestapo,' he said to the room. 'This woman is an insurgent. She is under arrest.'

'No,' Eliane shouted in German, pulling against the man who held her.

Their response was brutal, brief. A meaty slap to her face, and then she was hauled up by both men.

The German officers stepped aside but remained standing. Duchene could do nothing but watch as Eliane was dragged out of the room.

The black Citroën was parked on the street. Waiting at the driver's door, smoking, was the man with ice-blue eyes. He nodded to Duchene before pulling the passenger door open so his companions could bundle Eliane inside.

In a moment they were gone, and the silent restaurant burst into commotion.

Duchene was out on the street. Walking. Walking off the trembling that had seized him in the seconds after the Gestapo left. His whole body was shaking. He'd barely had the sense to drop the money he had onto the table.

He sucked air into his lungs.

He was so sure they hadn't followed him. Certain of it. He'd left the Gestapo on the street outside his apartment.

Perhaps he was meant to see his observer – a misdirection, so the real pursuers could follow him and Lucien when their guard was down. *An obvious misdirection*.

He stopped walking and grabbed hold of a lamppost. He tried to discipline his mind, let it track through the morning's events.

No. He had watched with absolute vigilance as they'd driven away from Saint-Ambroise. It had been too early for much traffic. There had been no one behind them for blocks. And they'd had no way of knowing where he was headed.

That's not the point.

He was right.

Why did they take the girl?

That was the real question. They'd said she was an insurgent, part of the Resistance, but this was clearly untrue. It was an acceptable explanation that would justify their behaviour to the German officers in the room.

Why did they take the girl?

Maybe they were using him as a harrier dog to flush out their quarry and then they would do their own interrogations.

Interrogations.

His gut welled up. He braced against the lamppost and bent forward.

Nothing came. Not even a dry retch.

A man approached him, concern spreading across his face. Duchene gave a weak wave, an open hand – *I'm all right.*

He sat at the base of the lamppost and patted his pockets for cigarettes. Nothing.

People were staring at him as they walked wide around him. He must have looked like just another crazy old man – incoherent and troubled, driven mad with age, his mind lost to time.

A waiter emerged from the adjacent café and walked towards Duchene. Waving him off failed, and he squatted at the lamppost. He had a calm, pleasant face. 'Monsieur, you should sit at one of our tables,' he said, offering Duchene a hand.

'I don't have any money.'

'I'll get you something to drink anyway.'

'Someone has to pay for it.'

'Don't worry about that. Come, Monsieur, sit.'

The waiter helped Duchene to his feet and led him over to one of the street-side tables. Within moments, a coffee appeared.

'Thank you,' Duchene said.

'Think nothing of it,' the waiter replied.

A moment of kindness. *Or to keep me from driving away their customers*.

He was so riddled with suspicion, so ready to think the worst, it was like a disease in his brain. His every thought was becoming tainted.

He sipped; he took another breath.

His distress at Eliane's arrest was passing, sliding off him. He had seen men die, explode into steaming pieces, and watched their entrails slide through their hands and into the mud at their feet. He had seen and survived worse.

He could survive this. All else was unimportant save for Marienne, Camille and, if he could manage it, himself.

He took another sip of the coffee. Swallowed. He could let his body guide him forward while his mind wandered.

Kloke was connected to the missing priest. Perhaps he had killed him. There had been a pistol in the hotel room, a Webley. It was common enough, the sidearm of enlisted British soldiers – but it was also one of the weapons Armand had listed as part of the cache. And who was this second man Eliane had described? A man who spoke French.

'Faber, perhaps,' Duchene said.

He drank. The caffeine moved through him. Stirred his mind into life.

If the second man wasn't Faber, Duchene was in trouble. Eliane's description didn't give him much else to go on.

But that challenge paled into insignificance when he played through a scenario where he was successful.

If he found Kloke and gave him to Philippe, Faber would feel cheated.

If he found Kloke and gave him to Faber, the Resistance would feel cheated.

Either outcome was bad for Marienne. The thought threatened to overwhelm him.

Except it was a problem that he didn't currently face. Right now, he didn't know where Kloke was. Right now, he couldn't satisfy the Resistance or Faber.

He checked his watch. Nine a.m.

He had twelve hours. Twelve hours to find Kloke and make a choice.

The Gestapo.

Perhaps there was another way. Lead Faber to Kloke? Betray the Resistance to the Gestapo? All it would take was an agreed meeting place and a phone call. He had their number on a card.

No.

Because then he would be a collaborator. Truly.

Even if he could willingly choose to help the Germans – push aside everything he'd fought for, push aside everything he believed in – as he had seen so many others do, the consequences would be deadly. To do this would be to sign his own death sentence. But at least Marienne would be saved.

It was a desperate option. If it were to play out, he'd need to build up a rapport.

He tapped the waiter's arm as he passed with a tray from the table he was clearing. 'I have a favour to ask, Monsieur. One last thing. A phone call.'

SIXTEEN

Duchene descended to the walkway that ran along the Seine. A chill rose from the cold, black waters. This was what he'd imagined the Styx to be, almost – it would be glassy and smooth, but all else would be the same. Even now, he could see the motorboat approaching him. Not the ferryman, but something close: three men, any of whom could be leading him to his death, although he sensed the only one he recognised, Armand, would be performing that role if it came to it.

The motorboat slid up to the jetty.

Duchene glanced over his shoulder. Along either side of the causeway. If the Gestapo were still following him, they would have to make themselves known to see this.

'Get in,' Armand said.

'Where's Philippe?'

Armand held a rusted iron ring that was embedded into the stonework. He kept the boat in position, his arms like a mooring rope, muscles straining under his grey jacket. 'Get. In.' He glowered at Duchene from beneath his oversized fedora.

Duchene stepped into the boat and grabbed one of its sides, steadying himself as he sat among crab pots. The pilot at the tiller revved the boat into motion, and they started across the river, cutting through the currents that moved over its surface. The spray that hit his face was briny, but it became less frequent as they motored down the opposite side of the river. They followed the Left Bank, passing large, flat barges. The motorboat slid under bridges he'd often crossed but never seen from below: the Pont de la Concorde with its dark bricks of Bastille rubble clearly visible, then the Pont Royal with arches that rose in gentle curves from the water. Soon they were cutting past the Île de la Cité, cluttered with its palaces, law courts and cathedral.

They slowed as they reached the next bridge and coasted up to another jetty. Philippe was waiting, and he jumped cleanly onto the boat. He used a leather satchel in his right hand as a counterweight to keep his balance.

'Where to?' the pilot asked from the stern.

'Follow the gardens, then take us along the Right Bank again. We'll find them eventually.'

Armand stepped back from his position at the bow and joined Philippe on the bench opposite Duchene. He hunched forward, picking at his tooth with a folded matchbook.

The motor spurred into action, and they continued downriver, sitting in silence while the pilot scanned the currents. By the time he adjusted their course, they were some distance from the centre of the city.

Philippe looked up at the pilot. 'Run past it, at a distance, then loop back. Make sure you see Casin before getting too close.'

The pilot nodded and took them wide, past a long canal barge. It lay high in the water, its deck free of cargo. Armand moved his attention away from Duchene and stood up, scanning the canal boat for signs of movement. 'I don't recognise the man at the helm,' he said.

'Casin or we don't go in,' replied Philippe.

They turned at the stern of the barge, cutting across its wake, before running down its starboard side.

A second man emerged from somewhere on the decks. Wild hair blew across a balding pate. He beckoned for them to pull up alongside. This satisfied Philippe, who nodded to the boat's pilot to move towards the larger vessel. Within no time they had moored to the side of the canal barge, and the rope-worn hands of Casin were reaching down to help pull Duchene on board.

'Good afternoon,' Casin said. 'Below decks, please, before we draw too much suspicion.'

Duchene climbed backwards down a slanting ladder, which seemed to amuse Casin, and ducked his head to follow Philippe across the hull. Thin shafts of light broke through the loading hatches on the deck above them. The few portholes that lined the sides of the ship glowed dimly in the darkness, covered over with stained newspaper – old copies of the *Pariser Zeitung*. The muffled call of the river lapping at the sides of the boat was answered by the sound of water moving somewhere inside the vessel. The dampness reached up the sleeves of Duchene's jacket and wrapped itself around him.

Philippe stood ahead of him, with Armand by his side. He gestured to a large, mouldy tarpaulin spread out at their feet.

Within seconds, Duchene could hear his heart in his ears. His hands started to tremble. 'What's going on?'

'Please.' Philippe gestured again as though the request was entirely ordinary.

Duchene walked over to the tarpaulin. Along one side

were large metal eyelets. Through these, a rope had been strung: one end securely tied to the tarpaulin, the other to a rusted anchor.

'I still have time,' Duchene replied.

Philippe made the gesture again, his face expressionless.

Casin and the two men from the motorboat moved to stand in a tight line behind Duchene.

He stepped onto the tarp as he struggled to control his breathing.

'You have something you want to talk about?' Philippe asked.

Duchene looked back over his shoulder as the men closed in on him. They were standing an arm's reach away.

He closed his hands into fists. It did little to stop the shaking.

'I need more time,' he said, his own voice strained and foreign. 'I'm not going to have the priest to you by this evening.'

'Actually, your time is already up,' Philippe replied. 'We met forty-eight hours ago. You never had until the evening. You're not what they said you were, Auguste. It's very disappointing.'

'I know who took your guns.'

The Resistance fighters stood absolutely still. The only sound came from the lapping of the water on the side of the barge.

Philippe's eyes were alert. 'Proceed.'

'I need a commitment before I say anything.'

'What for?'

'Marienne. Me. No harm. You must agree.'

'Why?'

'Because of this,' he said, pointing to the tarpaulin under his feet. 'You must guarantee.'

'Sure,' said Armand. 'We agree.'

'Not you,' Duchene replied. 'Him.'

'Fine,' said Philippe. 'Very well, you can have another twenty-four hours. Assuming you actually give us a name.'

'A German soldier, Christian Kloke, took the guns.'

Philippe raised both eyebrows, while Armand started glowering again.

'Bullshit,' said Armand.

'Elaborate,' said Philippe.

Duchene removed the photo of Kloke from his pocket. 'The man in the centre, that's Kloke. Somehow he learnt about your cache and, with an accomplice, managed to get into the crypt.'

'How?'

'I'm not sure. But they had access to the key overnight.'

'All right. How?'

'You have to swear you won't harm them.'

'Jesus, Duchene, what kind of people do you think we are?' Philippe asked.

'I think you're a man who believes you've got no other choice. Desperate times ... I think you're capable of anything.'

'Fine. I swear.'

'It was Madame Noirot, the church housekeeper. The woman who gave them the key was her niece.'

Armand sneered. 'Collaborators.'

'No. Think. If this man Kloke was acting on behalf of the Germans, they would have stormed the church and seized the weapons. Both the housekeeper and her niece spoke to me freely and in trust that they wouldn't be harmed.'

And now one of them is in a Gestapo cell on Rue des Saussaies.

Philippe ran a hand through his hair as he started to pace. 'So why did he take them, and where?'

'Both good questions. I'm still looking for Kloke. I have the name of someone, a lover, and I'm talking to them later today.'

Duchene tried to steady his gaze on Philippe, who was preoccupied with straightening his neck scarf. If Duchene remained still enough, the lie would pass.

Armand narrowed his eyes. 'I'll go with him. Talk sense to her.'

'No,' said Philippe. 'It's the closest we've been to the weapons. Let him continue his approach.'

'And the priest?' Duchene asked.

'Who cares?' said Armand. 'You're saying he didn't take the cache. Find this Boche thief. Find our cache.'

'Armand, please.' Philippe shook his head, then sighed. 'But I agree. I'm sorry for Father Ramelle. He is, was, a good man, but his safety is less important than that of the city. You've seen what's happening out there on the streets. The Americans, the Free French, they'll be here soon. The Germans know it. We know it. The citizens of Paris are getting ready to rise up, and we need those guns to help us do it.' Philippe waved a hand towards the ladder. 'Get him out of here.'

Armand gave Duchene a rough push to get him moving.

As he crossed the deck, Philippe walked alongside him and said, 'You think I'm wrong.'

'Who am I to say if the people will rise up?' Duchene replied.

'Of that I have no doubt. What I mean is that you think I am morally wrong.'

'Why would that matter?'

'You would have assisted me without the threats, if I had just asked?'

'Perhaps.'

Philippe smiled. 'Come, Auguste. When I spoke to Lucien about you, he tried to discourage me. He said you were too cautious – that you wouldn't do it – because of the risks involved. Tell me, would you have risked breaking curfew or discovery by the Gestapo so you could help find weapons? Guns are not the same as missing children – you're not saved the moral culpability. You're to find murder tools. To be used to overthrow oppressors, yes, but to kill people. People who have lives, yes, some of them souls even, if you like to think that way.'

'So you use my daughter to compel me? Threaten the life of an innocent?'

'You can't believe that. No one is truly innocent. She made a choice to collaborate, to fuck the enemy.'

'And that is punishable by death?'

'Only if you fail. I know you believe that the repercussions are extreme, but we live in extreme times. When we strike at the Germans, they will execute French patriots, but these punishments were decided by and exacted by an enemy. We are not responsible for their actions.'

'You're willing to make such a decision, because of what they did to your students three years ago?'

Philippe grabbed him by the arm and stepped in front of him. 'Not just my students. Me. It was no small thing – standing us naked in the rain all night only to line some of us up with guns to our heads. In retrospect it is so transparent, some theatre to break our will. Again, we didn't push them to this. It was one of the many foreseeable outcomes of the occupation that there would be protests, attacks, resistance. How could we not?'

'You're trying to justify your actions to me when you are threatening my life. My daughter's life. Even you must see that I'm not going to agree with you.'

'If you could see, truly, what is going on, I wouldn't have to threaten you. Wars have been fought in Europe for thousands of years, prisoners executed, lives cruelly taken. It's terrible, heartless, evil, but not new. What is new are these specific Germans, their specific ideology, this specific war. It is different. What struck me to the core, what changed it for me, wasn't my students – it was what the Germans did to the Sorbonne. They closed down a place of learning, of free thought. They are trying to drag us away from enlightenment and into darkness. Their whole regime was epitomised in that decision. I've seen your apartment. You love books. You've heard about what the Germans do to books?'

'I have.'

'That says so much, does it not? These are men who are afraid of words, afraid of free thought. And this is before we talk of rounding up Jews and communists and Gypsies. My question for you, Monsieur, is how can you possibly say that the end does not justify the means after all you've seen? They must be stopped, and I would take the lives of you, your daughter and these men around me if it gave us even the smallest chance of defeating them.'

SEVENTEEN

'Please, it's a simple question, and only you and I will ever know that it was asked and answered.' Duchene measured his words, spoke them simply and without emotion. Neither desperation nor demand would draw an answer from the restaurant's owner.

'You say this is a photo of three Germans, but you are a Frenchman,' the thin woman replied. 'Why are you looking for them?'

'I'm only looking for this man in the middle. He's stolen something from the Church of Saint-Lambert de Vaugirard. The parishioners have asked me to try to get their donations back.'

'Donations? Now I know you are lying. No one is making donations at church. Away, leave.'

'Please.'

'Go. Before I fetch my husband.'

'Madame …'

The woman's eyes were wide. Her face had reminded him of an English teacher he'd once had – brittle, uncompromising. But now that had changed. From the way she held her gaze on him, scanning his every movement for meaning, her arms folded across her chest, he could see he was frightening her.

'I'm sorry to have bothered you,' he said with a polite nod. 'Good day, Madame.'

It was between lunch and dinner, and without electricity or gas the candlelit restaurant was empty. Duchene had barely stepped inside when the woman had arrived, hopeful for business and disappointed when he came with questions and not barter.

It took a moment for him to turn and exit through the front door. Out on the street there was little activity, but at the patisserie a queue still stretched: women and children waiting with ration tickets at the ready. Madame Lyon was inside, trading the tickets for small bags of flour. As he watched, he could see one of her apprentices walking down the line, turning people away.

Duchene sheltered in the doorway of a closed-up milliner's and opened Kloke's Baedeker. He looked at the page that contained a small map of the streets surrounding the Rue Montmartre Métro.

He was desperate. He'd spent an hour walking back from the Seine to his apartment, where he'd been frustrated to discover that Florette had not tried to contact him about Kloke's French lover. He'd called in on Monsieur and Madame Junet to impress on them that he was expecting an important call and to please answer the foyer phone on his behalf. He then used his last can of sardines to catch a pedicab out to Rue de Castellane.

Kloke had circled many of the restaurants in the street with a pencil, and marked them with a tick or a cross. Duchene assumed that ticks indicated Kloke rated them well enough to revisit.

After finding that Maison Visk was a dead end, he looked down the list again.

La Festa was ticked twice.

This was a wood-fronted delicatessen two blocks further down Rue de Castellane. By the door, small clusters of herbs grew in a well-tended flower box – basil, rosemary and oregano. Above these, Italian cheeses, preserves and dried pasta were advertised in gold and red paint across the shop's windows. On entering, however, Duchene found that any potential customers would be disappointed. A woman was standing with a baby on her hip, trying to exchange vouchers. Duchene watched as she gave away most of her meal rations for three onions and a stale heel of bread.

He was surprised to see relief on her face as she left. It was well into the afternoon now and perhaps she'd been looking for food since morning.

Around a glass counter that would have once contained cheese and meat were tins of anchovies, cans of artichokes and tomatoes and a few packets of dried pasta. The owner waved to Duchene as he approached.

On the wall behind him hung a flag of golden fasces on an azure background. Beneath this was a framed photograph of Benito Mussolini.

The deli owner smiled at him.

'Good afternoon. What can I offer you? It might not look like much, but I can write down a recipe from my grandmother. Show you how she could make a wonderful meal in lean times like these.'

'Thank you, I was hoping you might help me with a question I have?'

'Of course.'

The deli owner came out from behind the counter. He had a thick moustache and stubble. His dark hair was peppered with grey and on his forearms were fading tattoos.

He placed a hand on Duchene's back and gestured towards a small circular table set with a sugar bowl and silver salt and pepper shakers.

Duchene sat and the owner reached out a hand.

'Giancarlo.'

'Auguste.'

Giancarlo tapped on the table. 'Your question?'

'I'm looking for this man,' Duchene said and held out the photo.

'Fine young men.'

'I was hoping you might recognise the man in the middle.'

The deli owner removed a pair of spectacles from his apron, then held the photo close to his eyes. 'Yes, this one I recognise,' he said, tapping the photo above Kloke. 'Christian. He comes here, perhaps twice a week. Usually a sandwich, sometimes an espresso. Pays in francs. His French is terrible, but at least he tries.'

Duchene sat back in his chair, surprised at the simplicity of the moment. 'Have you seen him recently?'

'Not for a few days. He's probably staying away like everyone else. Without an oven, without electricity, it's impossible to keep the refrigerator going or bake bread.'

'Do you know exactly when you last saw him?'

'Towards the end of last week. I'd brought up some meat from the cellar. We'd spoken about kaiserfleisch, and I insisted he try pancetta. He ended up buying a quarter kilo.'

Duchene held open the guidebook to the map section where La Festa was located. 'You can see here, he's placed two ticks next to your shop. Do you know if he spoke about any of these other places? Maybe he visited them with a friend, a Frenchman.'

'He only ever came here alone, no friends.' Giancarlo peered at the map. 'And as for the other places … Here. He did say he'd been meaning to visit Guillaume's charcuterie.' A large finger, tattooed with a crucifix on one knuckle, pointed to the spot. 'He said he'd been told to go there by a friend. I couldn't tell you if this friend of his was French.'

'Thank you,' Duchene said, shaking Giancarlo's hand. 'You've been very helpful. I'm sorry I don't have anything to give you to thank you for your time.'

'No need,' he said, standing.

Duchene also stood.

'You're working for the Germans?' Giancarlo asked, ducking behind the counter.

'Sorry?'

'This is why you're looking for him, for Christian?' he called back from under the counter. 'You're working for the Germans?'

'Ah, that's difficult to answer … Sort of.'

'This is what I thought,' Giancarlo replied, returning with a small parcel of waxed paper, *100g Pecorino* written on the side. 'Here,' he said, offering the parcel to Duchene, 'have this, and good luck.'

The chime above Guillaume's rang as Duchene stepped through the door into the dim shop. Candles in tin cans had been placed on shelves and nailed into doorframes. Almost twenty people were exchanging ration tickets or bartering with small valuables. There were no Germans in the shop, which lifted the mood. The dour Guillaume managed the queue and, from what Duchene could observe from a distance, his prices did not seem to have changed since the day before – no price gouging? Much of the stock had been depleted, but there was still enough preserved meat to go around.

'I knew this day would come,' Guillaume called to Duchene when he saw him standing in a corner.

'What day is that?'

'The Germans on the run.'

'Are they?'

The conversation paused while Guillaume served the next customer. An older woman in pearls was looking for dried saucisson.

'Aren't they?' Guillaume continued. 'Police on strike, Métro workers on strike, gas cut, electricity cut – this is a city running to a standstill, and the Germans are too afraid to lift a finger to restore it.'

A furtive cheer rose up from the customers.

'What if it's the quiet before the storm?' asked Duchene.

'But what if it's not? I've been listening to the BBC. The Germans have been completely pushed out of Normandy. Paris will be next!'

The next cheer was cut short as a German troop truck sped past and rattled the windows.

'Let us hope so,' Duchene replied. 'But let's make sure we stay safe until then. As the Germans get desperate, there'll be reprisals. Let's not give them a reason to make them.'

It was hard to tell if his response had affected Guillaume. The man's long face was as expressionless as ever. 'You're probably right.'

Duchene waited while the crowd thinned until the shop was empty, then he walked up to the glass countertop. Even though less than two days had passed, Duchene saw a noticeable change in what was being sold. Only a few pâtés and terrines remained. The other goods were less frivolous larder food, stored without refrigeration: dried sausages, candied pork belly, andouillettes in aspic. Other meats were notably absent too. 'Not selling German food anymore?'

'Put it back into the saucisson. I haven't seen much of their kind around in the past couple of days. They're thin on the ground.'

'I think they've just gathered in other places. Securing their headquarters, their barracks.'

Guillaume crossed his arms, relaxing while the shop was quiet. He wore several rings, most of them antique, one large and engraved with *Bordeaux 1918*.

'You fought in the last war?' Duchene asked.

'I did.'

'You trade fair.'

'We're all struggling.'

'Not everyone would. Rationing is one thing, but without gas only coal and wood ovens will work. That's a lot of the city left without kitchens, and without refrigeration.'

'I'm fortunate to have a well-stocked cellar. I've been planning for this. The people of Paris will have my support even if it sends me bankrupt.'

'Conviction and principle are rare these days. It's admirable.'

'I do what I can.'

'I have a question for you. Do you have a moment?'

Guillaume nodded.

'This man,' Duchene said, holding out the photograph with his finger above Kloke. 'I've been told he was a regular here.'

'A lot of Germans were.'

'Have you seen him in here recently?'

Guillaume shook his head.

'But he did come here?'

'I remember him. He spoke bad French. He liked kaiserfleisch.'

'So I've been told. Did he ever come in with a friend? A Frenchman?'

'How would I know that they were friends?'

'I don't know – talking together, sharing cigarettes.'

'I'm sure you've seen the city recently. No Frenchman would be a friend to a German, at least not openly. Some women, yes. But they do it because they are weak. Because they are looking for security in a time of uncertainty.'

'Aren't we all?' Duchene said, reaching inside his trench coat for the guidebook.

'But we don't take Germans between our legs.'

Duchene left the book in his pocket. He waited, trying to outlast the man's intent, to see if the comment was directed at him. But he sensed nothing.

They stood in silence for a moment longer, before Duchene said, 'Can you tell me anything about this man? Anything at all that might help me find him?'

Guillaume's face was motionless while he thought. 'The last time he was in, he wasn't in uniform. Had a lot of money in his wallet. He bought more than he usually would.'

'Do you remember when?'

'Maybe a week ago.'

'You can't be more precise?'

'No.'

Duchene sighed. 'Thank you for your help. Please take this.' He offered the wrapped cheese to Guillaume.

The charcutier shook his head. 'Keep it,' he said, lifting a parcel up from below the counter. 'And take this.'

Duchene reached forward and took hold of it. It was heavy, a kilo at least.

'Sausages and a few slices of bacon. Use it to feed the Resistance. And capture that German.'

EIGHTEEN

As Duchene stepped out of the pedicab onto the pavement, he passed some of the sausages, wrapped in paper, to the driver. The man tipped his hat, and Duchene watched as he rode back up the street.

The small aluminium and canvas pedicab had creaked and groaned for most of the journey. Had it been pulled by anything more powerful than a bicycle, it would have fallen to pieces. Its leather seat had barely fit Duchene, and several times he'd almost fallen out. He would have been better off in one of the horse-drawn carriages that had recently returned to the roads.

He scanned the street around him: no sign of hidden observers. Perhaps there weren't any. Perhaps their instructive purpose had been served when they'd arrested Eliane Payet. *Perhaps*.

He walked into the foyer of his building and tapped on the door to the Junets' apartment. The heavy shuffle of slippered feet betrayed the arrival of Monsieur Junet. He opened the door with a smile. 'Auguste. You've had that call. I left a message on your door.'

Duchene couldn't help but smile back at him.

'Thank you very much. Please take some of this bacon for Madame Junet and yourself. It's fresh from Guillaume's today.'

'This is too kind.'

'Not at all. Please. Take four pieces. It needs to be eaten.'

Duchene gave a quick farewell and ran up the stairs. He rattled free his keys and opened the door as he plucked off the note. Holding it in his mouth, he pulled out his trench torch to light his way to the dining table. He dropped the bacon and shone the torch on the note.

He said to meet at the Ritz at eight. Would not give a name. Sounded Swiss.
– M. Junet

Duchene crumpled the note and threw it across the room. *Faber.*

Kicking the nearest book stack, he sent it flying across the floor.

Duchene fumed all the way to the Ritz. He made the journey on foot after quickly eating half the cheese and three slices of bacon he'd cooked over the hotplate he'd rigged up last winter on the basement boiler.

He was no closer to finding Kloke than he'd been last night. He was relying entirely on a possible phone call from the man's French lover, a stranger with very good reasons for keeping his identity hidden, who had absolutely no reason to trust Duchene.

By the time he reached the hotel, bellhops were lighting hundreds of candles to coincide with the sunset. A few Parisians watched as he approached the guards stationed at the front entrance, and he found himself waiting beside a suspicious twenty-year-old with a rifle while his message was taken to Faber.

Hands patted across his suit and coat, and he was escorted inside. As the door closed, the heat enveloped him. The air was dry and smelt of wax. The faces of German officers in full dress gleamed with beads of sweat, while the few women who joined them wore light dresses and fanned themselves. The sound of a piano was coming from the bar to the right of the hotel's sweeping reception area, and Duchene crossed the marble to reach it.

Arrayed around the room were white Louis XVI tables and chairs. There was an improbability to their ornateness, with legs so thin it seemed they'd break under the weight of a man – let alone a man sitting with a Frenchwoman on his lap, of which there were several. Large glass steins were being carried to the tables by waiters, along with wine and cognac. Elaborate petit fours were also being offered, their dark chocolate and gold leaf glistening under the candlelight.

Every table was full, and the bar was standing room only. A few French civilians were present, probably from the Vichy Government: bureaucrats and envoys, those necessary experts who helped keep the city running. They looked uncomfortable for the most part – the lack of electricity surely a reminder of the strikes throughout the city, of how they'd lost control of those areas of their expertise. Most of the crowd were Luftwaffe officers singing along to a grand piano, fully opened, that stood on a low stage surrounded by the tables.

At this piano sat Camille.

Her face was flushed with colour as she sang with the crowd, hitting the keys with a force and precision that drove them to a peak of excitement. It was a lively version of 'Lili Marlene'. Duchene had never seen her play like this. She sat side-on to the Germans, rocking back and forth as sweat glistened along her arms. A lock of her hair had fallen loose, and she flicked her head to move it from her face. As she reached the chorus, she stood and raised a hand at the crowd, lifting her upturned palm towards the ceiling. The officers sang even louder, delighted and enthralled.

Duchene felt his body shiver at the sight of her compelling the enemy in this way. She was so much more than he was, and he thrilled at the thought that he had been with her.

All this evaporated as he saw Major Faber.

It didn't take much, just a cursory scan of the crowd. As the majority of patrons wore blue-grey Luftwaffe uniforms, he spotted the white of Faber's summer tunic quite easily despite the press of bodies. The major was sitting with his back to Duchene, watching the stage from a table he alone occupied. He was smoking. A whisky bottle stood on the table before him. Duchene squeezed his way, unnoticed, through the crowd; their eyes were moving between Camille and the companions at their sides, as they grinned in recognition of each turn of the song.

Duchene stood beside Faber. His blond hair, without a strand of grey, had been swept back with oil. He wasn't smiling or singing. In his stillness, he looked old and tired – as old as Duchene. Not even his finessed appearance could distract from the lines and shadows under his eyes.

Faber kept watching Camille and looked at Duchene sideways. 'You're late.'

Duchene struggled to hear him over the noise. 'No Métro.'

'Sit.' Faber poured himself a whisky. A good quarter of the bottle was already gone. He lit a cigarette and placed his mother-of-pearl lighter back on the table. 'So.'

'I haven't found him.' Duchene had to raise his voice and lean across the table so the major could hear.

'This is what I was thinking,' Faber shouted back. 'I thought, *Why hasn't he contacted me yet? Why am I still waiting to hear something, anything, about Kloke?*'

'Shouldn't we move somewhere else?' Duchene asked. 'There are a lot of people around. They might hear us.'

'So what? Hardly any of them speak French, and the ones who do are here to serve us – the men and the women.' Faber turned his head from Duchene and looked past his shoulder.

Duchene knew what was behind him. He didn't even have to look. But it was like witnessing an automobile accident – he couldn't help but turn and guide his eyes towards the incident, even though he knew what he'd see would distress him.

At a table right beside the piano were Max and Marienne. Max was in his uniform, sweating profusely, his pale skin bright red, Marienne in an evening gown, possibly new, with a low square neck, her dark hair in curls and her eyes outlined in kohl. They were singing along.

'It's always the same songs,' said Faber, 'the ones most popular with the high command. Last time there was a surprise vocalist.'

'Marienne.'

'You see, this is the intuition I've heard so much about. And yet, here you sit with nothing to tell me. Nothing.'

The song finished, and the crowd applauded, rising to their feet if they weren't there already. Camille stood, placed her hands over her heart and released them in acknowledgement. 'Thank you,' she said in German. 'Thank you.' As the noise dimmed to chatter, she spoke from the stage, 'Last time I was here, we had a guest.'

Some whistles from the crowd.

'Shall we do the same tonight?'

They cheered again.

Marienne, still in her seat, smiled but shook her head.

'Come, darling,' Camille said.

The cheering increased as Marienne got to her feet. 'You're all too kind,' she said in German to the crowd. 'How can I refuse an invitation like this?'

'She's too good for you, Max!' someone called out.

Laughter rippled, and Marienne stood beside the piano. Camille sat and placed her fingers on the keyboard, nodding the time to Marienne as she started to play, her fingers running up the keys. Marienne sang in French, her voice smooth and warm.

The Germans sat in silence as she looked across them and filled the room with her voice.

Duchene smiled briefly. It took him a few moments to recognise the song. She was fearless and bold and the Germans were none the wiser for her cunning. While she sang in her native tongue, the song was from America, Cole Porter's 'Night and Day'.

Faber finished his whisky and poured another. 'I'd really hoped it wouldn't come to this. She's an impressive young woman, as few are. But even they die. It's what happens when their fathers fail.'

'Your timeline was unreasonable. I'm getting close. I'll have him soon.'

The lie wasn't even a good one; he could see that in

the unwavering scowl on Faber's face. 'How are you close? Kloke has clearly deserted, and you've given me not even a hint of where he's gone. No details.'

'Details have consequences,' said Duchene.

'What was that?'

The Gestapo had been very specific. Duchene scanned the crowded room – even talking to Faber was a risk.

Marienne's voice soared. Those who had been speaking stopped, and there was absolute silence in the room.

Once Duchene had known all of her world, chosen the books he read to her, provided clothes for her, been the confidant for her concerns and her joys. Now he saw someone else, her world unknown to him. He'd never heard her sing like this, but he did know that she'd loved music as a child, and that she was always self-assured and never hid behind his legs. He'd taught her German, and English too, which she was translating to French as she sang a song from across the Atlantic.

No part of the hours he had left, however few, would be without risk. All he could do was play out each moment as it came.

'You want details?' he whispered back to Faber. 'How about the fact that the Gestapo are investigating you?'

Faber moved the glass down from his mouth. 'Pardon?'

'That's right. They picked me up outside Kloke's hotel, the Saint Clair. They're investigating him as well. They wouldn't say why, but I have my suspicions.'

The crowd were on their feet as Marienne finished the song. Their applause and whistling filled the room.

Faber leant in close to Duchene. 'You've made your point. We should go somewhere else.' He placed his cigarettes and lighter back into his pocket, then picked up the bottle and glass. 'Come,' he said as he started to thread his way through the cheering audience, who were calling for an encore.

Duchene followed, moving through the crowd as they called for an encore.

As they reached the archway that led back into the foyer, they passed the heavy blue drapery that lined the wall and framed its elaborate wallpaper. In the shadow of one curtain stood two men: a young Luftwaffe captain and Lucien.

Lucien.

The German slipped a roll of francs into the black marketeer's hand. Duchene couldn't slow down enough to see what Lucien gave him in return. But neither did Lucien see Duchene.

He kept moving forward and out into the foyer, where Faber was lighting another cigarette. The major approached the concierge, and they exchanged some hushed words. Within moments Faber and Duchene were being led behind the reception desk and into the concierge's office. The door was closed behind them, and Faber indicated for Duchene to sit, before leaning back against a large wooden filing cupboard. 'What do you mean, the Gestapo were outside Kloke's hotel?'

Duchene remained standing and eased off some of his weight across the top of the leather office chair. 'They were lying in wait. They knew who I was. They knew who I was looking for.' He showed Faber the letter exempting him from the curfew. 'Your letter from von Choltitz got their attention.'

Faber shook his head. 'Those fuckers.'

'They told me to go to them before I spoke to you.'

'And have you?'

'I'm risking everything by coming to you first.'

'Except you didn't come to me. I had to summon you.'

'That's hardly the point. I'm risking my life to help you, and my daughter's. I don't know if you've seen how things are going out there, but the Gestapo won't care all that much if I'm not able to help them. They'll just dismiss me as another informant who couldn't follow directions and put a bullet in my head.'

Faber nodded his head. His eyes were fixed on the bottle in his hand, which he placed on the cupboard beside him.

He looked up at Duchene. 'What do you know about Kloke?

'He stole some guns from the Resistance.'

Perhaps the drink had dulled Faber's responses, but he didn't seem surprised.

'You knew that?' Duchene asked.

'No. I'm just wondering what makes you think this ridiculous story is true.'

'Did you ever see him with a Webley pistol, a trophy taken from a British soldier?'

'No.'

'Well, he has one in his hotel room. You were stationed in the east. So, you haven't fought the British yet?'

'No. He could have been given one, as a trophy.'

'I also showed a photo of Kloke to a woman who helped him steal from the Resistance.'

'Let me talk to her.'

'You can't – she's been taken by the Gestapo. But there's another witness out there somewhere, the man Kloke was working with. A man who spoke French.'

'A Frenchman?'

'Or not?'

'What are you trying to suggest?'

'It would explain the Gestapo's interest in you – German officers, one quite senior, stealing weapons to sell for profit. That's bound to capture their attention.'

'It's absurd. Why would I send you to find Kloke if I knew you'd discover such a crime?'

'Perhaps you thought I'd never find out.'

'If this is true, it does make me wonder how you know that Kloke stole from the Resistance. Are you working for them yourself?'

Deflection.

'From where I'm standing,' said Duchene, 'it makes no difference if you know that I've spoken to the Resistance. You're already threatening to kill my daughter. You'll probably move on to threatening me too.'

'These Gestapo friends of yours will be interested to hear about it.'

More deflection.

'They probably already suspect it,' Duchene said. 'They've been following me.'

'And did they follow you here, tonight?'

'I've given up worrying about it.'

It was clear from Faber's expression that he hadn't. He stood and opened the office door just wide enough so he could look across reception into the lobby. 'So, what are you trying to tell me?' he said, closing the door.

'The one room I know the Gestapo aren't in, is this office. Other than that, your guess is as good as mine.'

Faber drew back on his cigarette. Exhaled. 'How do you know Kloke stole these guns?'

'That woman I spoke to, who helped him find where the

guns were hidden. She identified him from a photograph I found in his hotel room. The Gestapo have her now.'

'Show it to me.'

Duchene handed him the photo, and he stared at it as though he was looking for a hidden meaning. 'He's a terrible soldier,' he said, turning it over and scanning its back. 'Find him before the Gestapo get to him. I can still get him out of here. I can get him back to Berlin. I owe it to his family.'

'And what should I tell the Gestapo if they find me before I find him?'

'Whatever you have to, to stay alive. My command is stationed at the Majestic.' Faber plucked a pen from the desk and wrote a phone number on the back of the photograph. 'Call and update me on your progress at the same time tomorrow.' He returned the photo to Duchene.

'No deadline?'

'I can't see the point. Either you'll find Kloke before the Gestapo do, or you won't. You understand the consequences if you fail.'

After the German left, Duchene stayed for a few minutes in the office. Something in Faber's eyes had shifted when Duchene had mentioned the Gestapo. Something within him, a reflection, a thought, a memory – something that made him afraid. Duchene didn't let himself indulge in any satisfaction over this realisation. Faber had had the limits of his authority exposed. But where it had bought Duchene more time, it had also cost him in making the man afraid. *And a frightened man is a dangerous man.*

Duchene checked his watch: eight-thirty. Only half an hour until curfew.

Back in the bar, Camille was playing Beethoven while

the Germans continued to drink. He got the sense that many of the Luftwaffe were being redeployed. Farewells were being made, final drinks poured, home addresses and blessings exchanged.

Duchene moved through the room, looking for Lucien.

Camille, still at the piano, motioned him over. 'I saw you were talking with Faber,' she said as she continued to play. 'Is everything all right?'

'We're standing in the heart of Paris, surrounded by Germans. Nothing is all right.'

'Auguste –'

'Faber. Max. It's all too close to Marienne.'

'I need you to tell me about it. I need to know she's going to be safe.'

'That's what I'm trying to do. Make her safe.'

'Then talk to me about it later? Tonight?'

'I –' He saw Marienne speaking to Lucien at the bar, laughing as they sipped champagne. 'Yes. I will. Tonight.' He kissed Camille's cheek before rushing towards the bar.

'Promise,' she called after him.

Lucien was gone again, but Marienne was still there, smiling at an older, ruddy-faced German officer who had a hand on her shoulder and a glass of champagne in his hand.

Nodding, he tried to keep an eye on Lucien through the press of soldiers. He brushed past a German, knocking a swash of beer out of his stein and down his jacket. The officer called after Duchene, but he feigned ignorance and ducked around a table before walking up three steps from the sunken floor, back towards the bar. Behind him Germans came to the man's aid, mopping beer, helping to place the steins on the table and offering to buy more drinks.

'Where did Lucien go?' Duchene said to Marienne.

She turned from the German and laughed. 'This is something! I never thought I'd see you here.'

'I came to see Camille.'

She laughed again. 'You're a terrible liar.' She looked to the man next to her and spoke in German. 'General von Bühel, this is my father, Auguste.'

The general removed his hand from Marienne's bare shoulder and offered it to Duchene. 'Your daughter has a wonderful voice,' he said. His large, meaty hand held Duchene's with a steel grip.

'She does,' Duchene replied in German. 'Where's Lucien?' he asked her again, in French.

'How would I know? He went that way.' She pointed past the bar towards a corridor.

Duchene darted over. The hallway was empty but for two doorways, each leading to a bathroom. He jogged up to the men's and tried to regain his breath as he pushed open the door.

Sea-green marble lined the floors and walls, its veins matching the room's white furniture. An attendant was resting beside his trolley of pomades, colognes and polishes. He stood up when Duchene entered but resumed his seat when Duchene waved him back.

Two men were speaking German in a cubicle to Duchene's left: one in a drunken ramble, the other struggling to find the right words. Duchene pushed open the cubicle door.

Lucien was standing next to Max. He was placing something in his hand.

'Herr Duchene,' Max slurred, a bemused smile crossing his face. 'Did you see Marienne … see her sing?'

'What's in your hand?' Duchene snapped in German.

'Oh, this ...' Max pressed it against his chest. 'It's nothing.'

'Let's talk later, Auguste,' Lucien said, almost as though Duchene were a child.

Or senile.

'I said, what's in your hand?' Duchene pushed past Lucien and used both hands to wrench Max's palm from his chest.

In the next few seconds, thoughts sped through Duchene's head. He was seeing something that had been there all along, but he'd been too preoccupied with threats upon threats to view it with any clarity.

Falling through the air was a small rectangle of paper, brown and neatly folded.

Duchene knew, as it fell, that if he were to touch it, he would find that the paper was waxed. Waxed so that the white powder inside would stay dry and remain easy to consume. The white powder would be methamphetamines; it would spur on the mind of a pilot, or a soldier, or anyone looking to have a good time. Conversation would flow, thoughts would buzz, sleep would seem impossible, the party could continue, and all concerns would be forgotten.

The brown paper was the same kind that Duchene had in his pocket. The kind he had picked up in Kloke's apartment.

Kloke knew Lucien.

Lucien knew Kloke.

Lucien had been concealing it from him all this time.

The paper landed on the floor of the bathroom.

'Don't step on it!' Max shouted as he shoved Duchene out of the way.

Duchene hadn't anticipated the speed and strength of the younger man. He slipped backwards and fell out of the cubicle, his head hitting the marble.

Lucien stepped over him and was out the door before Duchene could get to his feet.

'Where is it?' Max shouted from his hands and knees as he scrabbled around in the cubicle.

Duchene pushed aside the attendant, who was trying to help, and ran to the door.

In the corridor, two women were giggling as they emerged from the ladies' toilets. Lucien was almost back at the bar.

'Lucien!' Duchene ran down the corridor, pushing the women aside. 'Lucien!'

He glanced at his watch: 8.45 p.m. Neither of them could make it home before curfew.

Lucien was swift as he moved through the crowd, winding around drunk soldiers, sliding past waiters. He was almost halfway to the other side, and there were several German officers between them.

Duchene spotted a waiter carrying a tray laden with full champagne glasses. With his arms up to protect his face, he stepped in front of the waiter and collided with the tray, moving aside as the man and glasses came crashing to the ground. On cue, the officers leapt into action, helping the man up from the floor and cordoning off the broken glass.

A space had opened between Lucien and Duchene.

When Lucien saw him, Duchene increased his speed.

'Are you crazy?' Lucien shouted back at him, before starting to run again.

In the next instant, Duchene was chasing him through the foyer. Lucien's feet slapped across the floor as he ran to one of the front doors and threw it open. The guards outside didn't have time to react as Lucien went flying past them, his coat flapping in the night air, his hand on his head to keep his hat in place. Duchene had to slow down as the guards moved in around the door.

'He took my wallet,' Duchene said in German.

Two privates held out their rifles to stop him. 'What is your name?' one of them asked.

In the still night air, Duchene could hear Lucien running along the far side of the square. He would be gone in moments if he didn't command the moment. Duchene thought of Camille, and her power over the Germans.

'Auguste Duchene,' he said without slowing. 'I was meeting with Major Thomas Faber. You can check for yourself but that would mean dragging him away from the young woman he's entertaining.'

The guards exchanged a glance.

Duchene could no longer hear Lucien running. Now he heard voices – Germans, somewhere in the darkness. Lucien, too.

The guards nodded and uncrossed their rifles.

He didn't have time to consider the ease of his success. Walking as quickly as he dared, Duchene tried to home in on the conversation. It was becoming heated. He could make out some of the words.

'Identification.'

'I don't speak German.'

'Raise your hands.'

Duchene broke into a jog. As he turned a corner, he saw two men in dark overcoats.

Gestapo.

They had Lucien against a wall.

'Wait!' Duchene called.

The men turned. Lucien started to run again, a plume of francs rising into the air behind him.

The Gestapo officers didn't hesitate. As Lucien increased the distance between them, one drew a pistol from his coat and fired. Three shots into the night air. The crack of gunfire reverberated off the stone walls around them.

Duchene screamed.

Guards from the Ritz began to run towards them.

Lucien's legs convulsed. And then he was still.

Friday, 18 August 1944

NINETEEN

The sage sat looking over a globe. His eyes were concerned, his hand cradling his head to help ease the turmoil of thoughts racking his mind. Despite his obvious wealth – the books, the well-appointed castle room, the gold and blue robes that fell from his shoulders – he was deeply troubled. Some might have said he was divining the future, but Duchene could see the truth of the painting. The sage was staring down upon that very moment, in that very day, grappling with the tragedy of mankind.

Duchene watched in the foyer of 11 Rue des Saussaies, 8th arrondissement, as the painting was wrapped in cloth and loaded gently into a crate by two Gestapo agents.

He would weep for Lucien. Again, perhaps. But his well of feeling had been spent. He barely noticed the Gestapo moving around him as they went in and out of the building, loading files and crates. At one point he'd heard three distant gunshots from one of the upper rooms. This had hardly stirred his senses – more pointless deaths, and there'd be more tomorrow and the day after that and the day after that.

He didn't notice the tapping on his shoulder.

It was the slap to his face that brought him back into the room.

'Up,' said Stahl, his ice-blue eyes fixing on Duchene's.

Duchene stood. This immediately relieved the pressure of the handcuffs around his wrists. They'd been locked behind his back, cutting into him, trapped between his body and the chair. His hands had started to become numb, but as the blood flowed back into them, he became aware of the pain.

He followed Stahl up the wide, curved staircase to the second floor. In the corridor, on the way to the Oberführer's office, they passed open doors. More Gestapo were either gathering papers or burning them. The men were moving quickly, and many pages were falling to the ground.

In the last room before the office, where the carpet and wallpaper had been stripped, were three bodies on the floor. Each was covered by a mouldy sheet, stained with blood around their heads.

He had no doubt this was intended for him to see.

Stahl moved him on, and the next door was opened. The Oberführer was sitting at his dining-table desk, authorising papers.

Sitting where he was placed, Duchene waited while the lean man worked his way through the stack. With a glance at the ticking mantel clock on the corner of the dining table, Duchene saw it was 8.13 a.m.

After five minutes of silence, the Oberführer placed his Montblanc on the table and looked up at Duchene, his body barely filling the width of his chair. 'Stahl tells me you've been busy. Getting around. Talking.'

'I have,' Duchene replied.

'And yet we've heard nothing from you.'

'That would seem to be a common complaint.'

'Pardon?' The Oberführer managed to find an even greater stillness.

'My daughter. She says the same thing.'

'Stahl picked you up last night outside the Ritz, chasing a man on the cusp of curfew. I do wonder, Herr Duchene, do you have a death wish?'

Duchene said nothing.

'This man, Lucien Martin – he was a colleague of yours?'

'He was. I was hoping he might have information that would help lead me to Kloke.'

'And that was?'

'The whereabouts of Kloke's lover.'

'And did he?'

'I don't know. You shot him before I could find out.'

'He was an insurgent.'

Despite the danger, Duchene felt his anger well. 'He wasn't.'

'We don't justify our actions. We are the SS,' the Oberführer said without expression.

'Lucien was harmless. You should have held him, at least, so I could talk to him.'

'Stahl has advised that's what he was trying to do. Until your friend ran.'

'I thought you didn't justify your actions.'

'We don't.'

'You're not making it any easier to find Kloke. There's also the woman you arrested the other day, Eliane Payet. She was helping me to find him.'

'Another insurgent.'

'Can I talk to her?'

'No. She was put on a train to Ravensbrück.'

The answer came too quickly. Duchene didn't dare challenge the lie. 'Your men need to stop following me.'

'That won't happen.'

'Then they need to do a better job of keeping hidden. The whole purpose of my looking for Kloke is that I can ask questions more easily than a German. When your men are seen arresting the people I talk to, that makes it very hard for me to do my work.'

'And your behaviour makes it hard for us to do ours.' The Oberführer raised a finger and pointed it at Duchene. 'You were found outside the Ritz. You'd spent some time in there. So had Faber. The two of you didn't happen to talk, did you?'

Here was a man practised in the art of discerning truth from lies. And here Duchene was, a poor liar who'd had no sleep. To spend too much time thinking of an answer would betray him, to reply too quickly would do the same. A partial truth was necessary to hide the lie.

'Of course we did. I couldn't avoid him. But I'd gone to meet Lucien.'

The Oberführer nodded to Stahl, who removed a notebook from his pocket. With the same care that his colleagues had observed loading the artwork in the lobby downstairs, he lifted out a scrap of paper.

Duchene recognised it immediately. It had been crumpled once; now it was spread flat from being pressed in the notebook. The handwriting was a tight cursive with extravagant flourishes.

He said to meet at the Ritz at seven. Would not give a name. Sounded Swiss.

– M. Junet

How had he been so foolish? All the elaborate manoeuvring to throw the Gestapo from his trail had come to nothing. They'd never followed him, just gone into his apartment building and read the notes pinned to his door – the meeting last night with Faber, the meeting yesterday morning with Eliane. They'd probably only retrieved this scrap to demonstrate the point.

'Then tell me,' the Oberführer said, 'why your French friend, Lucien, would run from you if he had invited you to visit him. Why would your elderly neighbour tell you he had a Swiss accent? I'm afraid what little trust we had in you has evaporated.'

Duchene's mind turned to the room next door and the bodies on the floor. 'I did talk to Faber. He wanted an update.'

'Did you give him one?'

'Partially.'

'That was not what we discussed.'

'I know. But I needed to give him something. He's threatening the life of my daughter.'

'Marienne.'

Duchene nodded. 'I told him some of what I knew, but not all of it. Not the important parts.'

'For example?'

'I told him Kloke was working with another man – whom I now know to have been Lucien – to steal guns from the Resistance.'

'That's a court-martial offence.'

'So I'd assumed. What I didn't tell him was why Kloke stole the guns.'

'Why not?'

Duchene paused. Faber was dangerous, but the Gestapo were here with him now. If they could see his value, feel that he was making headway, then he might still regain his freedom.

'Because at that time I suspected Faber was involved in the theft. I still do. I'm not sure. I feel he's hiding something, from you Germans too.'

'What makes you say that?'

'He distances himself from the role of an occupier, behaves as if he's morally and intellectually superior. He doesn't see himself as part of the Wehrmacht. Why else would he come to me to find Kloke? Why not the military police? He's taking steps unofficially, and I don't believe, as he claims, it's to help one of his troops.'

'Really?' asked the Oberführer. 'It's not possible for a German to show concern over someone in his command?'

'A major to a lieutenant? Perhaps. But the most damning evidence is you, the Gestapo. You wouldn't be investigating him if you didn't feel he was hiding something big.'

'But we're after Kloke.'

'But we both know you don't give a damn about him. It's Faber you're after, and something Kloke knows will help you catch him.'

The Oberführer narrowed his eyes. Duchene stopped breathing. Perhaps he had overstepped. 'There are other things you don't know about Kloke.'

As though he were standing before a cobra, he would need to retreat with caution. Too suddenly and he would arouse suspicion.

'Undoubtedly,' Duchene said.

'When you find him, he will have papers on him.'

When. A future.

Relief washed over Duchene. 'They're not in his hotel room?'

'He wouldn't risk leaving them anywhere but on his person. You're to bring them to me. You do this, and we'll take care of Faber.'

'And if I don't?'

'That should be obvious. We need to interview Kloke. You have until midday to find him.'

'I would do a better job of it if you weren't traipsing around behind me.'

'Very well, only Stahl will stay with you. With orders to shoot if you try to run.'

'That will make it harder for me to interview people.'

'I'm sure you'll adapt.'

Duchene shook his head. 'What about Lucien's possessions? Can I look at everything he had on him when you brought him in? Or is that too much?'

The Oberführer nodded to Stahl, who gestured towards the door. Duchene got up and started to walk out.

'One other thing,' the Oberführer said.

Duchene stopped walking and turned back to him.

'To whom were Kloke and Lucien selling the guns?'

'Like any good war profiteers, they were going to sell them to the people most desperate for them, the ones who'd pay the most. The Resistance.'

TWENTY

'How would they not know they were buying the weapons that had been stolen from them? Are you French stupid?'

'We are. But no more or less than you Germans.'

Stahl blinked at Duchene, his eyes vanishing for a second, only to resume looking at him with the same ice-blue intensity. It wasn't affectation or a practised art – it was biology. With his pale golden hair and square jaw, Stahl would have been the perfect poster image for his regime's propaganda. He stood out in a room, held the gaze of men and women alike when he entered. It made no sense that he was working for the secret police. Perhaps this was why he'd been relegated to the role of driver.

'The Resistance isn't ignorant because it's stupid,' Duchene told him. 'It's by design, in case they're caught.'

'Obviously.'

'The strength of a resistance is that one cell doesn't know what another one is doing. That way they can't reveal each other. Outside of their own cell, their membership is secret. Selling their own guns back to them is actually quite clever. They'd have almost no way of knowing.'

Duchene had lost track of which apartment he was in, and on which floor of the Gestapo building. Stahl's room contained little embellishment and few personal effects, just a photo of a young girl sitting on his shoulders in an alpine field. They were dressed in hiking clothes and had edelweiss flowers pinned to their shirts.

A clerk arrived with a box file and placed it on the table before Duchene. Stahl nodded and sat on the edge of the table. He flipped open the box and announced each of its contents as he dropped them in front of Duchene. 'Wallet. Keys. Lighter. Cigarettes. Brown paper bag with …' he opened it and counted the contents '… six bags of methamphetamines. And a handkerchief? What is this?' Stahl held out a small square of gingham, roughly cut. It was from the old apple box they'd used to carry the Vernier baby back to Paris.

Duchene shrugged.

'You know I had to shoot him. Your friend.' Stahl must have caught his expression. 'We have orders. If someone runs –'

'I ran the other day.'

'That was different. We were ordered specifically *not* to shoot you. You understand, yes? You were a soldier once.'

'Well, I'm not now.'

'I agree with what you said. You need to find Kloke, you need space. So, you work with me, and we can find a way to keep you and the Oberführer happy.'

'Germans are in my city, killing my friends. How can I be happy?'

'It's just talk. I don't really care if you're happy or not.' He lit one of Lucien's cigarettes and emptied the wallet onto the table: Métro stubs, business cards, twenty-two francs, a library card. 'Is that all of it?'

'He had a pen too. A nice one. The Oberführer kept that.'

'The thing I need, it's not here. We have to get going. Time is running out.' Duchene grabbed the keys and cigarettes from the table, and his trench coat from the back of the chair.

It took almost no time for them to cross the city in the black Citroën. There were very few cars and buses on the streets. The Champs-Élysées was almost empty, only bicycles and pedicabs at its edges. But what they made up for in time, they lost to conspicuousness. To keep German soldiers from challenging them, Stahl had placed two swastika flags on the front of the car.

It was 9 a.m. as Duchene unlocked Lucien's front door. He'd only been outside the building before, never inside, and had discovered the apartment number by testing the letterbox key on all the available options.

As the door opened, it pushed a pile of notes across the floor into the small living room. Stahl closed the door as Duchene bent down to flick through them. Without electricity, the apartment was dark. Stahl crossed the room to open the curtains, while Duchene pumped his torch to get a better view of the pages.

They were notes from the landlady, hastily scrawled. They contained initials, times and meeting places, all of them for that day. Nothing resembled a CK for Christian Kloke.

Duchene handed them to Stahl, who started to leaf through them. 'How did he keep track of all these initials?'

'That's why we're here,' Duchene replied as he unlocked the large double doors on a black armoire. It was filled with unopened boxes of stockings, bottles of wine and cognac, candles, inner tubes for bicycles, two cigarette cartons, three American first-aid kits, bags of flour, tins of tea, and a large sack of sugar ready for decanting.

He opened the nearest door. Lucien's bedroom contained an unmade double bed with a brass frame and two bedside tables. Duchene pulled the drawer from one of them and emptied it onto the mattress: broken cigarettes, spare lighters, a rosary, condoms, mismatched cufflinks. He did the same with the other drawer and found more trinkets, photos of male and female nudes, an old dog-eared copy of *Das Kapital*.

'Communist?' asked Stahl.

'Once. From everything you've seen so far, you can tell it didn't stick. Lucien might have dabbled in philosophy, but he was a committed capitalist.'

Beneath the photos was a dark-green block, crudely formed. Duchene picked it up and turned it over. It was made from hard wax, and in its centre was the impression of a large iron key. Six right studs protruded from the block. Duchene pushed around the trinkets until he found another block, almost identical in size and shape. It had the other half of the impression from the key along with six holes. A narrow channel ran across the top of the two blocks.

They made a copy of the crypt key.

'What's that?' asked Stahl.

'An answer. But not the one we're looking for.'

The remaining furniture in the bedroom was another armoire, which matched the one in the living room and was filled with Lucien's suits. Duchene started to remove them and dump them on the bed.

'If you want to search fast, I can help,' Stahl said. 'I have more experience than you. What are we looking for?'

'A small black journal. It's how Lucien tracked his incomings and outgoings, his customers. Are you sure you didn't find it on him?'

'Yes. He had nothing else in his pockets.'

Duchene stopped pulling out suits. 'How thorough were you?'

'There was nothing else.'

'What about his seams, hidden pockets, the lining of his jacket?' Duchene snatched up a jacket and felt around its edges until he found it. He held the garment up to the German to show him a small tuck pocket along the edge of a cuff.

Stahl paused. Blinked. 'Come on, then.'

It was almost ten, and the working day was well underway. But on the streets there was even less traffic than earlier, and very few bicycles and pedestrians. Aside from Stahl's Citroën, the only other vehicles on the road were a Kübelwagen filled with German officers and the six motorcycles that flanked it. This group hurtled past them towards the Avenue des Portugais, and Stahl slowed to watch them disappear down the street under a bright blue sky.

As the Citroën passed the Arc de Triomphe, Stahl slowed again. A few Parisians moved along the street. It was like a ghost town.

'Something is going on,' he said.

Duchene joined him in peering out the window. 'The police kiosk is empty.'

'Not a single policeman all morning. Not anywhere along the Champs.'

Stahl turned the car around and retraced their route until he found a telephone booth. He stopped right on the side of the Champs-Élysées. At any other time, this would have invoked the blaring of horns and the swift arrival of a policeman. Today it brought nothing.

'Get out of the car,' he said. 'And don't go anywhere.'

Duchene stepped out, lit a cigarette, and watched as Stahl lifted the earpiece from its cradle and leant towards the mouthpiece. He turned the rotary dial with swiftness and precision.

Gestapo headquarters.

It was the number the Oberführer had given Duchene.

Stahl turned his head from the car window and spoke into the phone. Duchene kept his eyes on his watch. The German spoke for about five minutes, before replacing the phone. He put his hand to his forehead and stood for at least twenty seconds before glancing at Duchene, his face locked in a frown, a sneer tracing its way across his mouth.

And then the expression was gone. He left the phone booth and got back into the Citroën.

Duchene offered him a cigarette. He took it and felt around his pockets for a light. Duchene held his own cigarette upright, offering Stahl the tip. The German lit it, drew back on the smoke and exhaled. 'It's starting.'

Duchene looked at him, frowning, to conceal his growing excitement. 'What is?'

'What we've been anticipating since the landings at Normandy. The insurrection has started.'

Duchene remained very still. He thought of the executed prisoners on the floor of the Gestapo headquarters. They were panicking, fleeing, covering their tracks. He held his breath and watched Stahl closely.

Finally, the German spoke.

'My orders haven't changed. Neither have your requirements.'

Duchene used as neutral a tone as he was able. 'How did it start?'

Stahl paused. 'Your police have occupied their headquarters on the Île de la Cité. They've seized the armoury. They're barricading the doors. Snipers have been observed on the rooftops.'

A thrill moved through Duchene – and left him just as quickly, as the logistical nightmare of a siege and street battles dawned on him. 'And the Resistance?'

'Nothing yet. But it's still early. High command is expecting they'll start emerging as the word gets out.' Stahl paused again, as if considering some other course of action, before turning his key in the ignition and accelerating into the empty street.

He drove the Citroën at full speed and ignored any traffic signals along the way. Duchene got the sense that Stahl wasn't racing for his benefit alone. His jaw was locked the entire drive. He crossed the Seine at the Musée de l'Orangerie and hurtled along Boulevard Saint-Germain. As they turned down Rue de Tournon, Duchene knew their destination: the Luxembourg Gardens.

They followed its edge past regimented landscapes and manicured lawns. The summer blooms were still bright in the garden beds, and the windows of its ornate palace gleamed under the early autumn sun. At the garden's museum, they turned onto one of its tree-lined pathways. At any other time, Duchene's Parisian sensibilities would have been outraged as lawns protected by law were furrowed under the spin of the Citroën's wheels.

German embankments had been set up in the gardens ahead of them. Stahl eased their approach. Sandbags and earthworks peppered the once pristine grass. These were clustered around Luxembourg Palace, an obvious strong point that the Germans could reasonably hope to defend. Several soldiers were reinforcing walls with more bags, cleaning weapons and staring intently down sightlines.

As Duchene's apprehension grew, he saw Stahl's jaw unclench. The German came to a stop, letting the motor idle, beside a confused-looking soldier. Stahl wound down his window. 'Scharführer Stahl, Geheime Staatspolizei,' he said as he held up his identification. 'I'm going to the statue.'

'Excuse me, Scharführer, but is it true?'

'You've received your orders?'

'Yes.'

'Then follow them. Why question them now when the moment is critical?'

'Yes, Scharführer. Sorry, Scharführer.'

Stahl wound up his window and continued to drive.

'This is what we've fucking got? Military clerks and raw recruits?'

Duchene remained silent.

They drove under oak trees, dappled light falling around them. As birds took flight from the pathway in front of them, Duchene was struck with a memory – Marienne as a child, riding a pony along this same path. She had laughed as the tiny horse was spurred into a trot by the carnival man who held its rope.

The memory fell away as they neared the Statue of

Liberty replica, and Duchene saw two German soldiers with handkerchiefs wrapped around the lower halves of their faces.

Stahl stopped at the edge of a large pit. 'Get out,' he said.

Duchene stepped from the car. The stench rose up at him, and he instantly clapped his hand under his nose. The rancid smell of rotting flesh seemed to be creeping into his skin.

He looked across at Stahl, his eyes wild.

Stahl seemed frustrated that he had to remove his hand from his face in order to speak. 'This is where he is. Your friend. Lucien.'

Duchene pushed himself forward, forcing his legs to take him to the brink of the pit. Dozens of bodies had been piled on one another and sprinkled with quicklime. Most had been executed with a bullet to the head. Others had ligatures around their necks, while some were unrecognisable beneath the gore. A thousand flies, like a sea of dark opal, glistened under the sun. And in that instant, what little misplaced empathy Duchene had felt towards Stahl left him.

'In you go,' Stahl said. 'We dropped him over there.' He pointed to a corner of the mass grave, and Duchene could make out the lapel of the light-blue suit Lucien had been wearing.

Duchene took out two cigarettes and lit them, holding both in his mouth. He drew in the heavy tobacco and exhaled it through his nose. It almost sent him coughing, but he managed to regain control. The smoke masked only some of the stench, but it was better than nothing.

He set his mind to Marienne and entered the mass grave,

gripping the earthen side as the two masked soldiers and Stahl watched. The pit had been cleanly cut by a machine, and Duchene slipped down its side, spreading mud up his trouser leg and almost falling onto the corpses.

He was standing on the back of a woman and felt a crack beneath him as he shifted his weight. His stomach roiled, and he drew in more of the smoke. Using the edge of the pit to help him balance, he took another step towards Lucien's body. His foot slipped between limbs; briefly, he feared it would become trapped. He pulled it free and resumed stepping on the backs and chests around him. Some bizarre sense of decorum took hold, and he tried to navigate via dead men only.

The Germans watched, their eyes transfixed and grim.

He slumped back against the wall as he reached Lucien, who was under two fresh corpses. Duchene's dead friend was missing a shoe – a red, white and blue striped sock was all that protruded.

Duchene returned the cigarettes to his mouth and drew back on them. The smoke billowed, and he let it waft over his face like incense.

Bracing against the side of the pit, he heaved a still-warm body off Lucien. It was a young man, somewhere in his twenties – no older than the guards who peered down. The dead weight pulled at Duchene's arms as he shifted it, and he felt a pain in his shoulder. The eyes of the young man stared directly into the sun, flies arriving at the bloodied wound in his head to lick and lay.

Lucien was lying face up. His eyes were closed. Duchene thanked fate for this small mercy and that there were no glistening wounds for him to see. These would be in Lucien's back, where the Gestapo had shot him as he ran.

His body was still locked in rigor mortis. Hours would pass before it became supple again.

Duchene struggled with Lucien for five minutes, trying to sit him upright, raise his arms, lift and pull him so he was in the right position. For a time, Duchene struggled to imagine he was with his dying friend in a hospice, where he would have treated him with humility and respect. But his corpse resisted each manipulation, held fast or moved into more awkward positions. *Still stubborn, even when you're dead*.

Duchene placed a foot on Lucien's chest and pulled hard against the jacket arm. It ripped free, and the seam at the shoulder broke loose.

Duchene kept ripping and tearing. He screamed. The cigarettes fell from his mouth as his nails bent back against the fabric, and he pulled and tore and tugged.

Finally, he stood still, the pieces of Lucien's suit jacket in his hands. Tossing them onto the grass at the edge of the pit, he reached up. Stahl nodded, and the two soldiers took hold of Duchene's arms. He scrambled up the side of the pit and lay back in the grass.

Stahl squatted beside him. 'We need to keep moving.'

'Go to hell.'

'Perhaps. In time. You too, probably.'

Duchene sat up and dragged what remained of the jacket towards him. He ran his hand around its lining and outer fabric, and within moments felt something small and rectangular. He took out the notebook.

Stahl leant in close as Duchene wiped the mud from his face.

'Lucien documented everything he traded, everything he exchanged, all the incomings and outgoings.' Duchene untucked the leather tongue that held its cover in place and cracked it open. He scanned random pages. Flicked to new ones, turned over others.

'What is it?' Stahl asked, frowning.

Duchene dropped the book on the grass and put his face in his hands. 'Useless.'

Stahl picked up the book and turned the pages. 'What is this? Arabic?'

'No,' said Duchene. 'It's shorthand. I don't read it.'

'No problem. We have clerks who do.'

'And do they speak French?'

'No.'

Duchene stood and dusted at the dirt on his trousers. It made little impact. 'Come on,' he said, holding his hand out to take back the book.

'Come where?'

'I know someone who can help.' He checked his watch, it was just after eleven. 'You need to drive faster. Or this won't get done.'

TWENTY-ONE

Again they crossed Paris, from the Left Bank to the Right. The afternoon had only increased in its glory, a perfect blue sky above them. The few clouds that had lingered since dawn were gone, and the sun made fountains sparkle.

All around them the streets were still. Cafés and shops were silent. *Fermé / Geschlossen* signs hung in every door. The kiosks that lined the popular pedestrian streets stood like silent obelisks while stray papers that had been caught by the wind now clung to the railings of bridges and dark Métro stairwells.

The stench from the grave clung to Duchene. It had seeped into his clothes, entwined itself through his hair. He wondered if he would ever be rid of it.

'What has Faber done?' he asked Stahl as the Citroën squealed around a corner. 'Why are you looking for him?'

'I can't talk about that.'

'What does it matter now? We could be dead in an instant. Or worse.'

'What's worse than dead?'

'You're Gestapo, and you're asking me that?'

Stahl thought for a moment. 'You were right, what you said to the Oberführer. Faber doesn't respect the authority of the SS. He was Abwehr once.'

'And they are?'

'*Were*. Military intelligence. They were abolished back in February, and Faber was reassigned to Paris to support von Choltitz. They were all the same. Egotistical. Untrustworthy. Full of defeatism. Infiltrated by anti-Nazi defectors and English agents. No good.'

'Don't sound so bad to me.'

Stahl gave him a sharp look. 'We will hold Paris against your pathetic uprising. We will turn back the Americans. We will wipe England from the –'

A gunshot rang out close by.

They both ducked. Force of habit, even in a hard-topped car.

Duchene scrambled to see where it had come from. While his mind struggled to catch up, his heart had no hesitation and started pounding in his chest. He pushed himself down into the passenger seat while Stahl hunched low and sped on.

There were no other shots.

Duchene pointed to the road ahead. 'Turn right at Rue Saussier-Leroy and pull up outside the green apartment building. Number twenty-six.'

Stahl followed the instructions and brought the car to a stop. 'We'd better do this back at my headquarters, where it's well defended.'

'That's not going to work.'

'Get up there, get this Frenchwoman who can read shorthand, and get back down here.'

'No, it will take too much time. Listen – the Oberführer wants Kloke before this place descends into a battle zone, yes?'

'Yes.'

'You don't want to get shot. I don't want to get shot. So we can't keep driving all over the city, not with these snipers. If the book points us towards Kloke's lover, where he might be holed up, we should get there as soon as possible.'

Stahl exhaled but continued to scowl at Duchene. 'Quickly, then.'

'Best you take those swastikas off the car. Don't want to draw attention to it while we're upstairs.'

On walls along the street were papers hastily daubed into place, their ink washed white by flour paste that was still wet. Duchene walked up to one.

To the barricades!
Organise yourselves neighbourhood by neighbourhood. Overwhelm the Germans and take their arms. Free Great Paris, the cradle of France! Avenge your martyred sons and brothers. Avenge the heroes who have fallen for the freedom of our Fatherland. Choose your motto: A Boche for each of us. No quarter for these murders. Forward. Vive la France!
– Colonel Rol, French Forces of the Interior

'What does it say?' Stahl asked.

'Colonel Rol is calling for civilians and insurgents to take up arms. To fight for freedom. Vive la France. Et cetera. We should get inside.'

'Read it all.'

More wary of Stahl than the snipers, Duchene read without edit, while the German listened without emotion. He nodded as Duchene concluded with the signature, then asked, 'Have you ever met him?'

'Rol? That's like me asking if you've ever met Hitler. People like us don't get to meet people like them.'

'Except I have,' said Stahl. 'Met Hitler. In the Lustgarten in 1933.'

'You would have been a child.'

'I was. We were at a rally. He shook my father's hand.'

Duchene pushed the buzzer, and within moments they were let in. He tapped at the door to the apartment. Only three days had passed since he'd been here; it felt longer. He was without sleep, stretched thin, brittle. His mind struggled to hold together all his vital thoughts and observations. They were slipping from him, drifting into that place of half-recollection, dream, memory and fantasy. The line between fact and illusion was blurring.

Had he made love to Camille? *When was it? Did it happen at all?*

He heard the light tread of bare feet on the other side of the door. There was a brief pause, then the sound of the brass cover moving over the spyhole. The chain was unlatched, and the door opened.

Marienne was wearing a floral robe. She wore no makeup, her eyebrows were unfinished, and her hair flared wild around her face. Her eyes were red; she'd been crying. 'Papa,' she said, kissing him once before sniffing.

'What's the matter? Is everything all right?' He instinctively put a hand on her arm – to his surprise, she let him keep it there.

Stahl stepped in behind them and quietly closed the door.

'It's Max,' she said. 'He's gone.'

Duchene's head felt light. He found himself joining her

on the couch adjacent to the door. She laid her head on his shoulder, and he placed an arm around her.

Max is gone. Had she actually said that?

He scanned the room. On the dining table was the Hennessy bottle he'd brought to dinner, now empty. A glass sat beside it, the rim covered in lipstick. Through the doorway to his left, her bed was unmade, the sheets tossed aside, a man's suitcase half-packed with items scattered across the floor. The cupboard was open, one half of it emptied with only hooks remaining.

Max is gone.

Duchene hadn't even been aware he was bearing such weight until it had lifted. 'Was he redeployed?'

Marienne stirred, moved off his shoulder and looked across at Stahl. 'Who are you?' she asked in French.

Stahl took out his identification and held it up. 'Scharführer Stahl, Geheime Staatspolizei.'

Marienne pushed away from Duchene and moved to the corner of the couch. Her face was contorted, hostile, her mouth downturned, her eyes driving fury at him. 'You judge me? My choices? You're no better than me.' Her voice was cold.

'Marienne, it's not how it would seem.' He shot a glance at Stahl, who shrugged.

'Calm her,' he said in German. 'Give her the book. We haven't got much time.'

'Calm me? What do you think I am, a child, a fucking dog?' She burst up to face Stahl.

'You speak German?' he said. 'Makes sense.'

'Marienne,' Duchene said, standing again, his legs stiff and aching. 'I understand. You're upset. Yes, Stahl's with the Gestapo, but that can be explained.'

'Then explain.'

'They're after Faber.'

'So?'

'Faber wants to find a missing soldier. He threatened me if I didn't help him.'

'What did he threaten you with?'

Duchene looked back at her.

'You can't be serious,' she said.

'He is,' said Stahl. 'Deadly.'

She started pacing. 'So what did you do, go to the Gestapo?'

'They came to me. It gets more complicated, but you have to believe I didn't choose any of this. It's because of what I do.'

'Find children.'

'Find people.'

'Hurry it up,' Stahl said.

'You need to go along with this, Marienne,' Duchene said in French. 'Obviously the Gestapo are dangerous. And if it's not them, it's Faber. I need you to help me, help us.'

She stepped back. Ran a hand through her hair. Sighed. And nodded.

They gathered around the dining-room table, and Duchene placed Lucien's notebook in front of them. He held it open. Across each spread of two pages were four columns with red ink along their headings and borders. In the rows that stretched across the columns were precise pencil marks of symbols in the shapes of hooks and curves.

'What does it say?' Stahl asked.

Marienne rubbed her foot on the back of her calf. 'This is French standard Duployan. Shorthand.'

'Do you read it?'

'Yes. It's a ledger – incomings and outgoings, with the names of customers and suppliers.'

'And in the back pages?' Duchene asked.

'These are names and addresses. In some cases, phone numbers. You can see they're matched with initials that aren't in shorthand.' She flipped between the pages, reading entries and turning to the end of the book. 'It's not alphabetised in the back. It seems as if the entries correspond to the order in which items were exchanged – it's chronological, starting with the oldest entries on the last page and then working back through the book.' She paused, her finger pressed to one of the ledger's entries. Her eyes narrowed, and she looked up. 'Where did you get this?' Marienne asked in French.

'It doesn't matter,' Duchene replied.

'In German,' said Stahl.

Marienne considered briefly, before complying with Stahl's demand. 'Really?' She kept her finger on the line and held it towards both men. 'Because it says my name here. *11 January – One bottle of Bordeaux – One packet of nylon stockings – Marienne Duchene.*'

Stahl smiled.

Duchene froze.

'Where's Lucien?' Marienne asked.

Duchene held out his hands as his daughter started to stiffen. 'Lucien's dead.'

Stepping back from the table, she hugged herself tightly. Her pale face seemed to turn another shade lighter, and a tear ran down her cheek. 'How?'

Duchene remained still. Stahl had stopped smiling.

'Marienne, I don't want to frighten you, but we're against the clock. We'll mourn Lucien, I promise – I already am.

But we need to know if there's any reference to Christian Kloke in the book. It's really urgent.'

'Why, because the people of Paris are rising up? Because the Germans are about to be overthrown?'

'Because an enemy who's afraid is dangerous,' he replied in French.

Stahl started to speak and Duchene raised his hand.

'Please,' he said in German.

Stahl nodded and Duchene continued in French. 'The Germans have tanks and artillery. They have trained troops. Our people might have the numbers, but we hardly have any weapons. It's not going to happen in an instant – it will take days if it happens at all. That's easily enough time for the two of us to lose our lives. And Marienne, my love, I don't want you to be killed. It would rend my heart.'

Another tear rolled down her cheek, and she quickly wiped it away. Duchene offered her his handkerchief, and she used it to wipe her eyes, her nose. Then she returned to the book. 'Christian Kloke?'

'We need to know if there's anyone listed close to him, maybe at the same address. Start from Friday the eleventh of August and track backwards.'

She thumbed to the relevant pages and started to flip through, her eyes scanning quickly down each page. 'I've got him and another man listed together. Olivier Manaudou, who traded a box of cigarillos for two fillet steaks and half a bottle of merlot. And I have Christian on the previous page, from two days earlier – traded a silk dressing-gown for three litres of gasoline.' She kept flicking through the pages. 'They're listed in here quite a lot – they seem to have been two of Lucien's regulars.'

'And in the back?' asked Stahl. 'Does it have his address?'

Marienne checked. 'Yes, one address for both men. Fifty-four Rue du Château-des-Rentiers, 13th arrondissement.'

'That's back across the Seine,' Duchene said.

'Let's hope he's in,' Stahl muttered.

Duchene held his hand out for the ledger, and Marienne passed it back to him. 'Please stay safe,' she said.

He gave her a hug and kissed her on the forehead. 'And you too. Try to stay inside. I'll call you soon.'

As he left, he cast one last glance at his daughter. She stood in her living room, the sun streaming in through the window, her wild hair lit like a halo.

TWENTY-TWO

Duchene had to rush down the stairs to keep up with Stahl. The lights weren't working, but there was ample illumination coming through the large glass panels on the entrance doors that led out to the street.

Stahl paused in the lobby. 'You've done well,' he said, reaching out a hand.

Duchene refused it. 'Is my life still under threat?'

'Kloke is almost found,' Stahl said with a frown. 'It's midday now, and it will take us fifteen minutes to reach our destination. You should be reasonably confident you'll live.'

'Well, let's keep the handshake until then.'

Stahl nodded and pushed the door open.

With a loud *crack*, Stahl's head erupted.

Duchene felt a warm spray across his face and closed his eyes. When he opened them again, he looked down.

Lucien was there spasming, trying to speak as blood gathered in his mouth. The spasming continued, and as though it were infectious Duchene started to do the same; within seconds, his whole body was trembling.

Finally, Lucien lay still, and Duchene could see it wasn't him at all. Stahl had been shot in the head.

An iron smell filled the air as blood coursed out of the wound. Duchene looked up, blinking through the blood on his face. He raised a hand to his forehead. Something sharp was lodged there. Pulling it free, he saw it was hair and bone.

Duchene dropped it on the steps as Armand rushed up at him from the edge of the door. The pistol in his hand still smelt of gunpowder, the muzzle hot as the maquisard pushed it hard against Duchene's head. 'Get inside,' Armand hissed.

'What have you done?' Duchene could barely form the words.

'Get the fuck up!' Armand shouted as three men ran across the street and pulled open the entrance door that was caught on Duchene's leg.

Duchene swayed as he stood, his legs giving way, and Armand pushed him back into the narrow foyer. He tripped and fell, sprawling across the floor. His chin hit the tiles, and blood flowed from his lip.

Turning around, he saw Casin and another man pulling Stahl's body into the lobby while Philippe kept watch from the doorway. A few faces had appeared at windows and balconies on the street outside.

Philippe waved a red scarf back at them and shouted, 'Vive la France!'

Duchene's hands were spreading blood – his, Stahl's – across the floor. 'What have you done?' he asked again.

'We killed that SS dog,' Armand shouted, 'and we'll do the same to you if you don't shut up. Where is the girl?'

Philippe slid the bolts on the door shut before walking back into the darkness. Casin and the other man had the mop cupboard open and were shoving Stahl inside.

Armand pushed his pistol hard into Duchene's cheek.

'Stand up,' Philippe said as he reached a hand down to

Duchene, before saying to Armand, 'He knows he's been caught out. Let's get him upstairs so we can find out what he knows.'

Armand took the gun from Duchene's face.

'Come,' Philippe said as he pulled him up. Blood was smeared on Philippe's hand and jacket cuff. 'You must have gotten a hell of a fright. We had to strike first.'

'I was using him to find Kloke.'

'Please, Auguste, you weren't using him. He was using you. Come, let's see if Marienne has something we can drink.'

It took only a moment for them to reach her door. Philippe tapped on it. 'Mam'selle, I need you to open up.'

'Don't do it,' Duchene called out, his voice sounding unfamiliar, and Armand slapped the back of his head.

'You can let us in, or we can come in,' Philippe said. 'Only one of those options leaves you with a door that you can still lock.'

Silence.

'Casin, Jean,' Philippe said.

The two larger men stood alongside him while Armand pulled Duchene back. The three men at the door counted down and kicked in unison, their boots crashing onto the panel nearest the handle. The door buckled under the force, and a fissure opened in the pine along the edge of the handle, a pale contrast against the dark grey of the paint.

'One, two ...' *Three*. They kicked again, splintering the wood and ramming the door open. The chain swung limply to one side, its mooring point buckled.

The men didn't move – Philippe had raised his right hand to call them to a stop, while with his left he'd reached into the room.

Duchene tugged against Armand to see what was happening.

'Mademoiselle, please, put down the gun,' said Philippe.

'Let my father go and leave.' Her voice was strong. Unwavering. Something about her resoluteness scared Duchene.

'That won't be happening. You fire, Armand will shoot your father and then you. Some of us might die, you two definitely will. Is that something you want? We're not here to fight you. We're here to fight the Germans.'

'Get him to put his gun away first.'

Philippe nodded. 'Of course.' He flapped his raised hand, and Armand slid the revolver into his belt.

Duchene glanced at it. It was still cocked.

Dangerous.

'Now, then,' said Philippe, 'we were hoping you might invite us in for a drink. So we can all talk.'

He led the others in, his hands still raised, and skirted around the side of the room, keeping an armchair between him and Marienne.

Duchene felt a surge of fear when he saw her, now in a floral dress, holding a gun towards Philippe. She glanced at him briefly but kept tracking the weapon across all the men.

It was a Luger. German. An officer's sidearm.

Armand pushed Duchene into the apartment.

'I'm going to open your sideboard now,' Philippe said as he bent down to its polished walnut doors. 'I'm hoping I'll find your liquor.'

'Who are these people?' Marienne said to Duchene in English.

'You're better off with German,' Philippe replied in English.

'They're Resistance,' Duchene said in French. 'Philippe is their leader. They asked me to find some missing guns for the insurgency.'

'An excellent summary,' Philippe said as he stood up, holding a half-finished bottle of whisky. 'Teacher's,' he said, examining its label. 'This will help smooth out the edges. Mademoiselle, please, the moment has passed. You can lower the weapon. We should all have a talk.'

Marienne kept the gun pointed at them.

'Please. There are only two outcomes – you do what we ask, or you die.' He unscrewed the lid and started to pour out six measures into glasses on the top of the sideboard. 'I'd rather talk to you than shoot you, but if you give me no choice, I will go ahead. We were all prepared to die when we decided to fight the occupation. Armand lost his family to the SS; they were killed in cold blood for capturing a Nazi officer. Casin saw his father taken off to a work camp last winter – he was sick with pneumonia. Jean lost two brothers, just the other day, shot in the Bois de Boulogne and finished off with grenades along with thirty-three other men. The Germans are indifferent and evil, but as you can see, we are ready. Can you say the same?'

Marienne lowered the gun.

'Thank you. Perhaps you could place it on the table?'

She paused.

'Armand?' Philippe said.

Without hesitation, the maquisard drew his revolver and fired.

The blast was right next to Duchene's head; his ears screamed, and he clapped his hands to them.

Marienne had dropped to the ground beside the table.

Duchene couldn't see her. He howled. His heart was

pounding in his chest, his head dizzy, tears welling in his eyes.

Look. Think.

The wall behind her – clean. Not a drop of blood. But there was a dark circle, a bullet hole, with the plaster cracking around it.

A warning shot.

'Not pleasant, to be shot at.' Philippe said as he passed a glass to Casin, whose eyes were wide, his hands trembling. 'Please put the gun on the table and slide it towards us.' Philippe handed a glass to Jean. 'For you.'

Duchene realised he was crouching. The ringing in his ears remained, but he got to his feet all the same, hoping to glimpse his daughter.

She pushed the Luger onto the table and slowly stood.

Philippe plucked it up as he handed her a whisky. 'Very good.' He circled the table and pressed a drink into Armand's spare hand. 'Let's put the gun away. Shall we sit, everyone? I really feel like I need to sit down after all that excitement.'

Duchene slumped against the table. Armand sat between him and Marienne.

'Are you all right?' Duchene asked her, and she nodded. 'I'm sorry about this. All of it.'

'Shall we drink?' asked Philippe. 'Vive la France.'

The partisans drank their whisky in one hit. Marienne left hers untouched. Duchene sipped from his, the alcohol stinging his split lip.

'Jean,' said Philippe, 'can you get something to clean up Monsieur Duchene's face? All that Boche blood is distracting.'

Jean returned from the bathroom with a damp

handtowel, and Philippe used it to wipe his hands clean before tossing it to Duchene. It was warm and eased some of the pain as he placed it across his face. It took off most of the blood but broke open the laceration on his forehead. Philippe threw over a handkerchief from his pocket, and Duchene held it against his head to staunch the flow. It failed.

'Ridiculous,' Marienne said and stood up. Armand followed her as she entered the bathroom and came back holding a first-aid basket. She wiped the wound with Dakin's solution and wrapped it in a dressing.

'I need to be clear about something,' Philippe said to Duchene. 'You are aware that the uprising has started? Today is the day we start to fight back against the Germans.'

'I'd noticed.'

'But what we don't have are the right weapons for the job. You so artfully summarised why we're here in your daughter's apartment, but have not updated us on your search.'

'Lucien stole your guns, in partnership with a German soldier called Christian Kloke.'

'Bullshit,' said Armand.

Duchene reached into his pocket and tossed half of the wax mould onto the table. It had broken in two, probably when he fell. 'This is the cast they made from the crypt key. I found it in Lucien's apartment. Think about it – the thief had to be someone who knew about the weapons. No one would just walk into the crypt of Saint-Lambert and walk off with six crates of weapons.'

'So the priest didn't move them?'

'No. He's probably dead.'

'So why would Lucien take our weapons?'

'To do what he did best – sell them on the black market.'

'To whom?'

'Back to the Resistance.'

'Bullshit,' Armand barked again.

'Who else would buy them? Civilians don't want to get deported or shot for having weapons. Only the Resistance would take that risk. But don't believe me – talk to Colonel Rol.'

'I have,' said Philippe, 'and he doesn't have anything from our cache. His first priority is securing proper weapons. That Vichy traitor Pétain was right about one thing – "firepower kills". We'd be taking more profound action if we had rifles and machine guns. We need to talk to Lucien.'

'He's dead. He was shot by the Gestapo.'

Marienne looked at Duchene, her eyes focused on his face, as though trying to read him, trying to make sense of this news.

Philippe shook his head, a bemused smile spreading across his face. 'The Gestapo? The same Gestapo officer we just shot in the foyer? The same one you arrived with half an hour ago?'

The realisation hit. 'You've been watching Marienne's apartment.'

'Of course,' said Philippe. 'We needed to make sure she didn't run off with her Luftwaffe lover. Makes it hard to motivate a man when we have nothing to motivate him with. Where is the lieutenant, by the way?'

'Gone,' Duchene said.

'A lot of people are gone, missing or dead,' said Armand. 'Where is the cache?'

'I was leaving to get it when you arrived,' said Duchene.

It might be true – and without that possibility, he had nothing to bargain with.

'With the Gestapo?'

'They wanted to arrest Kloke.'

Armand sneered. 'And leave you with the guns?'

'Why would I lie?'

'Why wouldn't you? Your daughter is about to lose her life. You too. I think a man in your situation would do anything.'

Marienne's eyes narrowed. 'Fuck you.'

'But,' Philippe held up his hand, 'if the Gestapo believed you, that would suggest there's some truth to it. Murderous scum they may be, but fools they are not.'

'So what do we do now?' Armand asked.

Philippe sank back into his chair and stared hard at the surface of the table. 'With Lucien dead –'

'*If* Lucien's dead,' said Armand.

'Is. Isn't. Duchene here says he knows where the guns are.'

'With Kloke's lover,' said Duchene.

'We go there. If we can't find the weapons … well, that will be the end of it. We won't waste any more time looking for them, and we'll need to move to alternative plans.'

'I can take you to them,' Duchene said, trying not to leap too quickly at the suggestion.

'In the meantime,' Philippe said, 'we'll take the girl somewhere else. We can't stay here with a dead Gestapo officer in the closet downstairs.'

'Take the girl somewhere?' asked Armand. 'We should all go to the cache.'

'It's too dangerous for a large group to cross the city,' said Philippe. 'Especially if we end up returning with weapons.

We lost too many patriots at Bois de Boulogne. We can't afford to repeat that mistake. The Germans are yet to make their move; they might come out in force, and we don't want to be caught in the open.'

Armand nodded. 'So how do you want to do this?'

'Armand,' said Philippe, standing up, 'you and Casin will go with Duchene to the weapons. Find them and call in. Jean and I will take the girl to a more secure location and wait for your call.'

'Where will you take me?' Marienne asked.

Philippe thought for a moment. 'Give me the keys to your apartment,' he ordered Duchene, who placed them in his open hand. 'This Kloke is a soldier. He'll be armed.' Philippe took the Luger from the table and passed it to Casin, who tucked it into the back of his trousers.

'What about you?' Armand asked.

'I've got Jean, and Jean's good with a knife.'

Jean pulled back his coat to reveal a sheath in his belt.

'Take the truck,' Philippe said to Armand, handing him a set of keys. 'I'll take the Citroën.'

TWENTY-THREE

Duchene sat between Armand and Casin as the engine of the small truck rattled to life. They waited and watched until Philippe appeared, Jean behind him with an arm around Marienne. They got in the black Citroën and started their engine.

Armand took the truck out into the street and pulled up alongside them.

'Be smart, stay safe,' said Philippe.

Armand nodded.

Duchene watched the car drive off down the street. He could see Marienne's face in the back window, staring towards him; she was probably fighting the same grim thoughts as he was.

'Where are we going?' Armand asked Duchene.

'Thirteenth. Fifty-four Rue du Château-des-Rentiers.'

Casin picked up a map from the cabin floor and folded it to the relevant arrondissement.

The sun had long since passed its zenith, and the silent streets of the morning were no more. Activity was commencing, furtive but dedicated. In the Place des Ternes, women, children and men were pulling up cobblestones and adding them to the beginnings of a barricade. At its centre was a park bench that had been dragged into the street and onto which two young men were placing a tree grille.

The further they drove the more makeshift defences they saw. A burnt-out Fiat reinforced with a street urinal. Kiosks carefully stripped, their wares shared out before they were deposited at strong points throughout the city.

'A tank will go straight through that,' said Casin as they passed a group of men sharing cigarettes on top of a downed tree piled with boards and stones.

'A tank will go through most things.' Armand's eyes were fixed on the road as he navigated around the barricades and slowed for pedestrians wandering in front of the truck. 'Except another tank. That's what we need to work towards. Like in the nursery rhyme – a fly, then a spider, then a bird …'

Casin shook his head. 'They've hardly got anything. Just one rifle between them.'

Deeper into the city, tricolores were being raised where once they had been forbidden: hospitals, schools, government buildings. And still no Germans.

'They're planning something,' Casin said. 'They have to be.'

'If you want to stay clear of Germans, you should cross before or after the Île de la Cité,' Duchene said. 'Our police have fortified their headquarters there. You can guarantee that's where the Germans will be headed.'

Armand opened his mouth, seemed to think better of it, and nodded.

They followed the Seine before crossing at the Pont de Tolbiac. Armand paused the truck in the centre of the bridge, and Casin took out a pair of binoculars. He climbed on the roof of the truck.

'Anything?' asked Armand.

'Not really,' said Casin. 'I can see smoke.'

'That's who we should be liberating,' said Armand. 'Thousands of police could all be fighting alongside us. That's the way to force out the Germans.' He hit the roof of the cabin, and Casin slid back in through the open window.

After an hour of traversing the streets, they found themselves on Rue du Château-des-Rentiers. Casin scanned the street numbers, calling out as the truck neared a small public park and children's playground. Directly opposite was fifty-four, a townhouse.

The street was blocked by a barricade, made up of play equipment and trees from the park, on which a few older children were climbing, while a mother nearby soothed two squabbling toddlers. The small crowd that had gathered to watch a group of locals bolstering the defences with an empty oil drum stared as the three men got out of the truck – unfamiliar people arriving in an unmarked vehicle when civilian automobiles of any kind were a rarity.

At the address, Casin swung the knocker. It echoed in the hallway beyond it.

'Pray he's at home,' Armand said, looking at Duchene.

Casin knocked louder and held his ear to the door. 'Silence,' he said.

The mother was watching them. Duchene straightened his tie and walked over to her. Her face soured as he approached, and the toddlers buried their faces in her skirts. He'd removed his jacket, but blood was spattered on his collar and shirt.

'I know, Madame, I look a state.' He tapped the gauze on his head. 'Fighting Germans. It's not always pretty.'

'You're with the Resistance?' she asked.

'Of course. These are my companions, Armand and Casin. We're hoping you can help us. Do you know where Monsieur Manaudou … where Olivier is? He's got some important supplies for us.'

She nodded and pointed at a young man in glasses, who was carrying the board from a seesaw across from the park to the barricade.

'Thank you very much.'

Armand and Casin rushed over and took the weight of the plank from Olivier, who mopped his tanned brow with a handkerchief. He wore a herringbone waistcoat and glasses that framed dark green eyes.

Duchene approached with his hand held out. 'Monsieur Manaudou?'

'Yes?'

'We need your help. It's quite urgent. May we talk inside?'

'What's this about?'

'We're friends of Lucien's. We have some things we'd like to discuss.'

'I'm happy to discuss them out here.'

Armand and Casin tossed the seesaw board onto the barricade and started to make their way over.

'I really think we should talk inside,' said Duchene. 'It's to do with another colleague of Lucien's – a friend of yours, perhaps? His first name is Christian.'

The blood rushed from Olivier's long face.

Duchene whispered to him. 'If Kloke is inside, say nothing. These men want to know about the guns he stole. If you have them, give them to us and say that the German has fled. I'll do what I can to protect you. Understand?'

Olivier nodded.

Armand and Casin joined them.

'Please lead on,' Duchene said and pointed to the door.

As they stepped into Olivier's house, Duchene listened for movement. A narrow corridor passed a staircase that led to the upper levels. Beyond this, he could see the kitchen and a window that looked into the back garden.

Build trust. And fast.

'Please,' he said to Olivier, 'here is good.' He pointed to the left of the main entrance, at a doorway that revealed a small sitting room.

'Check the house,' Armand said to Casin.

'Perhaps we don't need to just yet,' said Duchene.

'If there's a Boche waiting to surprise us with a machine gun, I want to know about it.'

Duchene smiled. 'If there's a Boche waiting to surprise us with a machine gun, there's not much we can do about it. He will have the element of surprise. We need to negotiate our way through this. I'm sure Olivier is ready and willing to help us.'

'I am,' he said, removing his spectacles and rubbing them with the corner of his handkerchief.

'You see?' Duchene said to Armand. 'Perhaps Casin could watch the corridor and you the street.'

This seemed to satisfy the maquisard, at least for the moment. He drew his revolver and took up a place by the window, looking through its Venetian blinds.

Duchene sat in a wing chair adjacent to Olivier while Casin stood by the wall, staring back down the hallway. He pulled the slide on the Luger.

Olivier shook his head. His hands were trembling but he managed keep his voice calm. 'Are you here to kill me?'

'We're absolutely not about to do that,' Duchene said.

'Perhaps we should,' said Armand. 'He's a collaborator.'

'Let's save the ammunition for the Germans.' Duchene nodded at Olivier. His jaw was starting to tire from forcing a benign expression onto his face. His shoulders were stiff, and he caught his hands digging into his legs. The fact was, nothing about him suggested he was relaxed or trustworthy.

Play it out. Build rapport.

'So,' he said, 'I'll tell you what we know, and you can fill in the rest.'

Olivier nodded.

'You had been using the services of Lucien Martin to buy from the black market, to trade for supplies. Nothing strange about that.'

'Is that true?' said Casin, looking over.

'It is. Was.'

'You also met Christian. Became friends – more than friends, lovers ...'

Olivier nodded.

'Again. Nothing wrong with that.'

Armand hissed.

'You introduced Lucien and Kloke, perhaps during a delivery one day. They hit it off – recognised something of themselves in each other. Is that true?'

Olivier nodded again.

'Now, this is the important part. Did you know anything about any schemes they hatched together?'

'They had a few.'

'Do you know they planned to steal a cache of weapons from a church?'

'Yes.'

'And do you know what happened to the priest, Father Ramelle?'

'Yes. Sorry, I'm afraid I do.' Olivier put his face in his hands. 'It's been like a pressure inside my chest. I knew something bad had happened. At first Christian wouldn't say what it was, but I wouldn't give him peace until he told me.'

'He killed Ramelle?'

Olivier rubbed his eyes. 'Yes. I don't think he meant to. They were surprised. No one was meant to be there during Mass.'

'This is very important,' said Duchene. 'What did they do with the body?'

'That's *not* important,' said Armand. 'Where are the guns?'

Duchene held up a hand. 'Do you know?'

'Where are the guns, fucker?' Armand said, stepping away from the window and raising his revolver towards Olivier.

Flinching, the younger man raised his knees and shielded his face with his hands. 'Please! I don't know. Christian never told me.'

'Where's Christian?' Armand said, slapping Olivier's hands from his face and pointing the gun at the middle of his forehead.

'I don't know. I haven't seen him in a week. Not since Thursday.'

Armand pulled the gun from Olivier's face. He bent forward and roared as though the earth would open up beneath him and his anger would draw out the missing weapons.

Duchene closed his eyes.

'Old man,' Armand shouted at him, 'you have wasted the last of our time. Where's the telephone?'

'Wait, please,' Duchene said, trying to control the desperation in his voice. He turned back to Olivier. 'Is there any chance, any chance at all, that Christian hid the guns in your house – under the stairs, in a cellar, the attic?' With his eyes, Duchene tried to make Olivier realise that every extra minute was critical to their chances of survival.

Olivier seemed to understand. 'Maybe ... maybe under the stairs? Or in the potting shed out the back?'

'Casin,' Armand said. 'Check them.' The maquisard started to pace, periodically looking out the window. 'Philippe was wrong to trust you.'

'We were all wrong to put any faith in Lucien. He knew the truth the entire time. I just assumed he was furtive because he felt guilty for dragging me into this. And he *was* guilty for having robbed you – afraid I might discover the truth.'

Armand snorted. 'There was never any risk of that. Pathetic.' He peered through the blinds.

The crowd on the street were cheering. A young woman in shorts, a blouse and a French Forces of the Interior armband cycled at speed down the road. She threw pamphlets from a sling bag and shouted a call to arms. The crowd clambered to the barricade as she rode by. Women hugged children, and men shook hands.

And then, in an instant, they stopped.

Duchene could see only a little through the window. He didn't need to.

First the light fittings rattled, dropping dust and dead insects. Then the ground trembled as the rumbling – steel on stone – became louder.

The crowd scrambled down from the barricade, shouting and pushing their way between bent iron and splintered wood.

'Casin!' Armand called.

From the street came the staccato crack of three shots.

The crowd rushed for the doors of their houses and struggled with keys as they hurried to get inside.

The sound of boots now, moving out from behind the protection of the tanks. Jogging up the street.

'Casin!' Armand rushed over to look down the corridor. 'Do you have them?'

Duchene leant in towards Olivier. 'If you want to live, you need to run. Now. With me.'

'Where?'

'The back. Away from the Germans.'

Duchene couldn't be sure if Olivier's grimace was an acknowledgement.

And he didn't have time to check – Casin had arrived at the living-room door. 'Germans. Armoured platoon. Four tanks.'

'You don't want to shoot,' Duchene said. 'That'll draw them in here.'

'I can kill a man in silence,' Armand said as he moved back to the window and made a sideways motion with his head.

Casin followed. 'They're gathering at the other end of the street.'

'Do they know we're here?' Armand asked.

Duchene let out a slow breath as he reached over to the fireplace. Olivier watched, his body seized in tension. Duchene took hold of the wrought-iron poker and nodded.

Olivier sat still. Duchene made his eyes wide and nodded again. The other man didn't move.

Duchene stood up and swung the poker, shattering the window so that shards of glass cascaded onto the footpath.

Armand and Casin stared, dumbstruck, at Duchene, their bodies seemingly incapable of movement.

'In here! Hurry!' Duchene shouted in German as he swung the poker back from the window.

Casin went white, Armand red.

Duchene's mind raced faster than his arm could move. He tried to spur it forward, increase its speed by thinking harder. He was swinging down; Armand was drawing his revolver up.

Milliseconds. Vital moments. His life held in the tick of a second hand.

The poker hit.

The revolver fired.

The men stared at each other as Duchene scrambled to piece together the aftermath. He had tried to hit the revolver but smashed Armand's hand instead. The partisan's wrist was bent like the neck of a swan. The gun was facing the ground, a cloud of wool still rising from a hole in the rug.

'Now!' shouted Duchene, and Olivier leapt from the wing chair and ran to the door.

On the street, the Germans were shouting.

Armand raised the gun again, his face contorting when his fingers refused to move. His injured wrist swelled as fluid gathered at the point of the break.

Casin was frozen.

Duchene ran.

In the corridor, he could hear a German barking orders outside. 'That house. Firing position.'

Duchene pulled the living-room door shut. He swung the poker at the handle, smashing it off the door, then used the tip of the poker to push the mechanism through the other side. He hoped it would slow down their pursuers.

Turning, he ran after Olivier, back down the house and through a well-stocked kitchen. Olivier was in the small paved garden, already pulling at the back gate, struggling with a latch that was stuck from disuse.

Duchene could hear gunfire as he caught up. 'Quickly,' he said, hoping a façade of calm would inspire the younger man into successful action.

'They'll come after us?'

'If they have any sense, they'll leave through the same exit. Let's not be here when they do.' Reaching up to the top of the gate, Duchene pulled; the wood shrieked, but the gate didn't open. 'Together this time,' he said.

Olivier tugged on the latch as Duchene yanked again. The gate burst open, and pain rushed through his shoulder. He held Olivier back from fleeing as he stuck his head out into the narrow lane behind the house. No Germans.

He could hear a hammering and splintering as wood cracked in the house behind him. Front door or back door? Neither would be good news.

'Show me how to get out of here, away from Château-des-Rentiers.'

Olivier nodded, and Duchene followed him. His heart was pounding as he struggled to keep up. Olivier skidded around corners, hurling himself forward without caution. At each turn, Duchene was certain they'd come face to face with Germans.

'Olivier!' he called, increasing his speed to get close enough to talk. His chest felt that it might burst; the air in his lungs burnt. 'A ... phone ... where?'

Olivier looked at the nearest street sign. Paused. Took his bearings. 'One block over. Opposite the square.'

Duchene nodded. Moved to wipe his hand across his brow and realised he was still holding the poker. He handed it to Olivier. 'Thank you. Do you have somewhere safe to go?'

The younger man nodded.

Duchene placed a hand on his arm. 'Sorry about all of this.'

Olivier stared at him. Turned. And ran.

Counting every second, Duchene pushed himself forward. Armand would find a phone – would call Philippe. Duchene had to call first. Explain what had happened. Sow doubt. Beg. Anything to keep that bullet from Marienne.

As he reached the phone booth, the streets were empty. The sound of gunfire had only just stopped echoing around the neighbourhood. He pulled the door open, fought to regain his breath and dialled his apartment building.

The phone kept ringing, so he tried again.

There was no answer.

TWENTY-FOUR

'Remain in your houses. Curfew is now in place. Disorder will be met with deadly force.' A German truck was patrolling the streets, the loudspeaker in the back playing a recorded message in French. The driver's eyes darted across the street, to the rooftops, towards blind corners, seeming to take in everything and nothing.

Duchene kept himself hidden, tucked into a doorway in an alleyway. The evening was upon him, still an hour from twilight, and every minute felt like an hour. The distance between him and Marienne was all he could feel, but he beat back his fears. He had a single objective, and completing it was all that mattered.

As the truck passed by, he glanced out again. He could see the soldiers sitting under its tarpaulin, their expressions a mirror of his own: fear, anxiety, concern.

He waited for the truck to turn off before he returned to the road. He'd seen a barricade ahead, so he jogged over to resume his search.

This barricade was shored up with stolen German sandbags, and filled mostly with old furniture and scrap metal. But mounted on top, in a gesture of defiance of the curfew, was what he'd been looking for: a bike.

Precious minutes passed as he struggled to pull it down. To his dismay, the front wheel was bent. He spent more time hammering it into a position where it would at least rotate while he pedalled.

As the pain in his legs grew, he knew he would regret this journey tomorrow. If tomorrow came.

Relief changed quickly to fear as Duchene turned onto his street. He dropped the bike and moved to the opposite side of the road, looking up at his apartment for signs of – well, anything.

Instead, he found nothing. No German convoy was parked on the road, and there were no soldiers, no signs of the Gestapo. By now they must have realised that something had happened to Stahl. But what would they do in response?

They have torture rooms. They're quick to kill.

Again, Duchene pushed these thoughts aside and focused on Marienne.

He crossed the road and went to remove his keys from his pocket. But they were useless – the building's front door had been broken open, its glass smashed.

His hands started to shake. His heart began to pound.

He walked inside, the glass on the foyer floor crunching under his feet. It was dark. The power was still out.

The door to the Junets' place opened slightly. Monsieur Junet stared back at him, eyes wild, jaw stiff with apprehension.

Duchene pointed a finger upwards, in the direction of his apartment. Junet nodded.

'Who?' Duchene mouthed.

Junet opened his door a little wider, raised his right

hand and gave a Nazi salute. Duchene nodded back.

His stomach turned, and adrenaline flooded in.

Gestapo.

Motioning for Junet to close the door, he started up the stairs. Each careful tread made the wood beneath the carpet groan, but he had no choice but to keep walking, even though the sound would alert whoever was inside his apartment.

Light was streaming from the open door as Duchene stepped onto the landing.

'You can stop creeping around. You're embarrassing yourself.' The voice spoke French, was slurred and had a faint Swiss accent.

He walked forward. 'Major Faber,' he said, summoning the courage to walk into the apartment with his eyes closed.

As he opened them, the fear leapt from him, making his head spin.

On the other side of the room, opposite his towers of books, in a chair beside Faber, was Marienne. Alive and well.

She and Faber were sitting at the old table littered with scraps of paper, empty bottles and a saucer for an ashtray. Her wrists were tied to the sides of the chair by fabric Duchene didn't recognise until he noticed his torn curtains.

'You're being painfully melodramatic,' Faber said. He was wearing civilian clothes: a waistcoat and trousers. A wide-brimmed hat sat on the table beside him.

'*I'm* the one being melodramatic?' Duchene said in German.

'Close the door as you come in,' Faber said, switching to his native tongue; he slurred his words less.

Duchene did as he was asked, but moved slowly, trying to

piece together this new threat. Slung over Faber's shoulder was an MP 40 submachine gun. In one hand he held a Luger, in the other a half-empty bottle of Teacher's whisky.

He's been to Marienne's.

There were no signs of the Resistance, of gunfire, of violence. But on the ashtray saucer beside Faber were two half-smoked Gitanes.

Philippe was here. But has gone.

At Faber's feet was a large German army radio wrapped in field-green canvas, and from one end rose a black antenna. On its front were a series of dials and a pair of headphones. But Faber wasn't in uniform.

The army doesn't know where he is. He's stolen the radio.

'Made sense of it all yet?' Faber asked, drinking from the bottle. 'Shall we jump to the end? I can shoot the whore now and be done with it.'

'No,' said Duchene, holding up his hands.

Marienne was making movements with her eyes. Something complicated; something that didn't make any sense to him.

'Where's Kloke?' Faber asked.

'I don't know. Hiding. Fled. Dead. All are possible.'

Faber's face shifted – it was a moment only, but an emotion was there. *Disappointment? No.*

'So you've failed,' he said.

'I've looked all over Paris. I found the last man who saw him – his French lover, Olivier Manaudou. He has no idea where Kloke is.'

Another shift. The upwards turn of a lip, the deepening of crow's feet. A twitch of anger.

No, something else.

'This man, Olivier, confirmed that Kloke had stolen

guns from the Resistance and was planning to sell the cache back to them. With the help of a Frenchman, Lucien Martin. Olivier was frightened, distraught.' Duchene paused. He had an idea. 'Oliver said he'd begged Kloke to take him out of Paris. Made him promise they'd build a life far away in Indochina, where they'd grow crops, grow old.'

No shift in Faber's expression this time. It was a full emotion, raw and loud; a souring of his face, a snarl on his mouth. Faber wasn't angry – he was jealous.

'Is that why the Gestapo is looking for him?' asked Duchene.

'What?' Now Faber seemed lost in drunken thought, irritated that Duchene had disturbed him.

'The Gestapo want Kloke so they can interrogate him. Get him to confess that you and he were lovers.'

Faber snorted. 'Too simplistic.'

'But you were. Lovers.'

'Don't push me, Duchene. A second is all it takes, and her brains will be spread all over your books.'

'They would have arrested you both. Your regime isn't so fond of homosexuals.'

'Obviously.'

'I'm sorry I couldn't find him. You don't have to follow through with your threats.'

'Oh, but I do. I'm still a man of my word, a soldier, a bringer of death.'

'If you're still a soldier, call the Wehrmacht. Ask them to pick you up.'

'He can't,' said Marienne.

'Shut up,' said Faber.

'They've stopped answering him on the radio.'

Faber dropped the whisky. Before it hit the floor,

his hand was wrapped around her neck, the Luger only millimetres from her eyes.

Rage. Fear. Duchene's hands started to shake. But he looked to Marienne, focused on her – not this enemy. Let his words flow as though he was talking to his only daughter.

'Wait,' Duchene said. 'What about the Abwehr? You must still have friends there, colleagues you can call. The old guard?'

Marienne's face was starting to turn red.

Duchene held up his hands. 'There's a phone in my neighbour's apartment, across the hallway. You can use that to call anywhere in Paris – in Berlin, even. Get help.'

'Look at you.' Faber turned from Marienne and spat at the floor. The spittle landed on a book. 'You're convinced you understand it all. You've sniffed around and dug up some old bones. So what?'

Tears were welling in Marienne's eyes, she was struggling to breathe.

'So, explain it to me,' Duchene said, his fists clenched so tight that his knuckles were stinging.

Faber snorted again. 'Confess? Don't be absurd.'

'You ... need ... to ...' Marienne's voice was thin and raspy.

'What?' Faber said, taking his hand from her throat.

She kept her head high, clearly refusing to splutter or cough. 'I said, you need to leave ... Paris. You're not in uniform. You'll be executed as a deserter.'

'She's right, Major. And the Resistance will shoot you on sight.'

'My father knows how to get you out from the centre of the city,' Marienne said, wiping the tears from her eyes.

'Oh? He does?' The major leant back in his chair as he watched Marienne.

Duchene was as intrigued as Faber to hear the answer.

'That man he spoke about, Lucien – he smuggled contraband past your roadblocks, into and out of the city. My father has been with him. He knows the way.'

'Your father has consistently disappointed me, something I understand you're familiar with. Why would I trust him with anything ever again, especially my life?'

'Because we'll be risking ours to help you,' she replied.

'And where is this miraculous smuggler's route?'

'The Catacombs.'

'The Catacombs?' Faber looked directly at Marienne, which meant Duchene was saved having to conceal his surprise.

'This route goes under the German roadblocks. It will bring you to the southern edge of Paris. From there you can make your way into the countryside.'

'To be shot by the Maquis?'

'You can pass as Swiss,' Duchene said. 'It's still a better chance than you have if you try to get out by yourself.'

Faber stood and walked to the window. He glanced down at the street. 'Can either of you drive?'

'I can,' Duchene replied.

'And we can? Drive there?'

'We have to cross the river,' Duchene said. 'Pont Marie has the fewest barricades, I crossed it on my way back here. We can get to the Left Bank there.'

'Then free your daughter. We leave now.'

Duchene didn't hesitate. With a paring knife from his kitchen, he cut the curtain fabric around Marienne's wrists.

Faber saw him holding it. 'On the table,' he said.

Duchene dropped it.

Faber slid the Luger into his hip holster and swivelled the submachine gun to face Duchene and Marienne. She rubbed her wrists as she followed Duchene to the door. He whispered to her, 'What's going on?'

'Oh, please, let's not end this before it's begun,' Faber said. 'If you try to talk to each other again, I'll shoot you both. Duchene, there's a blue Fiat outside. You will drive, and Marienne will sit beside you. I'll be in the back, and if either of you talks to the other, *bang-bang*. Got it?'

'And if the car crashes?' Duchene asked.

'Don't let that concern you. You'll be dead.'

Duchene opened the door, and they walked through darkness to the entrance. Before heading outside, they waited for a cyclist throwing leaflets to pass by. Although there were faces in the windows of the buildings around them, there was little other activity on the street.

Faber handed Duchene the car keys. The three of them got into the Fiat, and Duchene turned on the ignition. The car was small, its engine tinny.

'Not what I'd have expected you to drive,' Duchene said.

'Lucky for you, it's all I could get. This looks less like a German's car and more like a Frenchman's.'

'Right now it's not clear what we are,' said Marienne.

Duchene looked at her, and she nodded to him. Something had taken hold of her, something he couldn't quite establish. Was it anger, confidence? Some deep faith in her father to find a way out of their predicament? He had nothing, no strategy, only a vain hope that something would intervene and provide them an opportunity to escape. It was desperate thinking, and all too often desperate led to dead.

He couldn't let himself drift too deep into thought – he had to watch the road. Barricades and hazards were growing in size and number, and staunch Parisians were returning to the streets despite the curfew. On the main thoroughfares, convoys of Germans were rushing to defensive points.

In order to travel the four blocks from his apartment to the bridge, he had to double back and use side roads. It would have been faster to walk than drive. But the car made him feel more secure – encased in metal, able to accelerate should something happen – and for this, he was thankful.

The naivety of his optimism fell away as soon as they arrived at the bridge. He saw it first and let the car idle as Marienne and Faber took it in. Across the centre of the Pont Marie, four cars had been pushed into a line to form a roadblock. On their roofs stood three men, two armed with pistols and the other with an old hunting rifle. They wore black armbands. The crowd with them carried clubs and spades, and even some antique cavalry sabres.

'Go back,' Faber ordered.

'We can get through,' said Marienne. 'We'll tell them we're with the Resistance. If we turn around now, it'll raise their suspicions.'

'If they demand answers of me,' said the major, 'and I don't speak, that will raise their suspicions. And get us shot.'

Duchene didn't like it either, but he had to trust that Marienne had a plan. He just hoped that she wasn't doing the same and putting her trust in him. He put the car into first gear and moved across the bridge towards the barricade.

The sides of the cars had recently been painted with *FFI*, French Forces of the Interior.

'They're going to get themselves killed,' said Faber. 'Who would ask them to fortify this position? It's completely exposed. All it would take is a few soldiers, and they'd be dead. What do they think they're going to achieve?'

'For once, I agree,' said Duchene.

The three armed men climbed down from the cars. As they arrived at the Fiat, Duchene wound down his window. His palms were sweating; they had left damp marks on the steering wheel. He replaced them exactly where they'd been.

'Vive la France,' he said to the men.

The fighter with the rifle, his face like leather from years in the sun, nodded to him. 'Vive. Where are you heading?'

'Meeting the rest of our unit,' said Duchene.

'Who leads you?'

'Philippe Angevine. We were at the Sorbonne together.'

One of the other men tapped a pistol at Faber's window. Faber ignored him, and he tapped again.

'I think he wants to see your gun,' the fighter with the rifle said. He seemed to be the one in charge.

'I had to kill a Boche to get it,' Faber said in French.

Duchene's heart raced. Faber had impeccable pronunciation, but his accent was far from French.

The pistol tapped again.

'Let him see it,' Marienne said. 'They'll get their own soon enough.'

Faber wound down the window and handed over the MP 40.

The fighter slipped his pistol into his jacket pocket and held the gun up to his shoulder, pointing it over the Seine, then back towards the barricades and the crowd. His finger was on the trigger the entire time, and Faber and Duchene glanced at one another.

'There a problem?' asked the leader.

'Your man there is being dangerous,' Duchene said.

'No trigger discipline,' said Faber.

'Only place your finger on the trigger if you mean to fire,' Duchene said. 'I've seen too many men shot by their own hands – or their comrades' – from that one simple mistake.'

The leader grunted. 'It's a good point. Claude, give the man his gun.'

Claude shrugged and passed it to Faber.

'Any chance you can roll a car back for us?' Duchene asked. 'Help us regroup with our men?'

With a nod, the leader whistled to the crowd. Four men started to push one of the four cars in the barricade, their legs straining.

'Is that another gun?' Claude asked Faber.

The German pulled his jacket over the holster. 'No.'

The car was starting to roll.

'Looks like a Luger.'

'It's not,' said Faber.

Half the necessary clear space had appeared in the blockade.

'Hold up,' the leader said. He whistled, and his men stopped pushing, the car coming to a stop. 'An MP 40 and a Luger? How'd you kill the German, then?'

Duchene didn't wait for another bad answer. He pushed the accelerator to the floor and sounded his horn, and the three men fumbled with their weapons.

'Marienne, get down,' Duchene shouted as the crowd

ahead of them started to scatter. He flinched, ducking at the crack of a shot behind them. Putting the car into second gear, he over-revved the engine as they neared the gap in the roadblock.

Not enough space.

Another shot, and the glass in the rear windscreen shattered over Faber. He pulled the bolt on the submachine gun and held it out the jagged hole.

'No!' Duchene jerked the steering wheel to the left.

Faber slid across the back seat, his gun tumbling wildly and pointing at the roof.

There was the sound of shearing metal. The smell of hot steel. The Fiat jolted on impact, bucking Faber and Marienne forward, but it kept going.

Duchene accelerated and ground the gears to put the car into third. The bridge passed behind them as they sped onto the Left Bank.

TWENTY-FIVE

The glorious day made one final act of defiance as it passed into night. A rich sunset bathed the city in an orange glow, bringing warmth to grey slate and indifferent sandstone. This same light filtered through stained glass and narrow windows, breaking up the darkness of the Church of Saint-Lambert de Vaugirard. The faint smell of incense still hung in the air, while the flames of a few prayer candles lingered, burnt down to the sand in the tray beneath a statue of the Virgin.

Duchene had underestimated his daughter. Even now, her eyes were set on the other side of the church, probably scanning for the door to its lower levels. He was starting to fear her in some way – that she had so quickly recalled that Duchene had visited this place and built a story out of it suggested a sophisticated cunning. With a gun to her face, she'd managed to buy them another hour. She'd found moves still to make when all he could see was their inevitable failure.

The spirit of youth. The young never believe in their mortality, more so when it's presented clearly to them.

'The Catacombs,' said Faber. 'Which way?'

'Downstairs,' Duchene replied. 'We'll need the key from the office.'

Marienne nodded slowly. Was the crypt where she

hoped he would act? Perhaps she planned that in the darkness they'd escape – throw a lantern to the ground and run. But that would be rash. Faber's submachine gun fired so quickly that its barrel burnt, and its magazine contained thirty-two opportunities to kill. He held it at their backs, his finger on the trigger.

They walked across the church and reached the narrow door to the stairwell. To Duchene's relief, it was open, and he led them down to Father Ramelle's office. The narrow windows left more in shadow than light. There was no more whisky in the cupboard; an empty bottle lay in a wastepaper basket beside the oak desk.

He reached the desk drawer and scanned the room for something to break its lock. The letter opener would snap – what he needed was a crowbar or an axe.

'Why are we waiting?' asked Faber.

'It's –' Duchene said, pulling at the drawer. To his surprise, it opened. He reached under its lip and took out the heavy iron key. 'We're also going to need a light. I think there's a lantern around the corner.'

He had his torch, but he was looking for openings; a smashed oil lamp would be desperate, but a chance he might have to take to save their lives.

Faber nodded and jabbed the gun at Marienne. 'Then let's go.'

Duchene felt around the top of the cellar stairs that led down into darkness. The back of his hand brushed against glass, and he soon had hold of the oil lamp Madame Noirot had used. It took a few moments for the wick to catch from his lighter. He increased its length, and soon the lamp pushed back the darkness around them. Picking it up, he was surprised by its weight – not as heavy as he'd imagined, but perhaps it was running low on oil.

How quickly would it catch if he threw it at Faber? The glass cover would shatter, but the rest of it was metal, and its makers would have taken precautions against breakage. It all seemed unlikely.

He was back to the idea of plunging them into darkness. Not a good one, he realised as he saw the old wood and bric-a-brac stored at the edges of the cellar. Too easy to trip, to make a noise; too hard to find their way back to the stairs.

He nodded towards the door at the far end of the room. 'This way.'

Faber remained behind them both, gun still trained on their backs. 'Open it.'

Duchene walked over with Marienne close beside him. Her summer dress offered little protection against the cold under the church, and goose bumps had risen across her skin. 'Do you want my coat?' he asked her.

'No talking, just open the door,' Faber barked.

Perhaps the Catacombs were the answer. Could he lose Faber in the maze below Paris? If he held the distance, they might have a chance.

When Duchene turned the key in the lock, he felt no resistance. It wasn't locked. He glanced at Marienne, but she was already pushing hard against the door. He joined her, and the door started to move, scraping across the grit and bone that had collected in the chamber beyond.

It didn't take long before they were standing at the threshold to the crypt. Marienne's eyes were wide as she stared across the wall of tombs. The vein in her neck pulsed – her heart must be racing.

'Are you all right?' Duchene asked.

Faber moved up behind him and put a boot in his back. 'I said, no talking.'

Duchene stumbled forward, gripping the lamp hard as his right knee hit the ground. He slapped down his left hand to break the fall, and the sting from the cold stone floor shot through his palm.

Marienne was beside him within seconds. Before he could stand, she was pulling him further into the room, leaning her whole weight back against him while her legs scrambled to move him at speed. Without time to stand properly, he found himself stumbling to the floor as he struggled to keep the lamp from falling.

Faber rushed into the room, the submachine gun raised. 'Get up!'

As Duchene turned, he saw why they had come here. His eyes flicked to Marienne, her face set in defiance, then back to Faber as the German realised a few seconds too late what Duchene and Marienne saw.

They were not alone.

As Faber turned, trying to train his weapon on the threat, a shot filled the crypt with a noise like thunder.

Faber's legs buckled from under him, and Marienne rushed from Duchene's side. She was on the German while he blinked, seeming to struggle to make sense of the four men who had appeared from the darkness. He gripped the weapon in his right hand, but his left felt for the dark stain over his thigh. Marienne screamed as she grabbed the submachine gun, wrenching it from his hand.

Philippe walked forward and reached out to her. 'Marienne,' he said, as she held the gun to the ground. 'You've done an amazing job. The gun.'

She placed it into his hands.

Duchene closed his eyes. She couldn't have known.

Armand, his right arm wrapped in a bandage, strode forward and put a pistol to Duchene's head.

'Wait!' Marienne shouted. 'What are you doing?'

Philippe flicked a torch into light and sighed. 'You traded a German major for your lives. But I didn't have the complete picture – I didn't know your father had tried to get Armand and Casin killed by Nazis. That's more than collaboration, that's treason.'

The stain on Faber's trousers was growing. The colour was draining from his skin. 'What have you done?' he asked.

'Get him up on his knees,' Philippe said.

Casin dragged Faber beside Duchene. He pulled back the slide on his pistol.

'Please, don't do this.' Marienne's face was flushed, and tears were welling in her eyes.

Jean started to walk towards her. He held his hands up, still offering her choices but making the correct one very clear.

Philippe closed his eyes and shook his head. 'There's no other way, Marienne. I'm sorry.'

'Betrayal by a woman,' Faber said, as Casin put the pistol to the back of his head. 'It's so obvious. So inevitable.'

'Then maybe you should have been smarter,' Armand hissed.

Faber stared back at the maquisard. His face now white, the dark rings under his eyes seeming to darken by the second. 'I'm not talking about me, you cur. How do you think my tanks knew where you had gone? Which house you were in?'

Armand blinked, unsure.

'Let's make this quick,' said Philippe. 'Lingering is heartless.'

Faber's face twisted with rage. Duchene felt numb.

He tried to watch them all at once. It was as much as he could do to focus on the gun at his head, Armand's savage grin, Philippe reconciling himself to the role of executioner, Faber starting to chuckle beside him, the crypt, the smell of decay so close to the dead, Marienne fighting Jean's arms wrapped so tight around her, Marienne alive to the end, not like the bodies in the crypt around him.

The smell of decay.

Duchene threw up his hand. 'I know where the guns are –'

The thunderclap of a shot was followed by the lightning flash of a muzzle.

Duchene shut his eyes.

And opened them.

Faber's left eye was hanging out of its socket where the bullet had passed through his head. He lay in dust that was mingling with blood.

Duchene turned his head to one side and dry heaved. In this moment of retching and breathing, he was beginning to realise he was still alive.

Philippe's hand was wrapped around Armand's wrist, pointing the pistol into the air as he stared down at Duchene. 'Five seconds, then the bullet resumes its journey.'

'The guns. If I tell you –'

'You live, yes.'

'This is bullshit,' Armand shouted.

'Go. Where are they?'

'They never left this crypt,' said Duchene.

Philippe stared at him.

He scrambled to his feet. 'They're here – they're still here.' He started pressing his face against the capstones that secured the tombs in the walls around them. He was sucking air through his nose, trying to ignore the smell of blood rising from Faber's body. 'They're with the priest. Can't you smell it?'

Armand sneered. 'Smell what?'

'Death.'

'We're in a crypt.'

'Bones don't smell. Rotting corpses do. There's a body in the walls. I smelt it last time I was here but didn't realise, thought it was dead rats. If they couldn't move the body, how could they have moved the six crates? I think Lucien and Kloke only sold a few of the weapons – what they could carry out of here in their hands.' Duchene inhaled at the edge of a capstone, and the reek of the dead filled his nasal passages. He staggered back, pointing to the tomb. 'There.'

Philippe shone his torch at the wall. 'Jean, Casin.'

The Resistance fighters rushed forward and worked their fingers around the edge of the capstone, straining and pulling. Casin took out a knife and used it to loosen the stone, millimetre by millimetre. Then Jean put a leg against the wall, almost pushing his entire body at a right angle to the stone. With a crash, it fell to the ground, and the smell of death flooded the room.

What remained of Father Ramelle was lying on a large supply crate.

TWENTY-SIX

Armand ran forward and started to tug at the crate. Ramelle's corpse seemed to cling to it, his arms draped across the top. Even though his face was bloated, Duchene could see where a bullet had entered the priest's neck. The crate wouldn't budge, so Casin and Jean rushed to help pull it free, causing the body to peel to one side before sliding onto the floor and releasing new plumes of decay into the crypt. The stench sent a warning to some base instinct – stay away, death is here.

Covering their mouths, Casin and Jean lowered the crate to the floor. With his good hand, Armand flipped open the reinforced latches and threw back the lid. Wooden brackets held a neat row of rifles in place. They were stacked three rows deep, and only four were missing.

Philippe approached Duchene and put a hand on his shoulder. 'How did you know?'

'Where is Madame Noirot?'

'Upstairs. Alive. Locked in her room until the German was taken care of.'

His relief was lost in the river of emotions that was coursing through him, but he knew, intellectually, that this was good news. 'I came to visit her the other day. Some things didn't make sense to me, and I wanted to know if there was another way to enter and leave this crypt.'

'Yes? And?'

'There is. A false wall, a door, connected to the Catacombs. I made a brief search, looking for signs of Ramelle, and all I found was dust, bones and the smell of something dead. But when I spoke to Olivier, Kloke's French lover, he said Kloke had shot the priest in the church. This must have planted the seed in my mind. When I smelt the decay just now, it finally emerged.'

Casin and Jean had found a short crowbar among the rifles. It was the perfect size for opening the crates and, so it would seem, sealed tombs. Within moments another capstone crashed to the floor, revealing a second crate. Armand fell on it and tore off the lid. Grenades. Pistols. Some had been taken, but most remained.

Duchene crossed the room and placed his arms around Marienne.

'Did you know I'd bring us here?' she said, pressing her face into his shoulder.

He moved his face closer to her ear. 'Later. Right now we need to leave, before they realise what Faber was trying to saying to them.' Duchene wiped the tears from his eyes and took her hand.

By the light of the oil lamp, Jean, Armand and Casin were examining the contents of the second crate. Philippe was crouched beside Faber's body, going through his pockets, checking his wallet and recovering his Luger.

'We're going,' Duchene told Philippe. 'I trust you'll do the right thing by the priest.'

'Wait a moment,' Philippe held the Luger in his hand. Although it wasn't pointed at them, Duchene would have preferred if it was tucked in his belt. 'I have a question.

Did you tell the girl about the crypt? How did she know to bring us here?'

Duchene's mind was feeling spent. Slow. He knew the right answers were vital but he was having trouble forming them.

'He didn't need to,' said Marienne. 'I listened to the conversations around me and filled in the gaps. But how did Armand and Casin know where to find you?'

Smart.

She'd moved the conversation on. Guided them away from the details of their getting here.

'They called us at your building. You're lucky you made such a convincing case to bring the German to us. It was a smart plan. A lot rested on you, convincing him your father could lead him out of Paris.'

Philippe found the Roman cameo ring on a chain around Faber's neck, glanced at it, and tossed it into a dark corner.

'People can be misled when they're desperate and drunk,' Marienne said.

'People can be dangerous when they're desperate and drunk,' Duchene added.

'We could use someone like you,' said Philippe. 'This fight isn't over yet.'

Duchene shook his head. 'I don't have much fight left in me.'

'I was talking to your daughter.'

Marienne blinked. 'And if I want to, how do I find you?'

'The Sorbonne. In the library. We'll make our base there.'

With a nod, she took Duchene by the arm. They left through the door into the gloom of the cellar. He brought out his trench torch. Its glow was dim now, almost gone. He had used it more in the past four days than in the past four years. The bulb needed replacing. It was enough, however, to help them find their way across the cellar.

Marienne took hold of his arm – guiding him or seeking comfort, perhaps both. She waited until they'd ascended the stairs to the sacristy before she spoke. 'Did you know for certain where the cache was?'

'Not until I had that gun to my head.'

'You could have died.'

'I know.' He paused. 'The radio beside Faber, back in my apartment – did he use it to send those tanks to Olivier's?'

'Yes. I told him that Resistance members had gone to 54 Rue du Château-des-Rentiers and were going to capture Kloke.'

'It saved my life.'

'That's what I hoped.'

'Thank you.' He felt the expectation of her silence, that this was when he should stop and hold her, but he kept moving. Not everything had fallen into place yet. 'Was Faber in my apartment before the Resistance arrived?'

'No. Philippe saw him coming, from across the street. Drunk, with that machine gun barely hidden under his coat. I told them who he was and that I'd bring him to the crypt, where they could surprise him without risk of being seen by Germans.'

'You did well.'

'I'm glad he's dead.'

Duchene turned to face her. 'Marienne, where's Max?'

'Gone. Berlin.'

'But his suitcase was still being packed.'

'He said he couldn't take me.'

'Marienne?'

'Is that what it was like when she left? Did you feel the same towards one another, or did she love you less than you loved her?'

'I don't know. I don't think it works like that.' Duchene held to his point. 'What did you do, Marienne? Max wouldn't have left without his sidearm.'

'I didn't know you were in contact with the Resistance. If I had, then maybe I could have led them to him. He was leaving, deserting, and he refused to take me. He gave me no choice – I couldn't stay in Paris and be called a collaborator. So I called General von Bühel.'

'Von Bühel?'

'You met him at the Ritz last night. He sent them over.'

'Sent who?'

'Gestapo.'

'Marienne. Where is Max?'

When she returned his gaze, he understood a distance had grown between them. She was directly opposite him, but he felt as though she was a kilometre away. She didn't move. She didn't blink. Without expression, she said, 'Executed.'

They didn't speak as Duchene drove the Fiat back to Marienne's apartment, and a strange silence had fallen over the city. He watched as citizens moved back to their homes with the coming of darkness, so that by half past nine there was no one to man the barricades.

The Champs-Élysées was almost empty. Duchene

watched a truck of Germans drive along it, furtive and cautious. A civilian truck, its sides labelled with *FFI*, turned out from a side street. He stopped breathing as the trucks neared each other, but nothing happened. They passed by with determined indifference.

In the cupboard below Marienne's staircase, there were only traces of blood. Stahl's body had been disposed of. But unlike Duchene, she didn't slow down to look. She hurried up to her apartment and checked the door. The frame was still splintered and broken.

'You could stay with me,' Duchene said, walking up behind her.

'I'll nail it shut and prop it with a chair.'

'And if the Gestapo return?'

'Won't they come looking for you?'

'They will come for both of us.'

'What will you do? Turn over Philippe?'

'That would be a death sentence. I would have betrayed the Resistance.'

'So what will you do?'

He held her gently by the arms, and she stared at the ground. 'I can't know what you've experienced, Marienne. The decisions you've had to make. I've made my own decisions, many desperate. Many that served only one purpose – to survive. But when I stood in this apartment earlier today and thought you were dead, I didn't want to live. The thought that you would not be in this world, that you could be taken from it, was so overwhelming, so monstrous ... If turning myself in to the Gestapo now ensures you live, then it's worth it. If I can satisfy them – that Faber is dead, that Stahl was killed, that I can offer something more to them or simply let them satisfy themselves with my execution – then that will be good enough. You are my daughter, Marienne. I need you to survive. I need you to remain in this world.'

'Don't go.'

'It's the only way.'

She held him so tight that he felt as though she was trying to pull him into her. He wept as she did this. Her face was trembling but resolute. He kissed her and held her again before he finally turned to leave.

Outside, as he reached the car, he knew she would be watching him from the window. But he couldn't look again. If he did, his resolve would surely break.

He drove against the curfew, across the Seine and down to Rue des Saussaies. His was the only car on the road; the streets were empty, those Elysian fields spread into the world of the living now, ready for his arrival.

He parked the car outside the terraced apartment building. It was dark, but then so were all its neighbours. He stepped out into the road, drew in three deep breaths and tried to steady his shaking hands. They only trembled more.

Go through the gate and up to the door. Make the journey short, say what he could, hope for it to be quick.

He raised the knocker on the dark-green door and let it fall back. He could hear the echo in the hallway beyond.

Nothing.

A few more seconds and he raised the knocker again.

This time, the door pushed open.

Papers lay strewn across the floor.

His heart beat faster as he stepped into the building. The hope that he'd pushed low inside him started to emerge.

Hundreds and hundreds of pages, all typed in German, all stamped and signed, had been left behind.

Striding further into the building, he called out.

No reply came.

The Gestapo had left Paris.

Friday, 25 August 1944

TWENTY-SEVEN

'This is why the French vanguard has entered Paris with guns blazing. This is why the great French army from Italy has landed in the south and is advancing rapidly up the Rhône valley. This is why our brave and dear Forces of the Interior will arm themselves with modern weapons. It is for this revenge, this vengeance and justice, that we will keep fighting until the final day, until the day of total and complete victory.'

De Gaulle's voice was rising in passion and intensity. It crackled over the speakers that had been placed outside the Hôtel de Ville. He was somewhere inside, surrounded by generals and reporters, the speech being broadcast across the world. Outside the ornate hotel and in the surrounding streets, the crowd waved placards emblazoned with the two-barred Croix de Lorraine in celebration of France, the Resistance and of de Gaulle himself.

In the swelling crowd, Duchene stood close to Monsieur and Madame Junet, who cheered as best they could. They had insisted on coming to hear the speech.

An eager young man pushed past them to cheer, and Duchene used his body to shield Madame Junet.

'This duty of war, all the men who are here and all those who hear us in France know that it demands national unity,' continued de Gaulle. 'We, who have lived the greatest hours of our history, we have nothing else to wish than to show ourselves, up to the end, worthy of France. Vive la France!'

A roar rose up from the crowd as Parisians hugged one another and thrust their fists into the air.

In the days following the cache's discovery, the weapons had been used by Resistance fighters. The uprising had grown. The conflicts became more pronounced and Germans and French started to fall. Skirmishes had become battles, and battles had brought the war into the heart of Paris.

Duchene had, for the most part, remained inside. He read. And waited. He listened for the phone, which worked for the first three days when he still received regular updates from Marienne. After that, he made a daily journey to her apartment for signs of her return. The door had been badly repaired, and the neighbours said they'd seen nothing to suggest any harm had come to her. So, he occupied himself scavenging what little food he could find while looking after the Junets.

The three of them survived on meagre rations until word spread, just this morning, that Paris was finally free, and they joined the crowds.

De Gaulle's speech gave Duchene a sense of relief, and not only because their victory and freedom were being proclaimed to the world – it also helped to distract him from dwelling on Marienne's safety, along with the riddle of Camille's disappearance. He scanned the crowd, half hoping he would catch sight of his daughter holding onto one of the street lamps as a vantage point, or Camille waving a *Vive de Gaulle* banner while she watched the hotel with the rest of the throng.

The thrill of the speech quickly faded. The arrival of de Gaulle on the hotel steps, which stirred the crowd into further cheering, did little to reinspire him. Marienne and Camille's absences had pressed their way back into his gut and sat there like a lead weight.

Monsieur Junet, fragile and small, placed a trembling hand on Duchene's arm.

'Let's head back,' Duchene said. 'Before the streets become too busy.'

Duchene held the Junets' door open for them. A sour smell was rising from somewhere in their small apartment, so he'd come back tomorrow and offer to help them clean. It could be as simple as some old food that had fallen below their refrigerator, something they'd struggle to pick up.

He stopped in the foyer to check his letterbox before heading upstairs. Inside was a battered envelope – with no postmark, so hand-delivered – containing a letter. A crude cross of the French Forces of the Interior had been stamped onto the corner. It was written in English, and although the words were quickly scrawled, the handwriting was unmistakable.

C is at La Festa.
Love, Marienne

It was dated three days earlier, from before the arrival of the French and Americans, while the Resistance had still been fighting for the city. Remarkable that it had arrived at all.

Duchene rushed up to his apartment and retrieved the bike he'd taken all those days ago from the barricade – a valuable commodity that he kept locked in his bedroom. Without the Métro or petrol, bikes were going missing.

Next, he rode to Lucien's apartment. He still had the key from his visit with Stahl. When he opened the door, a swathe of telephone notes slid across the floor where they had been steadily accumulating since Lucien's death. The apartment was otherwise undisturbed. Dust lingered in the daylight that came through curtains, slowly settling on all that was left of a life spent in pursuit of wealth.

Duchene shook his head. He wouldn't let Lucien's death become a new obsession to torment himself with.

The large armoire to the side of the couch remained closed. After pulling it open, Duchene took out two cartons of cigarettes and two bottles of Hennessy. He placed these in a case he hauled down from a shelf in Lucien's bedroom, then locked the apartment behind him.

He rode to La Festa.

Rue de Castellane was quiet. The Paris celebrations had taken its citizens elsewhere, and the meagre delights of post-occupation delicatessens and patisseries seemed, on this of all days, an offence to the noble sacrifice of those who'd fought to liberate the city.

But there was something else, a certain tension in the street that Duchene noted soon after his arrival. There was a broken shop window, recently boarded, and a paint-splashed door that declared, *Collaborator!* It was no surprise: the street was a short walk behind the hotels that had been the base of operations for the occupiers. Here, Germans had pretended to be Parisians and enjoyed their delicacies.

A young woman wearing a simple dress was carrying a heavy basket of laundry towards the Italian delicatessen. Her hair was roughly shaved – some patches were bald, others glistened with fresh cuts and grazes.

When Duchene walked up to her, she bowed her head and started to pick up speed. 'Wait, Mademoiselle, please,' he said. 'I'm looking for a friend. You may know her. She's been, ah … the same as you.'

'I don't want trouble.'

'Her name's Camille. She's a good friend, and I was worried she was dead. I've been told she's been seen around La Festa.'

The woman slowed and turned to face him. 'What is your name?'

'Auguste Duchene.'

'Wait here.' She walked to the door of the deli and knocked out an irregular rhythm.

The herb-sprouting window boxes had been torn down, their windows boarded up. Where the Italian flag had been, only a broken pole remained. No light came from inside as the door was opened for the woman.

Five minutes later, another woman emerged wearing a shawl over her head.

It was Camille. Her lightness had gone. She looked tired and moved slowly against the world. It seemed that her age had finally caught up with her.

Duchene embraced her.

She let him hold her but held her hands tight around the shawl.

'I didn't know where …'

'That is a long conversation,' she said.

'Is there somewhere we can talk?'

'Off the street. Yes. Follow me.' She led him into La Festa and pulled the door closed.

The picture of Mussolini was no longer on the back wall; the food counter and shelves were empty. La Festa had been turned into a laundry. In the shadows of the unlit room, a few women were gathered, talking quietly as they washed clothes by hand in steel tubs. In a basket beside them, a six-month-old baby cooed at a doll suspended from the basket's handle.

Duchene spoke softly. 'What is this place?'

'A refuge,' Camille said as she continued to walk across the shop floor and around its counter to the office. 'Women have been coming here, those forced out of their homes.'

The office desk had been cleared, receipts and paperwork pushed into a rubbish bin beside it. The door to a small garden was open, and two more women, their heads shaved, were hanging washing on makeshift lines.

Duchene sat at the desk beside Camille. 'Are you coming back?'

'That's not a good idea. I've been accused of being a collaborator.' She dropped the scarf from her head.

Duchene had anticipated the revelation, but he found he wasn't prepared for its reality. Here was the shape of her skull, exposed. The hair had been cut with shears, leaving a patchwork of skin and stubble. He was relieved that there was no wound, no evidence of savagery.

Camille remained still as he felt a rage coming on. 'Are they rounding up every orchestra, every band, every cabaret girl who performed for the Germans?'

She placed her hands on her hips, her face without emotion. 'They accused me of having German lovers.'

'What proof do they have?'

'None. But we've both seen enough to know that doesn't matter. Truth is the first thing to fail when people are hurt and angry.' She sighed. 'They're looking to blame someone, anyone, for their own guilt at acquiescence. Women who took Germans for lovers or played piano for them in their bars and hotels – we're easy targets. And men who were too bold in their support, like that Italian who owned this place.'

'He was a fascist.'

'He was. But he should have been tried and sent to jail – not mobbed and lynched outside his own shop.' She shook her head. 'Although if that hadn't happened, we wouldn't have somewhere to stay. I'm hiding here while the anger subsides, until I can leave Paris.'

'But I can hide you somewhere better. Lucien's apartment is empty.'

'I can't leave the others. I've found a way for these girls to deflect attention. We wash clothes and sheets for nothing, sometimes handouts, to be seen to atone for our choices.'

'So, you won't come back?'

'In a few months. Maybe. Let's see how quickly the city moves on.'

Duchene looked into the yard, at the sheets rippling in the wind. A few lemon trees were growing in pots along one wall, some fruit still on the branches. Some of it had fallen to the ground – he assumed before the women had moved in – and was beginning to rot.

The rot had come to Paris.

And then it struck him. He turned back to Camille. 'Who accused you?'

'Does it matter? There were so many who could have.'

'Who do you think it was?'

'As I said, people were angry and afraid.'

'Camille?'

'It was the Junets.'

Duchene was out of his chair. The screech of the wood on the office tiles startled the women in the yard. 'I was with them only now. I've been looking after them for days.'

'Auguste. Please, sit down.'

'They know I've been looking for you.'

'You must promise me you won't do anything.'

'I'd never harm them.' *I'd make it quick . . .*

'Auguste,' she pleaded.

'They can at least hear my anger.'

'That's unwise. They've seen everything going on in your place too. Visits from Germans.'

'And the Resistance. Let's not forget I was helping the Resistance.'

'But also the Gestapo . . . they weren't very discreet. When the mob came to my apartment and marched me to the lobby, the Junets were there, waiting. They were about to accuse you too. So, I started howling and fighting. It wasn't my best performance, but it was enough to create a scene and turn their focus back to me.'

'I . . . You did that?'

She nodded. 'Would you have done the same for me?'

'Of course.'

'Then that settles it.'

He returned to his seat and dug his hands into his pockets.

'Say nothing, Auguste. Keep the peace.'

The breeze was bringing with it the smell of soap, of bergamot and lavender. For a moment, he let the flap of the linen lift the thoughts from his mind.

Until they returned. Inevitably.

'Will it ever go back to the way it was?' he asked.

'I think we both know that's unlikely. Paris was occupied. That is now in our history. The question is, how long will it take for the offence to be forgotten?'

He reached under the desk and pulled out Lucien's suitcase. 'I brought these for you. Cigarettes and two bottles of Hennessy. I thought we could barter them, so you could get out of Paris.'

'How did you know where I was?'

'Marienne told me.'

'I hear she's fighting for the FFI now.'

'She is.'

'I don't need to tell you the similarities.' Camille gave a weak smile.

'No, you don't.'

She pulled the bag towards her. 'Thank you for this. What we need now is food and some help trading it. You don't mind?'

'It's yours. Use it as you need it. Actually,' he pulled the keys out of his pocket, 'there's more to trade at Lucien's. Have these.'

'Are you sure?'

'More women will come. You'll need more than these can get you.'

'It's a generous offer, but there's a problem.' She gestured to what remained of her hair. 'This makes it hard to do anything. If we're lucky, we're ignored. Can you help us? Can you trade on our behalf?'

'Anything. What do you need?'

It was late afternoon by the time Duchene arrived at Guillaume's. He'd visited each store along the street, each time hoping to receive a different story. But after six days of fighting, there was very little to trade, even for sought-after luxuries. The gunfire of the past week had focused everyone's minds on survival.

As the celebrations had died down, the queues had grown. While this made it easier to find the places with food to sell, he was still disappointed by the amount they had to offer. He was trying to find enough to feed six people; the potatoes and sardines he had were barely enough to feed himself.

And then he'd remembered the charcuterie.

Its queue stretched out the door and onto the street. After an hour, he finally stepped inside the dim shop. There was plenty here – Guillaume's claims had not been idle. Sausages and hams hung above a counter that was now stocked with canned goods. The pates and terrines and rillettes were gone; now he sold only larder fare for lean times.

There were grim faces in the queue ahead of Duchene. Grim faces on those leaving the shop. It appeared that Guillaume would be neither rushed nor compromised. He had a rare commodity, and he knew its value.

By the time Duchene reached the counter, it was almost closing time. He watched as a woman traded a pearl necklace for a saucisson sec – three days' meat if she was sparing. She left, embarrassed and forlorn.

Guillaume seemed to take no pleasure in it, and Duchene didn't envy his role as provider to a desperate city.

'Good afternoon, Monsieur,' Duchene said.

'Monsieur Duchene. You've returned.'

'I have.'

Behind Guillaume, beside the meat slicer, an assortment of valuables had been arranged into groups: jewellery, silverware, ornaments. The charcutier had even managed to get hold of a jeweller's loupe, which sat on the counter beside him. Whether he knew how to assess such things or if it was for effect was unclear – regardless, its use would not be required with Duchene's goods.

He took a bottle of cognac and a carton of cigarettes out of the old flour sack he was using for a bag. He placed them on the counter. 'I have more like this. But right now, I'm after food for six. If you're reasonable and trade fair, I'll come back. I'll bring more.'

Guillaume nodded. 'But these are desperate times. I don't know when I'll next see a pig, let alone trade for one.'

'I can bring you cigarettes and alcohol. You can trade those more easily than heirlooms and dinner sets.'

'True. Let me see what you think of this.' Guillaume pulled three cans of meat out from his counter and pulled down a large sausage. 'I can't wrap it – no waxed paper left.'

'How about another can, and I'll promise to return tomorrow?'

Guillaume took out a small hundred-gram tin. He turned his head to one side and raised an eyebrow.

'Okay,' Duchene said, sliding the cognac and carton across to the charcutier. 'It's a deal.' He shook Guillaume's hand, then started to put the meat and tins into the sack.

Guillaume placed the cigarette carton on the counter behind him. As he returned for the Hennessy, he paused briefly to examine the bottle. Its amber liquid sloshed as his large hands splayed wide to cradle its weight. The rings on his fingers also caught the light.

A chill ran through Duchene.

On Guillaume's left ring finger was a lapis and ivory cameo ring – the profile of a Roman centurion.

One of a pair.

I had to have them both. Faber had said that about the ring on his finger.

Duchene tried to steady his shaking hands as he packed the sack, while Guillaume placed the cognac onto the counter behind him.

'I never found him,' Duchene said.

'Who?' Guillaume turned to face Duchene.

'That German I was looking for. I came here with that photo.'

Guillaume paused. And there it was: a flicker of recognition, a glance to the right. 'Well,' he said, 'I guess it doesn't matter now. They're all gone anyway.'

Duchene finished packing. 'You're right there, thankfully. All gone.'

TWENTY-EIGHT

'What does it matter? No one is making you find this man.' Camille watched Duchene as he searched the toolshed in the garden behind La Festa.

'People died because of Kloke. I was almost killed myself. Lucien died.' Duchene pulled out a rusted toolbox and popped the latch.

'From the way you explain it, Lucien and this German were stealing from the Resistance and selling the weapons on the black market. Lucien was shot because of that.'

Screwdrivers, a ratchet, a random collection of screws and nails – nothing of weight. Not what he needed. He dropped a flat-head screwdriver on the ground beside him. 'I've been threatened. Marienne has been threatened. I've been accused of being a collaborator.'

'Not just you.'

He stopped searching and looked up at her. 'Sorry. I know. But I need to find out how this ends. Too much has happened because of this hunt for Kloke – Lucien dead, a woman taken away by the Gestapo, Marienne almost killed ... If I can find him now, understand why, I can finish this.' Duchene dragged out a small wooden crate. It was heavy, which made him hopeful.

'Not every question needs to be answered,' Camille said.

'I've given away too much to get this far. I need to know the reason why.'

And there it was, sitting on top of a bundled chain: a small crowbar.

Duchene stood and brushed the cobwebs from his jacket. 'You said you had to leave Paris to move on. I need to find this man to do the same.'

It was well after nine and the sky was beginning to darken. From the corner of Rue de Castellane and Rue de l'Arcade, Duchene had an uninterrupted view of the charcuterie. He was as close as he could get without being seen.

Five minutes earlier, Guillaume had locked the door and sent the remaining queue away. Dissatisfied, the crowd had lingered briefly before making their way home. Guillaume had flipped the sign to 'closed' but was taking his time in the shop. Duchene waited five more minutes until the lights went out and Guillaume emerged with a bicycle, its basket packed high. He locked the door then started down the street.

After watching him turn a corner, Duchene waited for another five minutes in case he returned. It seemed unlikely, given the methodical way in which he'd exited his shop, but Duchene was methodical too. He needed to move with caution.

No sign of Guillaume.

Concealing the crowbar as best he could under his coat, Duchene crossed the street. He found himself checking his watch to count the hours until curfew: four years of ingrained behaviour. He wondered how long it would take him to shake it. He had as long as he needed – until Guillaume opened for business the next day.

Duchene didn't bother with the front door. Lots of people were relishing the opportunity to walk the streets into the early evening; not even the persistent rumours, sometimes true, of German snipers' nests were enough to deter Parisians. So he walked the length of the shopfronts, turning at the end of the block. Guillaume's was seven shops in from the street. Walking down the cobbled laneway behind the shops, Duchene counted back the buildings. Each had a small rear garden that shared its walls with the neighbours and featured a wooden gate for rear access – each except Guillaume's.

As Duchene approached, he saw the modifications its owner had made. An extension had been built, with an extra roof covering what would have been its yard. Rising from the roof was a tall tin chimney with a slanting cap: a smoke oven.

Guillaume's success during the occupation would not have gone unnoticed, least of all by Guillaume. To deter would-be thieves he'd salvaged razor wire and stretched this over the rear wall of the shop. To reinforce the point, he'd used mortar to place large shards of broken glass around the lip of the wall. This was a recent addition; rain and wind had yet to erode the sharp edges.

At the reinforced gate, Duchene checked the lock. Strong. Iron. He could lever it open, but that would make a noise.

He looked around. Each shop was on the ground floor of a townhouse, each four storeys tall. Similar buildings ran along the other side of the alleyway. Grey clouds were bringing the twilight to an early finish and darkness was filling the cobbled lane.

Now, later – it made little difference.

Duchene placed his coat below the lock and inserted the crowbar. He leaned his entire weight against it, straining hard until it tore loose. It fell onto the coat with a muffled clunk. Satisfied that no faces had appeared in the windows above him, he stepped inside.

The smell from the large smoke oven wrapped around him. He lingered just long enough to identify other fragrances: fresh-cut pine stacked against a wall, cedar on the table in front of him.

He pushed the gate closed and out of habit put his palm over the torch. It was completely unnecessary. The dull glow of its dying bulb cast little light. He removed his hand and used its fading beam to help him scan the room.

The oven was beside him. Along the walls, stacked on shelves, were empty jars and boxes, rolls of wax paper, and an assortment of hatchets, hand planes and saws. Ahead of Duchene was the heavy external door that led to the rest of the shop. Like the small window next to it, the door hadn't been replaced when the extension had been built.

Duchene tested its handle. Locked. Using the back of a hatchet, he tapped the crowbar deep into the space between the door and the jamb. There was no concealing this noise, but he hoped the sound wouldn't travel – and if it did, might be confused with a gunshot.

Strange times, when the sound of gunshots is ignored.

Steadying his weight, he leant back against the crowbar. The wood strained. He placed his foot on the frame. Pushed.

The crack of splintering wood echoed throughout the

room. He stumbled backwards, jarring to a stop as he hit a shelf behind him.

The door was open, and he entered the charcuterie. Using the torch, he looked over the room. It was a store. An open doorway led into the shop. He could see the back of the counter, the open till that had been emptied, several knife blocks and a few cans that remained on the countertop.

There were more of these in the storeroom with him. An entire cabinet was full of tinned goods: beans, meat, fish. A small fortune in times like this. Guillaume had made an art of the stockpile.

A table stood to one side, and on top sat a ledger for accounts. Flipping it open to the last entry, he could see it hadn't been maintained – the last date was over two years ago.

He flipped it shut and tracked the light around him. On a small preparation bench were the day's takings: all those traded items that could be deemed to have some value. Guillaume had grouped them into three collections, graded on the ease with which they could be exchanged. Silverware and costume jewellery in one pile, lamp oil and tools in another, and finally cigarettes, chocolate and alcohol.

Duchene looked through the rings. The cameo of the Roman centurion wasn't among them, but that wouldn't have made sense anyway. He was here to find something else, something that revealed what had happened to Kloke.

As he shone his torch across the floor, its light fell on a hatch with a recessed iron ring. It matched the surrounding floorboards. He leant down towards it and ran a finger along its edge. No dust – the hatch had been used recently.

He placed two fingers through the loop. A mechanism creaked from under the wood, and a pneumatic lever helped him to raise the hatch.

Within moments he was looking into a dark void. In the torchlight, he could see the first few wooden stairs leading down into the cellar. The smell of salted and spiced meats rose up towards him, carried on the chill air.

He glanced back over his shoulder one last time before starting down the stairs. There was no railing to help guide his descent, so he shone the torch on each plank as he descended.

When he reached the stone floor, he raised the torch to look around him. In the yellow light, he could make out contrasting colours: marbled patterns on air-drying meat, pale labels on spice jars, the curves of hooks that hung across the ceiling. At the bottom of the stairs, hanging from a meat hook, was a lantern.

Putting his torch in his pocket, Duchene unclipped a hinged pane of glass and opened up the lantern. Its wick was still high. He lit it, and warm light crept across the room.

Although he could now see better than with the torch, the lamplight cast shadows of the hanging meat across the room. This separation between soft glow and darkness meant it was still difficult for him to scan the room, and he ducked down to shine his torch under the many sausages and legs of ham.

As this was a place to preserve food, the floor was swept clean and well maintained, clear but for a single trunk on the far side of the room. His back hunched, he clambered across the floor below the meat.

When he reached the brown leather chest, he paused. It was old, worn on the corners and locked.

Putting one hand on the chill stone floor, he put the crowbar inside the loop of the lock.

His hands were shaking. He knew they wouldn't stop until he was out of this place. And he knew, deep within him, that the trunk held the answers.

The lock came free as he twisted the crowbar. Using its tip, he lifted the lid and pushed it back so it was up against the wall.

Inside was the grey cloth of a Nazi uniform. A jacket.

Duchene poked at it with the crowbar. It was soft. Folded.

He placed the lantern beside him but kept hold of the crowbar. Peering into the trunk, he slowly pulled back the jacket. Beneath it was the rest of the uniform, some watches, papers and passbooks.

Leaning over the trunk, he lifted up the uniform. It was the full dress kit for a private: boots, cap, belt, and all the pips and buttons. At a glance, it appeared to be about the right size for Guillaume.

With the uniform removed, the rest of the contents were more apparent. There were four watches, a wallet filled with Deutschmarks, and the passbooks for six German soldiers. Duchene quickly read the names on each one: Trautman, Jaeger, Roth, Scholz, Dietrich.

The last belonged to Christian Kloke. Proof that Guillaume had lied.

Underneath the passbooks was a fat envelope. Duchene took out the contents: a single-page letter on thick cream stock and a larger folded document the size of a map.

He opened the letter. It was in German, addressed to Kloke.

Christian,
So here we are, now, in the City of Lights. A place where we can be more like ourselves. A place that is not Berlin, or barracks or the slaughterhouse of the Front.

Paris is like no other city. It brims with potential, with passion and refined beauty. When I last visited, I bought this ring. One of a pair. One for us each to wear. Our hidden connection. Our hidden truth.

Last night, when the lust was dissolved and we lay together, I wanted to share my heart with you. I couldn't. You started laughing and singing and the moment moved on, and I let your joy be the accompaniment to the rest of our evening. But now I wish to share that with you. Now, while the muse and the drink have me. My lover, when I'm with you, I am fearless. When I'm with you, this war feels like it can't touch us. Let us not waste these precious moments. Better yet, let us plan to grow them into a life for us together. I don't know when that will be or how, but between us, I am certain we can make it come to pass.

Yours always.
T.

These were surely the papers the Gestapo had been looking for. Enough evidence to convict Faber at a court-martial.

Unfolding the three map-sized papers, Duchene reconsidered. They showed a schematic for something complex that looked like the inner workings of a machine. He couldn't make much sense of the labels, as they were in Russian. The machine had fins, a thruster and fuel tanks, so he had to assume it was a vehicle, but whether it travelled by air or sea wasn't clear.

It was within reason that the schematic was for a weapon the Germans wanted for their war efforts. Perhaps Kloke, the black marketeer, had hoped to sell or barter the pages to avoid becoming a prisoner of war. Either way, this was something that Duchene would never learn.

He refolded the schematic and placed it, along with the letter and Kloke's passbook, into the inside of his jacket. He shoved the uniform back into the trunk and shut the lid. He had his answers; it was time to leave. His knees aching, he crawled back towards the staircase.

Halfway across the cellar floor, he stopped. The flat of his hand had pressed onto the stone below him, and something was sticking to it, pliable and strange. He turned his hand over and shone the torch on his upturned palm.

At first he thought it was gristle or fat, fallen from the side of some pork. It was flat with curved ends, almost rectangular. He lowered the torch, and when he brought the light back onto it, he saw what it was.

A fingernail. A human fingernail.

Duchene shook it free from his hand. Bracing against the floor again, he slowly turned his torch upward. Hanging from a hook, directly above him, was a preserved human arm. The preserved hand attached to it was missing a fingernail.

The arm has been preserved for eating.

For eating.

Duchene fell backward, dropping his torch onto the ground. It spun in circles as he scrambled away.

His stomach heaved while his mind raced, drawing the

connections between the severed limb and the charcuterie in whose cellar it hung.

He questioned the ham hocks, the ribs, the other long meats that hung above him. Were they pork? The sausages filled with ground meat – the flesh of pig or man? How many had eaten from here? He had eaten from here. Marienne. Camille. The dinner with Faber and Max?

Duchene clenched shut his jaw, gritted his teeth, and refused to expel his meagre lunch onto the floor. Some bizarre propriety took over as he refused to contaminate a room of food while he was aware that it had been contaminated long before his arrival.

Heart pounding, he scrambled on his hands and knees towards the lamp. After he snatched it from the ground, he didn't stop until he was up the stairs and out of the cellar.

He sat for a moment to slow his breathing, but he couldn't slow his heart.

His instinct was to go to the police. Immediately. But when the letter and schematic rustled in his pocket as he mopped his brow, he reconsidered. They'd have questions. Why had he been looking for a missing German? Had he been a collaborator? Was he working for the Nazis even now that Paris had been liberated?

Any explanations would be lengthy. Not the simplicity of black and white. And even he was reconsidering his need to know Kloke's fate. He had the answer he was so desperate to find and he didn't like it.

There could be no police. He had set himself on this path, and he had no choice but to follow it to the bitter end.

TWENTY-NINE

Light spilled into the dim corridor as the door was opened. Guillaume peered through the crack. Duchene watched the subtle transition of his face from curiosity to recognition to realisation. 'I have a gun on the other side of this door.'

'I'm here to talk.'

'Talk?'

'We don't have to do it here. We could walk, in the streets.'

Guillaume drew a slow breath. Duchene waited.

'We can do that. I'll meet you downstairs.'

Duchene walked down the two flights of stairs from Guillaume's apartment back onto the street. Around him, Parisians were enjoying the night, strolling beside the Seine, listening to the buskers who'd returned to fill the air with music.

He stepped around the corner of a boarded-up brasserie and adjusted the cut-down belt on his left forearm. It needed to be tight enough to hold his trench knife in place, but also loose enough that the blade would draw freely from its sheath. Grabbing the handle, he practised pulling the blade from the sleeve of his jacket. He hoped he wouldn't have to use it but had no doubt Guillaume was making similar preparations.

Eventually the charcutier arrived downstairs, wearing a heavy coat despite the warm night. Duchene could feel the weight of the knife on his arm. He tried to compensate for it in his movements, limit how quickly Guillaume might notice something was there.

'You said we'd walk the streets,' said the charcutier. 'Where?'

'Up here, along the boulevard, with the crowds.'

'In case I try to harm you?'

'Safer for both of us.'

'After everything this city has been through, you think decorum has remained?'

Two young American GIs walked past, loose limbed and swaggering, their rifles slung to their backs.

'Who knows? Perhaps one of them will intervene,' Duchene said. 'They see themselves as heroes.'

'Our cowboy liberators? Perhaps.'

They paused at a marionette theatre. Children, out after ten for a special occasion, were seated on the cobblestones, watching as a knight on horseback fought an ogre. The knight's shield had recently been repainted with the Cross of Lorraine, the ogre with a swastika on its sizeable gut. The parents smiled and laughed as their children squealed and shouted while the battle raged on.

'You've been killing people, selling them as food,' Duchene said quietly. He didn't recognise his own voice. It was tight, wavering. Was it fear or anger?

'Not people,' said Guillaume. 'Nazis.' He turned his back to the marionette theatre. 'It was the ring, wasn't it? I was too bold in wearing it so soon.'

'It was.'

'Sinners will have their trinkets.'

'So you admit they're crimes.'

'Before God, of course. But I'd think the law, during war – well, that's another matter.'

'You were selling their meat to people.'

'As I said, not people. Nazis. I sold swine to the swine. Every slice and every terrine. They ate their own and they loved it. They should never have come to Paris.' Guillaume said and rubbed the back of his hand against his cheek.

'If you were only feeding them to the Germans, why do you still have a human arm in your cellar?'

'You won't be satisfied with that answer,' Guillaume said, reaching into his coat pocket.

Duchene moved his right hand towards the cuff of his left sleeve, touching the handle of the knife. 'Why?'

'Because collaborators still walk our streets. The same reason you didn't turn up on my door with the gendarmes.' Guillaume took out a packet of cigarettes. 'You're a collaborator,' he continued as he lit one. 'I'd confused you for Resistance – I thought you were hunting that soldier. But after you turned up on my doorstep, I realised you must have been working for the Germans.'

He held out the cigarettes to Duchene, who brought his hand away from the knife to take one. Guillaume offered him his lighter. Duchene remained still.

'Really, in front of these children? You think I'm a monster.' Guillaume flicked the flame into life and held it out.

Duchene lit the cigarette, drew deep and exhaled. 'You are a monster.'

'I did what I needed to survive. I couldn't have them in my city, eating my food without a way of defying them.'

'You could have joined the Resistance.'

'I wanted to live. You were the same. You made that same choice.' Guillaume turned back to face the play and to look out over the river, black under the night sky with golden eddies from reflected street lamps. 'So what are we going to do? You can't go to the police, as we've discussed. And you're not going to kill me. You're not that kind of man.'

Duchene sighed. Smoked some more. Looked for answers on the faces of the parents and their children. 'Things will never be simple again,' he said.

'Were they ever?'

'It has to stop. That arm – burn it. In front of me.'

'And then you'll be satisfied?'

'I will.'

'And if I don't?'

'Then we'll both be exposed. I'll go to the police and risk being branded a collaborator.'

'Why would they care if I fed our enemies back to them?'

'They probably wouldn't. But I can't see your business surviving if word gets out about the cannibal charcutier.'

Saturday, 26 August 1944

THIRTY

A column of tanks rattled into the city. The smell of diesel was thick in the air, pushed around on a breeze that brought with it the chill of autumn. The ground shook as the tanks rolled over cobblestones and down the Champs-Élysées, their heavy armour burnt and punctured by bullets and shrapnel. They showed signs of makeshift repairs, ablative plates replaced by scrap metal from enemy tanks. But among the patchwork and battle damage, one thing was consistent: three stripes painted clear and polished every day. Three stripes were worn with pride on the shoulders of the drivers and the smiling wounded infantrymen who sat on the hulls. Three stripes flew on flags in the swarming crowds along the roadside. The tricolour. Vive la France.

Last night Duchene had stayed at the charcuterie just long enough to see the arm go into the flames of Guillaume's smoke oven. As brief as that moment had been, Duchene could still remember the smell of burning flesh. Even though it had been spiced and preserved, there was something about the meat, perhaps the understanding it was human, that made his stomach roil. He'd spent a night plagued by bad dreams with no alcohol in the apartment to abate them.

A woman smiled at him. 'You're not happy?' she asked,

her voice hard to hear amid the cheering. There was a young boy at her side.

'I am. Just cost a lot to get here.'

'So it did.' She remained smiling, but there was distance in her eyes now.

'I can't believe those soldiers are really ours!' said the boy.

'Yes,' said Duchene. 'The Free French, who've been fighting for de Gaulle.'

'They're not dressed like they're French.'

'I don't care how they're dressed,' said the woman. 'As long as they fly the flag, I'll cheer.'

Despite running on little sleep, Duchene had been determined to come and see General Leclerc's Second Armoured Division. These were men who had risked court-martial to defy the Americans. Men who had rushed deep into enemy territory to support the liberation of the city. Men who had fought the Germans until they had, like a struck wasp nest, burst into anger and fought a battle on these very streets.

The tanks drove on, and soon the cheering grew again as a random collection of trucks, tanks and cars flowed in unranked procession behind the Armoured Division. Now came the French Forces of the Interior led by Colonel Rol in his handmade uniform. He stood in the hatch of a German tank, *FFI* painted crudely along its side, his wide mouth beaming under a hawkish nose.

Around and behind him, men of all ages marched out of formation, dressed in civilian clothes and unified only by their black FFI armbands and seized German weapons. A group of young FFI fighters waved from the back of a truck. A few women were among their number, dressed in trousers and shorts.

Duchene pushed forward as they came nearer, his instincts taking control of him as he recognised a smile within the group and called out, 'Marienne!'

The woman's eyes held his for more than a second.

It was her. Marienne. On the back of a truck, a German submachine gun at her side. She leant out over the street. 'Papa!' The truck was still moving. 'Papa!'

Duchene ran over, gripped the trailer with one hand and reached up with his free hand.

'Help me,' Marienne called, waving for two young insurgents to work with her to pull him up.

Duchene struggled onto the truck, already short of breath. He let his legs dangle over the road beside hers.

She held him, and he hugged her back.

'You're safe,' she said.

'I am. And you too.'

'I am.'

He nodded to the FFI fighters on the truck. 'You're with them now?'

'Yes.'

'Fighting?'

She nodded.

'So not entirely safe, then?'

'Safer than if I'd done nothing. I could have still been called a collaborator. You've seen what they've been doing?'

Duchene nodded. Already today, he'd witnessed two firing squads in an alleyway, and three women, one holding a baby, having their heads brutally shaved on the street. Even with the smell of burning human flesh that wouldn't leave him, he was relieved Guillaume hadn't pushed him to go to the police.

'Smart girl,' he said.

'Don't be sad. It's over now.'

'They're saying Rol will keep fighting the Germans, all the way to Berlin.'

She nodded. 'He will.'

'And you?'

'I'm not sure.' She frowned. 'Sometimes people look at me who knew me during the occupation. In the shops where I used to go with Max – the shopkeepers, the regulars. My neighbours. Sometimes I think this armband is all that's keeping me safe.'

Duchene looked at his daughter. She looked back at him without moving. A calm seemed to have found a place within her.

She reached out and placed her hand on his shoulder. 'It's all right,' she said. 'I understand now. She left because that was what she needed to do to survive this world. I can see that. I've lived it. I'm not angry anymore that you didn't stop her from leaving. But I need you to do the same for me. I need to go and fight.'

He touched her face. 'I don't think I could stop you if I wanted to. And I don't think it would be good for us if I did.'

Marienne smiled. 'Sometimes there's more strength, more courage, in letting go than in fighting to hold on. I can see that now.'

Duchene pulled a small photo from his wallet. 'Take this with you. Your mother.'

Together they looked at the picture. There she stood, on a hillside in Spain. Rifle slung. She too was wearing trousers and an armband, but the resemblance was only in how they were dressed. She looked nothing like Marienne; neither did his daughter look much like him. What ancestral features she had were from some other place in their family. She was her own self.

'You'll write to me? You'll try to call?'

She nodded. 'Yes. Of course.'

'I know you'll be busy. But just every now and then.'

She nodded again. Duchene put his arms around her, and she hugged him back so hard it was as though she was trying to press a permanent imprint of him onto her, and fill up on enough of his love to last her when he was gone.

He didn't want to let go. To leave her. But he knew that she needed his strength right now, as her parent, as her father, to show her that he could hold the pain of her leaving for both of them.

Sitting back from her, he smiled as the tears ran down her cheeks. He dabbed them with a handkerchief and passed it to her. 'Good for something,' he said, before he kissed her one last time on the cheek and slipped down from the back of the truck.

She stood and called back to him. 'Keep safe.'

He tipped his hand to his hat. A moment later she was too far in the distance to see, and he moved off the road and back into the crowd.

On the streets, Parisians walked arm in arm or in groups of revellers. Peals of laughter rang out from the banks of the Seine, while on the balconies above him people cheered as they looked out over the city.

There was no question about it: Paris was finally free. What was uncertain was whether they could forget what they had done to survive.

ACKNOWLEDGEMENTS

This book was written on the unceded lands of the Woi Wurrung and Boon Wurrung people of the Eastern Kulin nations, and the author pays his respects to their Elders, past, present and emerging. Always was, always will be Aboriginal land.

Many thanks to my publisher, Tegan Morrison, whose passion and insight helped to bring shape to the roughly hewn. To Kate Goldsworthy for her diligent editorial advice and for finding a way to reattach the missing fingers. And to the entire team at Echo for their work to bring this new edition to publication, including Juliet Rogers, Diana Hill, Anna Rogers for her deft editorial review and Debra Billson for her wonderful cover design. I am also grateful to my agent Fiona Inglis for her astute guidance and counsel.

Thank you to Ben Chessell for early reading and feedback and also for collaborating with me on many hours of narrative speculation and practice alongside Miles Browne, Rani Kellock and Patrick O'Shea. Thank you too to Jason Badower for being a ready ally in the war of art.

Numerous historical sources were used to research this book. I am indebted to two works in particular, Ronald Rosbottom's *When Paris Went Dark: The City of Light Under German Occupation, 1940–1944*, (London: John Murray, 2015) and Douglas Boyd's *Voices from the Dark Years: The*

Truth About Occupied France 1940–1945, (London: The History Press, 2015). I also greatly benefited from the cultural and linguistic advice of Pierre Proske and from eleventh hour WW2 fact-checking by Mark Angeli – any mistakes are my own.

My family have stood beside me throughout this writer's journey, always with encouragement and optimism. Thank you to my sister Claire and my parents, Carol-Anne and Terence, to whom this book is dedicated.

Finally, as always, I am humbled and amazed by my wife, Berni – thank you for your inspiration, advice and unfaltering support. And to my daughters, Francesca and Genevieve, who are a constant revelation.

THE BERLIN
TRAITOR
BERLIN HAS FALLEN. THE WAR IN EUROPE IS OVER.
HIS FIGHT HAS JUST BEGUN.

'Highly evocative... a totally engrossing read.'
MICHELLE WRIGHT
A.W. HAMMOND

If you enjoyed *The Paris Collaborator*, don't miss the second Auguste Duchene novel . . .

The Berlin Traitor

July, 1945. The war in Europe is finally over. But Auguste Duchene, who survived occupied Paris at great personal cost, cannot escape his past. He finds himself helping the Allies to pursue a Gestapo war criminal through the ravaged and dangerous streets of Berlin. Duchene soon learns, however, that although one global conflict may have ended, another is beginning, and he is in a deadly race against the Russians as they hunt the same man. And, once again, at the heart of all he does, are his extraordinary wife Sabine and his beloved daughter Marienne.

With its vivid evocation of the post-war hardship and desperation of Germany's capital, *The Berlin Traitor* pits a man of principle, who hates war and all it stands for, against relentless nationalism and self-interest. Tense, terrifying and compelling, full of twists and turns, this riveting page-turner is a worthy successor to *The Paris Collaborator*.

Available now, read on for a sneak peek . . .

The sudden events that blind us with their light
had roots in the slowly-turning decades.
Mick Herron, *Spook Street*

PARIS
Tuesday, 31 July 1945

ONE

The man stood beside him, too close for it to be accidental, even in a crowded bar. Auguste Duchene could smell the brandy on the stranger's breath. If he was lucky, it was just a swig for confidence. If he was unlucky, the better part of the bottle. Drunk is hard to reason with, and reasoning was what he needed to do right now. Now that he had a gun held to his ribs.

He should have been paying closer attention, should have noticed them entering the small brasserie by the Bateau-Lavoir. Although it was well attended tonight, he had chosen this vantage point at the bar so he could keep an eye on the door. But he'd been a fool to let his guard down, if only for one hour, one hour in eleven months. Since Paris had been liberated from the Germans, and the rumours of his role in the city's occupation had begun, he had remained vigilant.

But he'd picked this place specifically because it was away from his new apartment, not the old one he couldn't return to. Here he was, halfway up the Butte Montmartre, two arrondissements away, at a restaurant he hadn't been to in over eight years. Not since the Paris International Exposition had sought to assure everyone of a united Europe.

All it had taken was a letter and a photograph of

Marienne, only recently returned to his worn black wallet. Contact, after so many months of travelling, and the confirmation of a location – Sétif in Algeria – would have been cause for a celebration at home, but the letter contained bigger news – her return to journalism, her decision to put the war behind her and seek a new future.

'Auguste Duchene?'

The man wasn't alone. He had arrived with two others, about twenty minutes earlier. Their worn raincoats, battered caps, out of place in summer, were not uncommon for black marketeers, which is what he'd assumed they were from their furtive movements. They'd gathered at a small table and ordered only coffee – or coffee substitute. The return to civilisation was long and Paris was still troubled with food shortages. His meal had been a simple one too, moules frites and a young, acidic sauvignon blanc.

The two men at the table started to stand.

Duchene glanced at the maître d', whose attention moved elsewhere, although his brow furrowed and his eyes grew wide.

'Monsieur, we can assume your guilt from your silence and I can pull the trigger now,' said the man beside Duchene. His voice was tight and forced but betrayed his middle-class accent. His shirt had worn cuffs and the skin on his ring finger was pale from a missing wedding band.

'Witnesses?'

'They will understand.'

'And the owner? His restaurant will now be the site of a murder.'

'An execution.'

The pain was shocking, almost overwhelming, as the man brought the back of the gun up against the side of

Duchene's head. It flooded across his forehead as blood ran down his face. He began to fall, grabbing the bar stool so he wouldn't land on his back. But he'd only slowed his fall. In a moment the man planted a foot on his chest and completed Duchene's journey to the floor.

The restaurant erupted into noise and movement. Some diners headed for the door while others stood to get a better view, their faces distorted with fear or excitement.

The maître d' was out from behind the bar. Dropping his charade of ignorance, he helped the man to haul Duchene to his feet. 'Apologies, all. No harm done. Too much to drink. Please return to your seats and I'll refill your glasses. On the house.'

Were his head not spinning, Duchene would have been impressed by the speed with which the maître d' had sought to secure the night's takings.

'This way,' he said in softer tones to the man with the gun, gesturing with his head towards the kitchen door.

As Duchene was dragged into the kitchen, a ruddy cook shouted, 'Trouble?' without looking up from the filet he was searing.

'I have it under control,' the maître d' snapped.

Duchene tore an arm free and grabbed for a pan. The maître d' shrieked and recoiled, but the blow never landed. One of the men behind Duchene bludgeoned the back of his arm with a heavy cosh and a new pain raced through his bones.

The pan clattered onto the floor, the cook swore and an apprentice scrambled to retrieve it. Moments later, Duchene was out into the warm night air, sprawled on the cobblestones where the men had thrown him.

Knee on Duchene's chest, rough hands pulling through

his pockets, the maître d' seized the wallet and pulled out its few notes. Far from a fortune but more than the cost of his meal.

He slapped Duchene across the face. 'Bring trouble into my restaurant?'

'Them. Not me.'

'No. *You*, Monsieur Duchene. There are those of us who know what you did. Not many, but just enough to make it right.'

He got up and nodded to the other men. 'Away from here, so the customers don't hear the noise.'

For the third time this evening Duchene was hauled to his feet. But this time they knew better. Following the initiative of the maître d', they patted him down, removed the knife from his boot and tied his hands with his own belt. Then they marched him deeper into the darkness, away from the lights of Boulevard de Clichy and its dance halls and cabarets.

The adrenaline spike had been replaced by a growing chill through his hands and his face. For a moment it seemed he was outside his body, watching himself being led through a grimy alleyway with, at the end, an unparalleled view of the City of Lights. From up on the hill, the grandeur of Paris so easily cancelled out the struggle of the day to day – the ration lines, the new graves, the shorn women, the returned prisoners with their haunted eyes.

Confused and desperate, he started to shudder from the pain. 'What is it you think I've done?'

'Think?' said the man with the gun. 'We know.'

'I can't plead my case?'

'We're not without mercy. Pleading won't make this quick.'

'Good to know you have my best interests in mind.'

This was no justice. It was gossip and rumour dressed up as evidence. Likely they had done things to survive, and had compromised themselves.

His fear was becoming anger, and this was a good thing. Anger could be a weapon.

'Your wife,' Duchene said.

The man stopped for a moment.

'Your wife. She left while you were fighting for France?'

'What?'

He had to get him talking, distract him, find an opportunity.

'The pistol you're holding. It's a Free French service revolver, supplied by the Americans. You were in England with de Gaulle. You fought to liberate France after Normandy.'

'So?'

'The pale stripe on your finger. You used to wear a wedding band. You don't anymore.'

'She could have died.'

'Perhaps, but then you'd probably still wear it – in her memory.'

'Shut up. Want me to shoot you here?' The man raised his voice. A moment later a light in a ground-floor apartment went on.

Duchene stopped walking. 'You know this isn't the same. Killing unarmed Frenchmen isn't the same as killing Nazis.'

'You're a collaborator.'

'Are you sure? Why not round up the maître d'? He would have served German soldiers as they strolled around the Butte. He made money from them, fed them and chose not to poison the first one who crossed his door.'

'That's different.'

'It's complicated. And it was complicated for me too. Killing me won't bring her back to you.'

'Shut up.'

At an apartment up ahead, the back door opened and an old man in threadbare slippers stuck his head out. He held an ornate walking stick.

'I'm sorry. She shouldn't have treated you that way,' Duchene continued.

'Quiet!'

Duchene could feel the blood on his face, sticky now.

The old man looked them up and down.

'Go back inside,' said the gunman. 'You need to go back inside.'

The old man's grip on the stick tightened.

'Not out here,' he said. 'I've seen the bodies in the streets. You just leave them for the rats and dogs. You never clean up after yourselves.'

The gunman shook his head. 'It's a warning to others.'

'It's a disgrace. We're not the Germans. We're French. We respect the dead. *Our* dead.'

'Get back in –'

Duchene rushed forward, driving his legs so hard that his feet stung as they slapped on the cobblestones. His instinct was to close his eyes, waiting for the shot, but somehow, with his hands bound in front of him, he needed to steer his course right. If he fell, he wouldn't be getting up again.

The old man reached for his door handle, but with the stick in his hand, the movement was awkward and slow. This gave Duchene the necessary seconds to hurl himself, shoulder first, through the doorway and into the old man, who toppled to the floor. An instant later, he let go of any guilt as a shot splintered the doorframe. Duchene's heavy-handedness had been justified. The old man might be bruised but he wasn't shot. With a kick, Duchene slammed the door shut and hit the hallway light switch with his arm.

The darkness wasn't absolute but it was something.

As he bent low to grab the cane in both hands, Duchene felt a sharp pain in his back as his body rebelled against the sudden movement. Putting the walking stick between his knees, he slid its metal tip between the belt and his wrists. Just as he loosened the knot, there was a smashing of glass behind him.

By now the old man had hauled himself up and was leaning against the wall. 'Fuck off. All of you!' he shouted.

Duchene, more than happy to obey, threw the front door open and ran out into the street, clutching the walking stick. Hoping instinct would guide him, he turned right, before reaching a narrow set of stairs that cut between two terraces and down to brighter streets below. With one hand on the central railing that divided the steps, Duchene risked taking them two at a time. He could hear the shouts of the men echoing through the canyons of buildings around him. As he slowed to risk a glance over his shoulder, he saw only a few night-time strollers.

When he reached a wider, well-lit street, he stopped briefly to draw breaths of relief into his lungs, then ran on. His legs were burning, his vision blurring, his back jarring with every foot pound on the street – but he was alive.